QF

HOW WE

REMEMBER

HOW WE REMEMBER

J.M. MONACO

RedDoor

Published by RedDoor
www.reddoorpublishing.com

ISBN 978-1-910453-62-9

Cover design: Clare Connie Shepherd
www.clareconnieshepherd.com

Typesetting: Tutis Innovative E-Solutions Pte. Ltd

Printed and bound by Nørhaven, Denmark

For my mother

One

My father insisted on paying for the flight, the limousine from the airport and whatever extras. He knew I would prefer to stay at my old friend Beth's place and not with him at the house, but I needed a car, so he offered my mother's. My dead mother's. Her flash, maroon 2011 model Ford Mondeo, the prize baby she loved so much. She used to marvel at how fast it moved from twenty to seventy coming onto the highway.

'It's so smooth, Jo, you don't even know you're moving,' she'd say. 'But watch out, those state police will get you for going over by just five miles an hour, so best be on the safe side.'

I used to worry my mother would fall asleep at the wheel on interstate 90 on her long journeys to visit my uncle Tom, the priest, who lived in upstate New York near Albany. Not much skill needed to drive these things. Americans meander along happily on automatic pilot, cell phones, travelling coffee mug in hand, music blaring, their own private oasis until – *wham*. It only takes a second and it's over. No, that's not how she died. Lung cancer was the unsurprising culprit, but after Ma passed away Dad discovered she had taken out another life insurance policy that covered accidental car death. She was pretty thorough in planning for the future.

The route out north from Boston Logan Airport is as tedious as ever, in spite of the tempting mid-March clear sky that shakes and shimmers along the edges of the urban landscape. After passing a few local news billboards, flawless anchormen and women smirking with perfectly made up complexions that you want desperately to squeeze till there's nothing left, my driver moves farther away from Boston and onto Route 60 where the shopping plaza strip soon begins.

Revere's International House of Pancakes is a stop I knew well during my high-school years, a popular hangout on Friday and Saturday nights after cruising the beach. The IHOP has survived in this same location for more than thirty-five years. I shouldn't be surprised at the longevity of such places around here. A few years ago, to my parents' great disappointment, the Hilltop Steakhouse restaurant up on Route 1, well-known for its gigantic cactus sign and several large plastic cows that hovered out front by the entrance, closed down after serving the community for over fifty years. Who needs fancy urban food innovation for lactose-intolerant and gluten-free snobs – that just translates into small portions – when you can rely on the old gas-generating favourites? After all, you're not getting value for money unless you're taking a doggy-bag home. Still. Fifty years. They had their time, just like Ma.

Still going strong, The Squire, a local strip joint that's had its fair share of shootings with drug deals gone wrong, looks cleaned up. The place sells itself as the 'Premier Gentlemen's Club,' but don't be fooled. You won't spot any gentlemanly-squire types around here.

By the time you hit the mini plazas, gas stations, Italian-American and Chinese restaurants, the all-day breakfast diner, Dunkin' Donuts and yet another Papa Gino's, you can be sure you'll never have to worry about starving. America. Land of the free and the home of the obese.

I can't claim the taxi ride from home in north London to Heathrow is much more exciting. But somehow the slog through the outskirts of that rain-sodden, grey capital doesn't generate the same aversion in me, that wave of nausea way down in the gut when I'm emerging out of Logan to the place I used to call home.

Match all this with the conversation I have with the oh-so-friendly Italian-American driver, Dino. His perfected, rocket-speed small talk with characteristic Bostonian whiny shortening and stretching of vowels would win him a gangster-film Oscar in a flash. If only he knew he possessed such talents. It appears Dino has become some kind of personal escort choice for my parents.

'Jimmy's old school, but that means he does things right. Yeah, your father, Jimmy,' he pauses, as if to contemplate the enormity of Jimmy O'Brien's transcendent qualities. 'He's good people,' he says, glancing at me in his rear-view mirror. 'I'm sorry to hear about your mother. She was a nice lady, she was.'

Dino picked me up a month ago, when my mother was dying, after Dave phoned to tell me about the hospice. 'You better get here soon,' he said with an urgency I hadn't heard until that point.

I rushed over on a flight the next day and saw her later that afternoon. My mother was sitting upright scanning a newspaper in the sun room of the renovated colonial mansion, now her hospice, and offered me a bright, toothy grin. For someone who was so close to the brink I thought she looked pretty good.

My visit lasted three weeks and while I was there she decided to postpone her death. My brother brightened up fast, said we should get together, catch up with a brother and sister night out. But Dave never brought up the subject again. Two days after I arrived he went away for the weekend with a friend. A woman friend, I thought. *Oh, that's strange, wasn't our ma just about to die when he called me*, but I stopped myself from saying anything. *Be kind.*

'So you have a girlfriend now, that's nice.'

'No, no,' he said. 'She's just a friend… a friend with benefits.' He belted out his trademark laugh, reminiscent of an excited seagull. 'You know that kind, right? They're the best, those friends with benefits. Right? Am I right?' And off he went to have his fun.

After my mother had pressed her doctor to tell her how long she had left, she shopped around for the perfect surroundings where she could say her goodbyes. The website described it as 'a home away from home,' but I knew from first glance it was much grander than the old homestead. 'I really like the look of that bedroom fireplace,' she said in her email. 'And it has wifi.' She knew she couldn't die in the house where my brother and I grew up. 'Your father can't cope with all that,' she said on the phone, her voice fading. 'And the last thing I want is to be worrying about *him*.'

Dad complained about the long drive, the cost. 'Greedy sons of bitches. Making money from dying people.' He kept his visits to Ma's hospice short.

It took her longer to go than we all imagined. After my second week there, with each day that passed, it looked as though her body was getting more ready, beckoning her closer to that eternal light she sometimes talked about. Her eyes began to look glazed as if she was in a trance. Her mouth appeared frozen, cracking slowly when she tried to smile.

'I'm not afraid,' she told me. 'It's going to be beautiful when I'm up there with my maker. They're all waiting for me, you know. My parents. Sisters. My brothers.'

But something kept holding her back. I'm sure now the something must have been me.

I was the only visitor who saw her daily from morning till evening during that three-week stint. She felt bad, she said, about the inconvenience she was causing me, the busy academic with my important work.

'You know you don't have to stay so much. Aren't you bored? All this hanging around when I'm sleeping? I hope you brought some work with you.'

'Hey, Ma,' I said, leaning towards the bed from where I sat in the armchair. I noticed the red fleece blanket by her feet and started to unfold it. 'I'll decide for myself what's boring and what isn't.' I covered her feet and legs with the fleece. 'And I can tell you,' I continued, patting her arm, 'there's lots of times when I'd like to grab some rest and relaxation. Yup, I wouldn't mind a chance to just sit and do nothing.' I nodded a few times, pursed my lips and sighed. 'All comfy now.' I glanced up with a smile and caught her eyes for a few seconds before returning to smooth the blanket over her knees.

'Oh, Jo. I knew you'd come. You know I appreciate it, don't you?' she said, with moist eyes. 'I just want you to know that. You know that, right?'

I sensed that staying alive was an effort for her. There must be nothing worse than opening your eyes to another day, knowing it's going to be the same as yesterday; the pain, the disturbed sleep, the retching, more sleep, waking up again. She was on standby at the gate with her boarding pass and she was pretty pissed off with all the delays.

'My doctor said three months, max. Look at the calendar, Jo. Now it's four. I've had it. Enough already.'

The old man across the hall kept her awake day and night.

'Waitress? Waitress? Anyone? Can I have some service here? What kind of a place is this? Never coming back here again. Oh, please. *Please!* Why are you doing to this me? Can't any of you hear me? *Hello?*'

But one night the man stopped screaming, my mother said, and the next day he was gone.

There was a shouty nurse who would bounce into my mother's room, all chippy-chirpy, and call my mother hon or honey. 'Heya, hon. Aren't you looking good today?'

In spite of my mother's irritation, she offered a polite response. 'You think? Maybe better than I feel, but thank you. Must be all the weight I lost. Cancer's the only diet that ever worked for me. Hah, hah.'

And more laughing and singing and dancing from the nurse until Ma puked up her breakfast.

Dino the driver remembers me from that recent trip, but still runs through the same barrage of high-pitched questions. 'What you do for a living? You married? Kids? How long you staying? Did you sprain your ankle, sweetheart, is that why you got the cane?'

I remind him that I teach art history at a university in London. I lie in my efforts to keep it brief. I actually run this course called Critical and Contextual Studies in Art and Design. No one on the outside really gets it and I'm not in the mood to try to explain. I tell him again, yes, I'm married. No, I don't have kids. No, not even one.

'Oh,' he says in a consoling tone, and shuts up. He doesn't stop yapping for long. The sad fact about my mother's passing and any normal assumption that I may be a grieving daughter, not to mention jet-lagged, doesn't stop Dino.

When he mentions the cane I wonder whether I should retell the boring story of my failing body that's been taken over by MS. I've managed some feats in my lifetime that I never thought were possible for someone like me, but I can't seem to conquer this one. I tried to explain it to him the last time but regretted it after detailing the different types. But like others, he didn't know how to respond except to say, 'Hey, that's a real bummer.'

'Yeah, it's just a little ankle sprain,' I lie. 'Not too bad.'

His shrill rattle continues. 'And what'll you be doing for fun after all the family business? You're staying with a friend? What's her name? I got a good business you know, my cars are the best in Boston. I work too much, but I like the karaoke over in Chelsea. Does she like karaoke? Here's my card. That's me, Dino Palozzi.'

At a hundred dollars for a twenty-five minute airport trip he must be doing OK, but I'm pretty sure he's not Beth's type.

We reach my parents' house, a small two-bedroom 1950s house that would benefit from a good scrub-up. Some half-decent perennial flowerbeds and shrubs out front wouldn't go amiss either. My mother's Mondeo, recently washed and sparkling, waits for me in the driveway.

Dino takes out my suitcase and surprises me when he stretches his stumpy arms to offer a hug. While it feels a bit weird, his shoulders and back are soft and somehow this is comforting. He pulls back and hovers, a sign it's time to tip, even though my father told me his pre-payment included an extra ten dollars. I throw another ten at him as I don't have anything smaller.

He smiles and says, 'Take care of that ankle, sweetheart. Hey, let me know if your friend needs a ride to the karaoke.'

As he drives away I remind myself not to feel begrudged. *Let it go, Jo. Let it go.*

Two

I find the keys to the house and the car, along with the sat nav, in the glove compartment of Ma's Mondeo as planned. I sit in the driver's seat and inhale the smell of the car. I wish Jon was here. I've never met anyone who's better at mastering exotic dinner recipes for two from nothing. He's the kind of guy who slaps on rubber gloves when washing dishes, always sets down the toilet seat, and even wipes the floor clean afterwards. And he still has a sex drive that I can't quite keep up with. If he didn't snore like a hog, expel dead-animal-scented farts, or spend his waking hours seeking physical activity in his efforts to avoid boredom, he might even pass as a picture of middle-aged male perfection. But hey, who am I to complain? My grandmother always told me if I could find a guy who kept a full-time job, didn't have a criminal record and wasn't a drunk, I'd be onto a winner. In the end I scored a senior social sciences academic at an old London university, a prestigious Russell Group establishment, kind of the equivalent of the US Ivy Leagues.

As I'm trying to orientate myself with the unfamiliar controls there's a hard knock on the window that jolts me. Dad's seventy-five-year-old mourner's eyes look tired, heavy bags underneath and half-moon circles with a twinge of deep purple in the creases. His black four-wheel-drive Ford pick-up is parked on the drive.

'I had to take a truck delivery for the day out to New Hampshire, but I'm back early,' he says. On his head sits that same Boston Red Sox cap he's always worn, sunshine or not, wiry-white sideburns creeping out near the ears. A toothpick dangles from the left corner of his mouth, his oral fixation since he quit smoking a decade ago. He likes to chew on it, move it around, feel it under his tongue. It makes him speak with a bit of a lisp, an observation he's always rejected.

'I talk just fine,' he used to shout when my mother teased him. 'How about worrying about your own business for a change and not me, huh?'

'Hi Dad, how are you?'

He nods. We exchange a few words about the car. I get out, he takes a step back, no hug offered. Still, I remind myself to be forgiving. *Must remember to be a better person today.*

I follow him inside the house to use the bathroom and get a drink of water. I notice straightaway the usual build-up of dust on the floor in the corner, on the two-tier bookcase filled with my mother's old nursing magazines and crime novels, a newer pleasure of my father's. Layers also cover the coffee table, the television, the top ledges of the crowded photos that sit on a table next to the TV. After I urged my mother several months back to find a cleaner to help she reported a big improvement, but since her final exit Dad has got rid of her. He doesn't trust anyone in his house, claims he can manage himself.

The perennial smell of cigarettes pervades the place. Some of it may never go away. My mother exhaled her way into the porous walls that had no choice but to absorb her. Maybe Dad, even as a non-smoking toothpick-sucker prefers it this way.

It's a means of holding on to her. He's already decided not to take her voice off the answering machine, a rare decision that I agree with. Since she died I've sometimes called when I know he won't be home just to hear her. *Hello, you've reached Jimmy and Terry. We can't come to the phone right now but if you leave a message we'll get back to you as soon as we can. Have a nice day.*

Dad mumbles through a list of things he wants me to do. Go through Ma's clothes, shoes, do things he has no time or patience for. Cancel credit cards she didn't tell him about, call her more distant friends and relatives who don't know about her passing.

When there's a pause, I say, 'OK, Dad. Don't worry. It'll all get done. Why don't you tell me how you're doing with all this? How are you coping?'

'Fine. I'm fine,' he says quickly. He takes off his cap, checks the inside, gives it a shake, checks again. Gazing into the cap again, he says, 'Did all the crying. Got it out of my system. It's done. She was dying for a long time. So. That's that. Nothing more to say.' There's a long silence, his eyes still lowered. 'Oh, before I forget,' he says, suddenly, 'I want to show you where I keep our will. So you and your brother know where it is in case something happens to me. I'm the one and only executor, remember.'

He leads me to their bedroom. My eyes are drawn to the warped venetian blinds that cover the two small windows. They are kept closed, but the beams of light creeping through the top and sides with their surrounding dust motes emit a strangely pleasing halo, even after Dad has turned on the light. My mother's bedside table is clear, empty of life, while dad's

11

reveals his ongoing attempts to keep afloat. A pill dispenser box and several orange bottles of prescription meds cover the surface, note pad scribbles indicate his pill schedules. A large digital clock, keeping Dad on time, casts a white glow over them.

'Everything's in this little filing cabinet here, black and white. Even split. No arguments,' he says, with a waving gesture. He opens the bottom drawer and locates the envelope, labelled WILL, in large, carefully handwritten capital letters and thick-red marker pen. 'See? Right here.' His index finger taps the paper hard three times.

He shows me some papers my mother kept in her bedside drawer; to-do lists, nursing-related things from before she retired, postcards, some old photos from her visits to London to see me. With the exception of the will he hands the stash over, then remembers another item he's put aside. 'And I found this under some of her old magazines in there. It's a diary. Yeah, she kept a diary,' he laughs, avoiding my eye. 'I don't want to know what she said about me. You take it.'

This takes me by surprise. She wasn't exactly the kind of person who would set time aside for written reflection. Back in London when I was packing for this trip I found some letters my mother wrote to me years ago after I left the States. Most of them started with an apology for not writing back to me more often.

Later, she made her emails short and to the point; two- or three-line messages with photographs attached, requests for setting up times for phone calls or Skype chats. Her subtle energies, the anxieties that found their way into her pre-internet letters written in Catholic-school disciplined penmanship, all but disappeared.

I linger a bit over the paperback diary's cover. A simple print of a colour-pencil illustration of daffodils, framed with delicate green leaves on a burgundy background. At the top and printed in hand-drawn calligraphy is the word Mother. My mother would have liked this sort of thing. She always sent me those bland Hallmark cards with cheesy passages and poems printed inside. She'd never add anything else except, 'Love Ma and Dad.' I open the first page and see there's a handwritten note from my younger self, and I begin to laugh and well up as I read it.

> Ma, You have been so good to me, I would never be able to make up for your consideration, kindness and love! There is more than one kind of word for you. I see myself as the luckiest girl in the world to have a mother like you. You're terrific! I hope this day is as special for you as it is for me. Thank You for being you. Happy Mother's Day, I Love You Always, Jo

There's a heavy sadness first, in knowing that I have no real memory of giving her this gift. The memory space around purchasing this thing, writing the note with all its hyperbolic sentiment, giving it to her, is empty. I can *imagine* this is the kind of gift I would have given to my mother back in 1983 Mother's Day. But could I have been serious about being 'the luckiest girl in the world'? Or was I just a lot more naive then?

I flip through the diary and see she filled about half the pages, but my father stops me before I can settle into it.

'OK, so there's something else that came up from the lawyer,' he says, and pauses. His tone has a nervous tick to it. 'OK, I haven't told your brother yet 'cause I know what he's like and when he hears it he ain't going to be happy. So your mother, you know what she was like with money. Yeah, well apparently when Ma got the news about the cancer being terminal she went to the lawyer a few days later and told him she wanted to add something to the will, but didn't want me or anybody else to know. She thought that would just make things easier. So, here's the thing. She sold some shares, some she bought years ago. She invested in some drug company or something like that years ago when she started working at the hospital, and she ended up closing the deal with around $300,000.'

By this point he's building his voice to almost a shouting level, while he stares at the ceiling. 'And she told the lawyer she sold them because she didn't want us left with shares having to make decisions about whether to keep them or not or lose money, so to make things easier she wants the three of us to split it. The problem is your brother. Because she was always sick with worry over him and his money problems she wrote it that he'd get his batch in instalments over the next five years, and that's the thing he ain't going to like. But, Jo,' he says, sitting down, now looking straight at me for at least five seconds, unflinching. 'This is the thing, Jo. David, he can't do a damn thing about it.'

I join him at the table, palms spread. I think my mouth is still open. 'I can believe it and not believe it. I mean…I mean, shit, Dad, I know she was a saver and all that, but how the hell did she pull it off? The stock market's something else, and she never showed any interest in stocks, of all things. How could you not know anything about it?'

'Look, it don't matter what it is, what it was. And she always did her own thing with her money, you know that. Fact is she left you and your brother a shitload and you should be, and me too, we should all be grateful. But I know your brother. He's going to throw a fit. We got to see the lawyer, get everything figured out. Got to fix a time to see this guy.' Dad breaks into a quick coughing fit, recovers and says, 'Right now I need a drink.'

He sets out his usual Budweiser before him and partners it with a shot of Jim Beam.

While Dad eases his worries with his usual panacea, his news begins to sink in. Split three ways. That's about £70,000 each, give or take. It's not enough to buy a place in London but it's still a lot of money. Before this point in the day, the tiredness, the jetlag was hitting me. If I had the inviting prospect of a nice bed and a comfy pillow I'd be out cold in five minutes. But suddenly the talk of so much cash falling into my lap, money I haven't worked for, money I certainly didn't expect to inherit, is giving me palpitations. I'm trying my best to hold back a bizarre urge to laugh.

'She always had her own separate accounts. That's how we did things,' says Dad. 'And on her days off, what was she doing, huh? Working at the hospital with those doctors, the managers, they all know what to do with money, maybe they helped her, found her a good stockbroker, who knows?'

I picture my mother making careful notes on a yearly basis about how much profit her investment is making, and working herself into a muddle about what to do with it. *Best to leave it for now*, she would have told herself. *Tuck it away for a rainy day*.

Dad pulls the toothpick from his mouth, swigs the shot with his head thrown back and eyes closed. He releases a hissing sound through a small gap between his lips and slides in the toothpick. 'While you're here I might as well show you where I'm hiding something else. Yeah, I got my own secrets,' he says. 'I know this ain't the kind of thing you like. I know you won't like it, but you should know about it,' he pauses, 'just in case something happens to me.'

He carries a chair from the kitchen and positions it near their bedroom closet. He slides opens the closet doors, climbs up, takes out a shoe box from the top shelf and pulls out a hand gun. While I'm certainly not expecting this, I guess I'm not too surprised. The glass cabinet of rifles he's had in their bedroom for the last forty years or so still gleams from the other side of the room, in spite of needing a good cleaning.

'This I have because I want to be ready for anyone who comes in and tries to rob me. The neighbourhood ain't like it used to be. Sorry, but I gotta protect myself. So there it is. You won't need it, but if anything happens to me, there it is. Oh, the other thing is this.' He pulls out an envelope from the box. 'I keep this here too with around a thousand bucks in it. That's my spending money. You know, play money, should I ever need it.'

The first time I saw my father with a gun other than one he used for hunting trips was sometime during the 1970s.

Maybe I'm nine or ten. I am watching television. My older brother isn't in the room watching with me, he always seems to be somewhere else. Dad is somewhere else in the house too, maybe in the basement. My mother sits in the kitchen. There aren't too many options, being such a small house. The living room has only enough room to fit a small couch, a reclining chair, television and two side tables. My brother and I share the one bedroom upstairs. My parents have the little bedroom off the kitchen. A box room next to it holds a chair and small desk where a telephone sits with a notepad and pen, waiting for important messages. Filling the walls of the box room are fluorescent graphic posters of Jimmy Hendrix and Janis Joplin. Their glow-in-the-dark yellows, lime greens, pinks and purples are printed with a soft, velvety-black background, which I love to caress with my fingertips. I catch my dad lying on his back on the floor in the dark sometimes listening to Hendrix, gazing at the posters, while he blows perfect smoke-rings. *Your dad looks so cool*, all my friends say, with his long hair and moustache. That leather jacket. *Your parents are so young*. My friends' parents are much older than mine. This is something I don't like.

The doorbell rings and my mother says, 'Who's that?' as she walks through the living room to open the front door. I have a quick look up and see two policemen.

'We're looking for Jimmy,' one says, in a way that sounds like he knows my father. It's not a big showdown. It's all quiet. Maybe they're being careful not to frighten the innocent-looking little girl who's watching TV. After a minute, with the police waiting outside, my mother finds him. As he moves toward the door Dad mumbles something incoherent under his breath. He's talking to them for a long time outside now in lower, nervous tones that I struggle to hear. He steps back in quickly and passes me, in a huff about something, swearing in loud whispers, *fucking* this, *fucking* that. *Cocksuckers*. He rushes to their bedroom, returns with something in his hand. He's trying to keep it wrapped in a black cloth but I catch a glimpse. A hand gun, suitably named because of the way it fits so easily into your palm. Small and powerful, hits with a punch, smashes with a good kick. He's outside with them again. Hands it over. More nervous chit-chat, murmuring, some raised voices that settle down. Is he off the hook?

He closes the front door, flashes past me, this time not holding back the loud swearing. My mother stays quiet in the kitchen, waiting, then takes her chance, keeping her voice low.

'But how'd that happen? Who is this guy, Jimmy? Who *is* he?'

I hear him slam their bedroom door. Long silence. Is she in there with him? Opens it again, hurries past me. Out the front door he escapes into the darkness. This happens frequently. Where does he go?

'Ma,' I shout from the living room. 'What were those cops doing here? What did they want?'

She ignores me.

'Ma… *Ma*?' I persist, standing tall now, moving into her view at the doorway. I want to be seen, to be heard. She casts me a quick glance from the kitchen table where she's sitting with nothing but a pack of cigarettes and an ashtray in front of her.

'Nothing,' she says. 'Just asking Dad about something, someone he knows.'

'It looked like he gave the cop a gun. Did he give him a gun?'

She says nothing.

'Ma?'

'Nothing. It don't concern you.'

Three

I arrive at Beth's, about forty minutes north of Boston. It's a neat, three-bedroom ranch-style house with a double garage that could easily house a young family. At the back is a lush, evergreen tree-lined garden. The expansive decking area and lawn allows you to imagine endless possibilities of domestic pleasure; hours of play with children and dog, volleyball and badminton competitions, family reunion egg and sack races, birthday parties, anniversaries, high school and college graduations. Barbecues galore. Still, since Beth and Paul divorced, it feels pretty big for two people.

I let myself in with the key that Beth left inside one of her primrose flower pots. It's a spacious but cosy place with a modern, open-plan kitchen diner and living-room area. The mantelpiece is covered with pictures of Beth's daughter, Danielle, at various ages, her niece and nephew, her parents. There are some other shots of her old black and white collie dog, Bailey, in his younger days, one with him sitting in front of his fifth birthday cake wearing a red bow on top of his head. Her sweet boy Bailey died about six months ago and she's not over this tragedy yet. Cancer, again, was the killer. Even dogs can't escape it. At least they don't have to suffer like people. Say your goodbyes and put them out of their misery. A quick injection and off to a nice long sleep. Lucky them.

Beth is a clean and neat freak, in a way that is far more fastidious than Jon's tidy habits. Not a thing is out of place and soon after her cleaners have been, she's getting out the broom and duster. Her interior design choices and tastes are quite different from mine, which is pretty much anything goes. Beth favours traditional furniture accented with things like Tiffany lamps, and she collects Waterford crystal from her trips to Ireland to see family. Her smaller items, like the reproduction Fabergé eggs, are displayed carefully in a glass cabinet bought for the purpose. The combination of everything generates a slight feeling of suffocation, a sense of being spun too rapidly inside a tight web of perfect suburban domesticity. But there's something irresistible about the fresh lemon smell of that furniture polish, Bailey's dog smile.

Beth's parents were the kind who put money away for college. The Connellys had a nice big house too. The first time I had dinner there I sat next to Beth at the dining-room table and stroked the beautiful surface of the wood.

'This looks nice,' I whispered to Beth, but her mother heard me.

'That's solid American maple,' she said. 'We bought it to celebrate our anniversary last year.'

And I remember looking around the large space and thinking, *Wow, imagine that. And they have a whole separate room just for eating.* They were the kind of family who went away every winter on skiing vacations and every summer rented a big house right on the beach in Cape Cod for a month. Their mother didn't have to work and prepared home-cooked meals most evenings. Over their kitchen sink she placed a decorative wooden placard marked with the inscription, *God bless this house*.

The Connellys welcomed me like I was one of them and I loved them for this. At the same time I couldn't stop myself from questioning the nature of their kindness. Did they take pity on my sorrowful state? What did they say about me when I wasn't there? What did they *really* think of me and my family? What did they want in return for all the meals they provided, for all those times I joined them for summer vacation? Over time I would learn that folk like the Connellys expected nothing. How is it that some people are capable of this when others are not?

While I waited at Heathrow for my delayed flight to Boston, I thought about the Connelly family and their successes. That led to mulling about my own hard-earned accomplishments and in a moment of boredom I made the mistake of Google-searching myself. Aside from spotting a few academic citations of my work, my browsing led to my recently updated faculty webpage, the one with the uninspiring photo, that head and shoulders shot revealing my weight gain over the years. For many of us in middle-age we find our bodies have transformed in surprising ways. Men turn doughy, women grow more facial hair as their waistlines expand – before you know it, men, women, it's hard to tell the difference between us. I used to offer the line that at least my extra facial flesh was a healthy-looking alternative to the sunken-in faces of other women who decided in their fifties to take up marathon running as a hobby or drink their own urine in their quest to live forever. But you can only fool yourself for so long.

Beth and Danielle won't be home for hours. Beth has one of those unpredictable, high-stress schedules in IT sales that would finish me. Danielle is sixteen and has some cheerleading competition practice after school. She never gives her mother a hard time. During one of our chats on my last visit I asked her what she might want to study after leaving school.

'I think law school's a good idea. Lawyers make amazing money and I'm going to need a profession like that to pay off the student loans I'm going to have. I don't want to end up like my friend's sister, Joy. You remember Joy, right, Mom? Becky's older sister?'

'Oh, that one,' Beth said, squinting from across the room where she sat with her TV guide. 'I sure do remember her. She was kind of a wild one.'

'Yeah, well, she's still working as a waitress a year and a half after graduating from Boston University with liberal arts or whatever she got there.'

'Waitress, huh? I guess that doesn't surprise me. She was always a bit mixed up, wasn't she? Nice enough kid,' Beth said with a bit of a laugh, shaking her head, looking my way, then glanced down again at her magazine.

'Anyway, I get top grades at school and I know I'll get good grades at college, so it kind of seems like the best thing to do. I know I can get my head down.'

Beth looked up and said with a smile, 'That's my girl, Danielle. *Stay focused.*'

I know I can get my head down. Just what those yearning parental ears want to hear. *I don't want to end up like her.*

23

Danielle is the type of all-American girl who sets up ideal expectations. Girls like Danielle make it impossible for all the other lesser, imperfect souls, who may not have had her advantages, and are, of course, in great danger of being despised.

There's no kettle in sight to make tea, and I remember Beth puts her cup in the microwave to boil the water. I think about what Jon would say. *You're joking. She microwaves her tea?* I make a weak tea and wander into Danielle's room where Beth has insisted I stay. It's a well-organised space, overall; cheerleading trophies proudly displayed with fairy lights running along the walls and around the bed's headboard. A good-size desk in the corner is covered with tidy stacks of school books and papers. Two overhead shelves are filled with a mish-mash of items including paperback copies of *The Scarlet Letter* and *To Kill a Mockingbird*, alongside a carefully arranged collage of images. Danielle features in many wearing her cheerleading outfit, surrounded by other cheerleaders and boys in football gear. Some are selfies she's taken at pop concerts. But it's a new pic that catches my attention – an innocent-faced, quiff-haired, acoustic-guitar-holding character called Shawn Mendes. His eyes seem to follow me around the room. I unpack a few things, go for the diary and get cosy in bed.

Many of the first pages are short, with entries for different dates appearing as though they were written together when she was catching up. I picture my mother, she would have been around forty-one years old then, sitting in bed, blue ballpoint pen in hand, a cigarette from the nearby glass ashtray burning soft waves of smoke around her.

I open it randomly in 1985.

Josie was saying she felt like she was in the middle between me and Peggy. I told her that I thought she was pulling away and I felt that it was hard talking with her. In regards to Peg it's been about 9 months since she's talked to me, even at Maureen's daughter's Shower and Wedding in April it was obvious to everyone there that she was ignoring me. I'm having a real hard time with it, but it's something I'm going to have to deal with. I've been praying a lot and asking God to lift it from me. I'll try not to wait so long before I wright again. Time is just going by so quick…

I stop reading momentarily, and close the diary shut. Shawn Mendes catches my eye. It's the content of what the latter section of that page implies, but never states, about the trouble between her and my aunts Josie and Peggy – that awful, sick time. Like the tip of a sharp blade prodding at my chest, it forces me to close my eyes and take a deep breath before reading on.

Can't believe it's 1985 already. Jo's been working lots of extra hours now trying to save up for the school year. She's already taken a loan but needs more to get by. I've been having some counselling with Wendy the therapist (Ron). This stuff with Peggy and the whole business with that husband of hers and Jo is hard. I still pray to God for help. I'm tired now, Got to get up extra early to let the car warm up for work. Need to buy stamps this week.

I stop reading, confused then shocked. My mother's handwriting has a break in the middle of the word *therapist* so it reads as two words: *the rapist*. Or has my brain done its own editing? Even after reading it twice I still see the same thing, *the rapist (Ron)*, then, *the whole business with that husband of hers and Jo*.

I think of Uncle Ron when he took me home in his truck that time, still a blur even now. I flip fast through the rest of the pages, re-read the letters she sent me over the years in search of more, but it's the last of any mention of the troubles between her and Auntie Peggy. And that husband of hers.

Four

1985

I'm twenty-three years old when I pull into the driveway of the little brown, two-bedroom family home where I grew up. The flawless, powder-blue sky shines through the dusty windshield of my mustard-coloured, two-door Gremlin. It feels like spring, a welcome time after a hard New England winter, although it's still only February and the temperature is an unusual 55°F.

I step out and pause, breathe it in. It's been a good afternoon at my part-time job, but it's not long after I'm through the front door when I sense something is different about Ma. She smiles too much, is a bit too interested in hearing how things are going with me, her eyes fixating on mine as I offer up details of the mundane. Her usual stoicism, aided by the calming effects of her smoking habit, is absent. My mother is most at ease with a cigarette in one hand and its best friend in the other, an alcoholic drink – a frosty beer at a summer barbecue, after work at the kitchen table. As years pass this will change to a large wine glass filled with her favourite, a pretty pink Californian Zinfandel. I too enjoy my cigarettes. A drink or two. Or three, even more. We are a family like many others around us who cosy up over cheap booze within the confines of smoke-filled rooms. On this occasion her speech is quick and her hands shake when she lights up. She opens up eventually.

'Now, I want you to know first that I'm always going to be behind you. In whatever you say, whatever you do, OK? I don't want you ever to forget that I love you, right? Please, Jo, just tell me you know that.'

'Well, yeah, OK, but what do you mean, Ma? Understand what?'

'I just want to say that first because I don't want you to feel bad with what I'm going to tell you. OK, so please promise me, Jo, that you will always know I love you and I'm behind you all the way. Always.'

I guess this may have something to do with her ongoing troubles with my father. Will they stay together? Will she divorce him? But she's quick to dismiss my assumption.

'It's not about Dad. He's something else altogether, he is,' she sighs, looking at the ceiling, then returns her gaze to me. 'I haven't told you that I've been having counselling with Wendy. You know, Wendy, the one who did the family sessions with us when your brother was in the hospital? You remember her, right?'

It would have taken a lot for me to forget the pale, stick figure of a woman whose love of shorter skirts drew attention to her bowed legs. We – my mother, my brother and I – spent a few years in weekly family therapy at the fancy private mental hospital, paid by my mother's work health insurance plan, with bendy-Wendy-the-therapist trying to steer us out of our mess. My father stormed out on the third session, never to return.

At this later point, we are done with the family therapy stage but it looks like my mother has now found a way to attend to her own issues. This seems to me a good thing.

'Wendy? You've been seeing her for therapy on your own? That's great, but why didn't you tell me?' I have turned on my encouraging voice.

'I've been going a few months now, just for me. You know, I've had trouble with stuff, like knowing what to do about my sister. I've been wanting us to be sisters again. To be close again.'

I nod. I've assumed, after seeing Auntie Peggy and my mother together at various times over the last few years, that their troubles are over and everything has resumed to its previous state of absurd normalcy. I've played along too, trying to pick up where my aunt and I left off, acting as if nothing ever happened, like we were as close as we were before, smiling over coffee or tea, but it's never been the same.

She hesitates at points to take long drags of her cigarette. I do the same. She sips her instant coffee then continues. 'So, Wendy's been good for me because I've needed to work some things out, figure out what to do. You know, I've been feeling really bad about everything. But Jo, what I'm going to say doesn't mean anything about the way I feel about you. You know that I've always believed you, right?'

Ma's words take me back, fill me with dark thoughts. My body feels heavy suddenly. I feel my mouth drop open, I bring my elbows to the table, sink my head into my hands and keep it there a minute. I fight back the urge to cry.

'Oh, Ma.' I let out a heavy sigh. 'What are you trying to tell me, Ma? What do you have to figure out?' I ask with growing impatience, head and eyes still lowered. 'I thought everything was OK now.'

'Well, your Auntie Peggy said…she said she wants me to apologise to her, to say that everything you told me about Ron was a misunderstanding. She wants me to say this to her as a condition for us to be sisters again. She wants me to sign something, an agreement between me and her. Peggy will write it. But Wendy said I should talk to you first. Make sure it's OK with you.'

She's looking at me with questioning eyes, waiting, trying to read my expression, but I can't hold her gaze. I'm aware of an odd physiological change, the sort of thing that might preclude a speechless moment. A pull at the throat, a tight banding sensation across the chest. An increase in body temperature works its way up to my neck and face.

Ma sets her unsteady cigarette hand onto mine. Her pale, blue-grey eyes are now watery and almost fearful. Her upturned brows cause slight wrinkling in her otherwise smooth forehead. She wants my blessing, my permission to say it's OK to sign an agreement, one that my aunt will write. It will be my mother's admission that her daughter, Jo, when she was fifteen years old, told an untrue, imagined story about her sister Peggy's husband.

Everything happened gradually over a few months in 1976 when fifteen-year-old me was babysitting for Auntie Peggy and her husband, Ron, who had three boys. The story went something like this:

Auntie Peggy had to get going fast with babies as she married later than the other sisters at the ripe age of twenty-nine. The little ones are sweet, lively things, all born around a year after each other, age three, four and five. Billy is the oldest, Matthew or Matty is the middle, and Christopher, Chrissie, is the littlest. Their faces are flawless in their innocence, but it's Chrissie who stands out. He's the one with the curious big-brown eyes, long eyelashes, and delicate curls. He doesn't seem to resemble the others at all, not even his parents, and I make up all sorts of stories in my head about why this must be, an angel sent from heaven. But they're all special when they're this young, when they look up to me in awe, tell me I'm so pretty, and are captivated when I read to them. It will all change, I know, but just to hang on to the way they are now is enough.

Over the past month or so it becomes apparent that Uncle Ron has his eyes on me. His interest grows obvious over a series of provocative looks and gestures. *Hey, you look nice tonight, got a date later? You got a boyfriend? Why don't you have a boyfriend? What do you do for fun on weekends? You wanna beer? I won't tell. It's nice and cold. There you go.*

This all occurs while I wait for Auntie Peggy to return home from her weekly bowling night. They don't have much money, can't afford to pay too much, so they like having me to babysit because I help them out on the cheap. Uncle Ron arrives earlier from his job as a mechanic fixing eighteen-wheeler trucks and Auntie gets back around thirty minutes later, although sometimes he tells her to take her time, have a drink with the girls, he says. Then when she's home Uncle Ron usually drives me back and he's ever so friendly and interested in me and all I have to say about the world, and sometimes he takes the long way just so we can finish talking. But it's an unexpected visit from him one Saturday afternoon on an unusually hot day in May at the local pharmacy where I work one day after school and on Saturdays, that confirms he's up to something. He's never bought anything there before.

'Just passing by,' he says, all smiles, hovering by the register with some shaving cream. 'Hey, I can give you a ride home later. Got some errands to do. Can take you home at two when you finish.'

I smile back, wondering what kind of errands he has to do. I spend a quick second with this, but the question leaves my mind when I think how nice it would be to get a lift home, no one's ever offered before. And it's only a few minutes away by truck.

'OK thanks Uncle Ron.'

'I'll be right outside,' he says, holding his smile.

Later the ride home turns into a longer detour out to the quiet, tree-lined streets of the pleasantly fragrant suburbs to get an ice-cream, where large, luscious green parks are in abundance.

'What's the big rush?' says Uncle Ron. He pulls up to an ice-cream stand next to the corner shop that displays three old-fashioned gumball machines in the window, all full of pink and blue gumballs. I remember chewing mouthfuls as a child and having competitions with friends to see who could blow the largest bubble. Without looking at me, he says, 'What kind do you want?'

I pause for a second. 'Chocolate's my favourite. And I like sugar cones. Can I have it with jimmies?'

He turns to me with a little grin. 'You can have anything you want. You wanna sundae? Banana split? Anything you want. My treat.'

'No. Chocolate's good. The soft kind with jimmies. In a sugar cone.'

He catches me watching him hand over the money, then winks. He returns with the ice-creams, his a soft vanilla in a small cup that he passes to me.

'Hold that for a second.' He starts the engine, puts on his sunglasses. 'Let's go somewhere nice and eat these things.'

It only takes a few minutes to find a secluded spot off the main road near the woods. There's talk about what I'm studying at school and what I usually do during my leisure time, and I feel a strange uneasiness and a sense of freedom simultaneously. Following this, as I relish the smell of clean air, indulge in the taste and cool relief of my ice-cream with jimmies, Uncle Ron begins to tell all. It appears he and Auntie Peggy are having troubles. I am now his confidante.

'It's this Irish-Catholic thing of hers. She's like that, wanting all these kids, right? Kind of uptight, doesn't want to do things that are natural for couples.' Then, in a slightly deeper voice I don't recognise, he says, looking straight ahead through the windshield, 'Why can't people just express their love in the bedroom?'

A rush of heat travels to my face as I imagine my aunt and uncle in bed together. I blush harder when I think of my drive-in date Tommy Stewart's reaction last weekend after I told him I wouldn't give him a hand job.

Uncle Ron turns to face me now, takes off his sunglasses so I can see that his dark eyes mean business with those deep laugh-line creases surrounding them, but I try not to look. He's quiet, waiting for an answer, then reaches over me, slowly, opens the glove compartment, searches for his cigarettes, touches my knee with his other hand, accidentally of course, but lets it sit there for a few seconds. Maybe longer. I respond a bit too late with the nervous laugh I have now mastered.

'Huh,' I giggle. 'Wow. I don't know what to say.' I try hard with my tongue to catch the melting chocolate ice-cream as it drips over the sides of the cone onto my fingers.

He sits back and lights up. After a quiet few drags he passes the cigarette to me and I look at it in front of me, surprised. He's teasing. He'll pull it away when I reach for it. 'Go on. I won't tell,' he says.

Cone in one hand, I take the cigarette in the other and try to look cool, but Lucky Strikes aren't like the Marlboro Lights I usually smoke; harsh against the back of my throat, it hits me like a sudden wildfire and I cough uncontrollably.

He laughs. 'Gimme that thing.'

But I hang onto it and our fingers touch as I recover and try again, show him what I'm made of. A long inhale, slow exhale. A wave of dizziness. I close my eyes. When I open them I see he is staring at me. He searches his cigarette pack again and now he takes out a joint.

'Hey,' I say, surprised. 'How'd you get that?' He doesn't respond. 'That's not a cigarette.'

'Yeah, I bet you can tell the difference, a grown-up girl like you.' His eyes are steady on the joint, only casting a quick, knowing glance and smile my way. 'I got my ways.'

'*You* smoke pot, Uncle Ron? Wow. Bet Auntie Peggy wouldn't like that.'

'No. She sure wouldn't, so don't go telling her. I only do it now and then. Just a little buzz. Nothing wrong with that, right?'

When it's my turn I inhale deeply and hold it down as long as I can. We pass it between us until half is gone.

'Can't smoke the whole thing,' Uncle Ron says. 'It's way too potent to do it all in one go.'

And I laugh, my head feeling lighter. What a riot. Uncle Ron, getting high with his niece. More laughing. I can't stop myself.

After he stubs it out, he moves closer while reaching over me again to put the cigarette pack in the glove compartment. His arm brushes against my left shoulder and breast. This tickles just a tiny bit, but I manage to hold back the giggles. He closes the compartment door and lowers his hand to my knee again. This time he doesn't take it away. Then he moves it slowly up my thigh and down again.

'Nice legs.' His eyes study them. 'Nice.'

He coughs a little, clears his throat. His hands are clean but I notice his fingers are oil-stained under the nails and at the tips. I'm wearing a short denim skirt and feel the heat of his hand on my skin when he squeezes my thigh, and it's so, so hot in the truck, even with the windows open, even after eating the ice-cream. He's wearing a T-shirt and it's the first time I've noticed the muscles in his arms, the way they flex when he squeezes me.

I'm feeling weak and giddy. The remnants of the ice-cream, Lucky Strikes and weed, settle, sticky and dry in my mouth. There's a force holding me back from forming coherent words.

'No,' I giggle. 'My legs are fat. They're fat.' I let my head fall back and my eyelids flutter shut.

'Don't have to stop the fun there,' he says, sitting back. 'Got me thirsty now. I got some cans of Coke in the back. And some whisky.'

He doesn't wait for an answer, puts on his sunglasses and makes a move outside to the back of the truck. It's a two-door pick-up, the same kind my dad drives with a closed back storage area to keep tools and things like a cooler box. I close my eyes again and hear him fumbling, but it seems to take him a long time. I giggle some more and think, *whisky sounds good. With Coke. I like the sound of that. Why not?* I'll try anything once.

He shows up at my passenger window and without speaking hands over my drink in a tall plastic cup. I watch him sweep his free hand, the one that's not holding his drink, through his hair as he saunters in front of the truck on the way to his side. I think to myself how those sunglasses make him look so much younger.

'Just what we need,' he says, getting in. 'Go ahead and try it. Bet you've had whisky before.'

'Yeah. Sure. Sure I have.'

In a quiet, serious tone, he says, 'Bottoms up.' When he reaches to tap my cup with his he holds his there for longer, his face still and expressionless.

The drink is strong, but mixed with the cold, sweet Coke, it goes down easily. *Wow*, I think, *he must have just bought the cans nice and cold before picking me up.* And while I'm pretty stoned now, I know I'm always up for an alcoholic buzz.

'Yeah, this is good,' I say, licking my lips, looking into the cup. I take another couple of swigs. 'My friends would…they would really, really like this.'

He says nothing, leaning back on his door, and continues to stare at me.

I knock back more and say with a noticeable slur, 'I really… yeah, really like it.'

It doesn't take me long to finish. Uncle Ron goes to the back of the truck again and returns with another one for me, not him.

'This is soooo good, Uncle Ron. Ron. Ronny! Hah. Ronny. Does anyone ever call you that? That sounds funny.'

I notice he smiles a little but keeps quiet while he watches me laughing hysterically over nothing, almost to the point of tears.

'Oh, God, I'm totally wasted now,' I laugh.

When I finally stop, he says, 'You know you shouldn't go putting yourself down. What you said about your legs. You're a beautiful girl.'

'Huh. Yeah, right.' I down more of the drink and then finish it. I close my eyes and let my head fall back.

He shifts closer and touches my cheek, moves my chin to face him. Now his hand slides down to my neck, across my breast, my stomach. He takes my empty cup and sets it on the floor. I feel his mouth on my lips, the tickling sensation of his razor stubble on my chin. I can hardly keep my eyes open now, I am suddenly so, so exhausted. My slightly doubled vision through heavy lids catches glimpses of his older-man face, his dark hair, close to mine. Then I'm blinded by spots of bright sunlight, crystallised white circles flashing and vibrating through the gently swaying tree branches outside. It's mesmerising, these beautiful moving lights, but now it's sickening too. I need to get off this rollercoaster and stop this crazy urge to laugh. But I can't move. I can't do anything but close my eyes. After a while they stay closed and I drift off into a dream.

Before dropping me off at the end of our road he leaves me with a plea. 'Keep this between us, OK? No one will understand. They'll only get the wrong idea.' He looks at the quiet street.

I look around too and say, with some uncertainty, but knowing he's right, 'Yeah, OK. Sure. OK, bye then.'

He says nothing else and watches me open the door. As I step out of the truck I sway with a feeling of leftover drunkenness, or is it more of a hangover? How much time has passed since I got stoned? Since I drank that whisky and Coke? Some seconds pass before he revs the engine and drives off.

When I walk into the house, slightly unsteady, it is empty, dark and cool. My afternoon encounter with Uncle Ron has left me feeling unsure and shaky. I check my reflection in the hallway mirror, picture what I might look like to him, wonder about all the things I might have said. The ice-cream. The joint. The whisky and Coke. All the laughing. Something about my legs. But everything's fuzzy.

I hold one shaky hand in the other and tell myself to calm down. My mouth is dry, my tongue feels sandpaper-rough, and I remember the strange feeling when my friend's cat licked my face last week. I drink water, glass after glass.

In my bedroom I undress, feeling an odd soreness between my legs. When I touch myself I see there's a bit of blood on my finger and it starts to trickle down my thigh. Then I take a shower, the hottest I can stand with lots of soap to rid myself of that overly heated fleshy smell that's just hit me, scrub away the dirty, hazy web that's clouding my brain. It must be one of those funny period times, I tell myself it's a bit of spotting, that's all. It has to be that, I've just finished my cycle a few days ago. But some other part of me, the part that senses it should remain silent, tells me it could be something else. But that can't be. I dozed off, couldn't keep my eyes open. And when I opened them again – didn't I only sleep a few minutes? – I felt different. Aching groin, sick stomach. But weed and whisky, those two things together, can make you feel really weird.

Uncle Ron was driving, all quiet and serious. As we approached my street, he said, 'Hey there sleeping beauty. Time to wake up.' I try my hardest to remember more, so hard my head hurts, but nothing comes. If I went to sleep, maybe Uncle Ron did too. Still, I have the strangest end-of-the-world feeling. After I get out of the shower I hover over the toilet and it's not long before I puke up what remains of the chocolate ice-cream. And jimmies.

I console myself with the comforts of the old couch, a light blanket, my routine of Saturday afternoon TV and fall asleep again.

As the next babysitting night approaches that following week I begin to worry about Uncle Ron. It seems it's the turning point from which this forty-something relative transitions from the realm of the unnoticed into something else. Something real. Something visceral.

These days my mother works as a nurse assistant while she attends night school to help her get onto a nursing course. The shifts are set around her night classes and vary from 7am-3.30pm and 3.30-11pm, including so many weekends I lose track of when she'll be around. It's just my mother and I living in the house. My parents are split, though not divorced, and Dad lives across town with the new girlfriend and a fancy new leather couch and waterbed. My brother, a couple of years older than me, is in the hospital *again* after another stint of trouble that's led to long-term treatment for his drug problems and his other mental-health issues. By this time he's officially a high-school dropout and there's no sign of return.

It's difficult to recall how much time I actually spend with my mother at this point in our lives, a time when I'm fifteen and can look after myself. *I'm so easy, just leave me in the corner and forget about me.* But something about the prospect of Uncle Ron sends me to her door. The one thing I know I can rely on is the regularity of the beloved naps that follow her day shifts.

Late Tuesday afternoon, the day before my Wednesday night babysitting, I go into her bedroom and nudge her shoulder gently, but with persistence, then hear a murmur. I can't hold it in any longer, so I tell her about some of Uncle Ron's comments, *why haven't you got a boyfriend*, the ice-cream ride. The troubles Uncle Ron and Auntie Peggy are having.

'He said some weird things, like they weren't getting along and stuff.'

Ma continues to lie still, turned on her side facing me in the darkened bedroom with her eyes closed, but I know she's listening to every word.

'I can just say I'm sick this week then I can stop after that, say I got another part-time job or something.' It's a nice, clean way to end it with Uncle Ron. I have it all figured out. There's only silence and I assume she doesn't hear what I say, or she's fallen back to sleep. So I poke her shoulder with my forefinger.

In her groggy voice, eyes still closed, she mumbles, 'Did something happen?'

I breathe in. If I say what really happened, Auntie Peggy might find out and I'll get all the blame. 'He wanted to talk, I guess.' I say nothing about the joint, the booze. About his hand on my knee, his lips on mine, his fingers squeezing my thigh. About the things I don't remember. 'I just don't want to babysit for Auntie Peggy again.'

She sighs. 'You know it's your auntie's only chance to get out. It's her bowling night and she doesn't have anyone else. I'd hate to let her down when she couldn't find anyone else.'

'But Ma. Ma… I told you I don't want to. It's so boring there.'

'Boring?' she says. 'They're your cousins.'

I shrug and look at my nails. She waits for me to say more but of course I don't. I stomp out the room and slam the door instead.

It feels like I'm being tested, placed like a rat in a complicated maze-like structure as an experiment to study problem-solving, patience, and endurance behaviour. Which way will Jo turn? Will she figure out how to get to the other side? How long will it take before she resorts to gnawing at her own tail?

That babysitting night holds no surprises. He makes his next advance in the renovated basement family room where they watch TV, where there's a bar in the corner all set up and ready for mixing drinks. He smiles as he walks towards me.

I tell him I don't need to wait for Auntie Peggy to come home, I can walk with it being so close by.

'No, no. I'll take you home. Don't need to go running off so fast. Auntie Peggy's not coming back for a while.'

Then he moves in fast with a mouth-to-mouth kiss which isn't wholly unpleasant. As he holds my upper arms firmly in his hands, his body reveals a combination of odours I hadn't noticed on our Saturday afternoon ice-cream ride. Up close the smell from Uncle Ron's overalls resembles my father's work shirts, with their layers of unwashed dirt, car grease and oil. My father's a mechanic too, one who likes to wheel and deal on weekends when he buys, repairs and sells second-hand cars.

'There's no point washing them,' Dad says. 'It'll never come out anyway and they'll get just as bad again.'

Uncle Ron's perspiration after a hard day at work creeps through the mask of scented hair cream that makes his straight black hair look shiny and slick. He has, after all, just gone upstairs to *clean up*. From his breath I catch a hint of the Schlitz beer he opened. I get a taste of that and the Lucky Strikes.

It's the first stage of my test. I can react by pushing him away. I could shout, *Stay away from me*. Over time I will re-imagine the catharsis of this scenario, asking myself repeatedly, *Why didn't I do that? What would have happened if I had done that one simple thing?*

But then nothing more would have happened if I hadn't babysat that night. Nothing would have happened if I had refused the ride home on Saturday, if I hadn't worn that short skirt, if I had taken his hand away, if I hadn't smoked that joint, drank all that whisky and Coke. If I hadn't laughed. If I hadn't passed out. None of it is clear in my head. I can't remember what was done or said next and it doesn't matter because none of it would have happened if I was someone else. Nothing would have happened if I could have just disappeared.

As he's driving me home he says he needs to stop at the liquor store for some cigarettes.

Without hesitation, I say, 'I'll walk from there.'

'I'll only be a minute,' he says, a look of concern in his eyes.

'No. I'll walk,' I snap. 'I want to walk a bit. It's fine, I want to.'

I move fast out of the truck and as I'm walking my legs begin to weaken. My knees feel like they may buckle and yet I pick up a faster pace, just about breaking into a clumsy run at one point. I turn around and he is still in the truck at the wheel, just watching me. Is he going to follow me? And suddenly I'm crying, a little baby whimper that turns quickly into a full-blown sob. I pass an elderly couple walking arm in arm together. They look at me with suspicion as if to say, *What have you done?*

'He kissed me this time,' I tell Ma that night. 'Then he drove me home some of the way and I walked from the liquor store.'

'On the lips?' Her face is one big exclamation mark. 'Did he kiss you on the lips?'

'Yes. On the lips. Please, Ma,' I beg. 'Don't make me babysit again. Tell Auntie I have another job or something. Just tell her anything. I can't go back.'

Ma looks breathless. 'Is that everything, Jo? Did he do anything else to you?'

'No.' I can't look her in the eye. 'But, Ma, I'm not going back.'

Then she makes, for her, an unexpected move. It's bold, but naive; she hasn't planned for any of the consequences.

It's later the next day when I discover she called Uncle Ron at work that morning. 'I told him to back off,' she announces to me over supper.

Over the years I've considered what this was supposed to mean. What kind of outcome did she imagine? Did she expect me to continue going there to watch his kids if he did as she instructed, so Auntie Peggy wouldn't lose her bowling night? Was this my mother's own test to herself, her first experiment with a feminist assertion of late 1970s personal-political power? Was she offering herself up as a figure of strength in defence of her youngest born female child? Or, did she now have a dislike, perhaps even an unspeakable hatred, for Uncle Ron for thinking he could take advantage of her Jo? Was it time to show this no-good brother-in-law? *Watch me, Ron. I'll show you who's boss.*

I learn the hard way about my mother's phone call when I am stretched out on the couch after school watching my favourite soap, *General Hospital*. I'm obsessed with the Luke and Laura romance, but I hate the rich-bitch and her sense of entitlement. She doesn't deserve him.

The phone rings. It's Auntie Peggy, for me.

She starts the conversation with a soothing voice. She speaks in such a nice way that I remain reclined and keep one eye on my show. 'Everyone knows he jokes around a lot. That's Uncle Ron,' she says. 'Can you try to tell me everything, Jo? Just think about it, OK?'

In spite of her attempts to limit the damage she asks for more details. I try to find a nice way to recount the oddness around the Saturday ice-cream ride.

'I don't know. He offered me a ride home and then we went out for ice-cream and he told me you and him were having some troubles.'

I don't tell her about the other detours from the nights he drove me home after babysitting. I don't tell her about the joint, the booze or the way he left his hand on my knee where it shouldn't have been. But I should have moved it. Why didn't I move it? *No one will understand.* There's no way around it. Too much is now known.

Auntie Peggy's tone soon grows cold and our conversation doesn't end on a good note. By the end of the call I'm sitting up, bawling as I make my final, pathetic appeal to be heard. *But I didn't, I didn't do anything, Auntie.* To be believed. *I can't remember. Not everything.* It is going nowhere.

Some years later Auntie Peggy will present her ultimatum, the agreement my mother will feel compelled to sign.

Five

'This is all crazy, Ma. She wants you to sign this...this *thing* she's written? She's out of her mind.'

'Oh, I know, I know it's really crazy stuff,' she says, nodding enthusiastically. 'And this is just to make her happy, Jo. I don't believe any of what she said about you. You need to know that, right?'

'Then why, Ma? Why?'

The smile switches off and within a couple of minutes she is weeping quietly through her words. 'She's my sister. It's family. It's so hard. I go to family get-togethers and we're all there and things aren't right. Peggy's different to me, ignores me. And now she's saying she's finished with me if I don't do this.'

It's the first time I've seen my mother cry so much. But rather than feel sorry for her, I'm seething like a frustrated mother when her teenage kids get into a mess and can't find a way out of their own stupidity. Except that I don't want to be kind. All I want to do is thump her. Hard. And what pisses me off the most is the revelation that my mother's worst fear is not that her daughter might have been assaulted by her uncle, or that her depressed, messed-up son might be found dead one morning. No. Her biggest worry is that one of her sisters or brothers will disown her, throw away their history as though they never breathed the same air.

46

But I know that nothing I do will ever change my mother's need for her sister's approval. Ron's never going to try this with me again, that's clear, and signing the stupid disclaimer will somehow make Ma happy. Whatever happens, I know I'm screwed.

'OK,' I say finally. 'Fine. Whatever you want.'

'Your daughter's the one who came on to me,' Uncle Ron had argued in his defence, according to my mother. 'You won't have to say anything to your sister because I'm going to tell my wife the truth about your daughter.'

Apparently he told Auntie Peggy I'd been coming on to him for months; when I waited for her return from bowling I approached him, nestled up to him, tried to kiss him. He tried, like a good, caring uncle to talk some sense into me, he said, to guide me like a loving father, offer me the kind of role model I was lacking. It was all my father's fault, you see, Auntie Peggy said to my mother, for ignoring his responsibilities, and it was my mother's fault for going off to work, night school, by focusing on a career and not her family, which was in a big mess. After all, look what had happened to my brother David. Where were her priorities? Peggy even accused my mother of not being a good Catholic.

The night after my mother's lethal phone call to Ron, her other sister came over to our house.

'It's funny though,' I heard Auntie Josie say in the kitchen, when I was upstairs in my room. 'When I told Phil he said he had always thought Jo was a bit of a flirty type, with all the make-up she wears and those pretty batting eyelashes of hers.'

When I made my way downstairs before going out that evening I saw my father hovering quietly near the stove in his work clothes. On the other side of the room by the fridge stood my mother, seething, pursed lips, jaw clenched. A few years later she would have to wear a mouth-guard at night to stop her from grinding her back teeth down to nothing.

'He's just such an asshole,' my mother said. 'Bastard.'

I looked in my father's direction, expecting to catch a sign of anger, some kind of a reaction. When people pissed him off everyone knew about it.

Our small, mouldy basement housed a hanging punching bag in a corner for his use. When he still lived with us you could often hear the far-away, steady thump of his fists hitting the leather. Sometimes I went down there on my own when my mother wasn't home. I would thwhack the bag hard, build up to a fast whirling momentum that sent sharp electricity through both arms and once broke the skin of my knuckles, drawing blood. My mother's bedroom door near the kitchen had a large dent from where my father's frustrated punch landed one night after my brother was arrested for violent, drunken behaviour and possession of marijuana. It wasn't unusual for both of us to get hit with his back hand or the metal end of Dad's belt when we misbehaved.

Maybe she hoped Dad would save the day, go over to their house, threaten Uncle Ron with a decent, manly heroic fight. Show him who was boss. But none of that was to come. Dad stood there by the kitchen stove wearing his flattest expression, his empty gaze fixed in the direction of the floor, not once casting a glance my way, the girl who was the start of all the trouble. Sweet little JoJo, the storytelling liar. The tease with those pretty batting eyelashes.

When I leave my mother on the evening she tells me about the agreement she wants to sign, I meet my then-boyfriend Mike and tell him the story about Uncle Ron for the first time, the condensed version.

'That's sick, Jo,' Mike says. 'A guy that age taking advantage of a young girl?' Then he adds with a smile, 'Where's he live? I'll mess him up. I can find someone, you know, to mess him up. I don't like the idea of some creep doing that to you.'

'Well. Too late for all that. But that's sweet. You wanting to defend me.'

We hang out at his house, another place in the quiet suburbs, where he lives with his nice parents, sister and brother, but everyone's out for the night. Mike is my first real love, the one who teaches me how to love back. He is the first boyfriend I trust enough to experience an orgasm. Even though he makes me feel uncomfortable when he says, 'I love to watch you when you come,' at the strangest moments in my day I fantasise about him saying this over and over.

That night we agree to take our minds off things, drink a few beers and when we get through those we finish a bottle of white wine, then smoke a joint. I indulge in the gradual loss of myself and embrace the attention he gives my body when we make love on the couch. I am dying the best death I can imagine, as a tender tornado sweeps me up and takes me away to a place where I don't have to look back.

We are so out of it that we wake up later, half dressed, to the sound of his parents coming in at the front of the house.

We are in the extension to the rear where they won't see us. Mike escapes quietly to his bed. I fall into a deep sleep in the spare room and dream I am fifteen years old again, standing outside Auntie Peggy's house. I am screaming, 'Please, Auntie. Please, let me in.' I end up in a battle with a faceless, dark, long-haired girl who is blocking the door. Both of us swing baseball bats frantically as we try to strike each other. Finally, I manage to perfect my aim. With full force, just as I hit her in the face, I see she has turned into me and I wake up.

Six

My eyes open in the evening to the sound of Beth's voice in the kitchen as she speaks loudly to someone on the phone. In spite of the usual discomfort in my bad leg, I leave the cane for the moment. As soon as I open Danielle's bedroom door I catch an inviting smell of something cooking in the oven. Beth comes to the hallway. I give her a quick wave letting her know it's OK not to hang up just because I'm there, but she uses me as her getaway.

'Ma, OK, OK. I have to go now. Jo's up. Yeah, well, she can decide how to manage her own jetlag. I'll see you when you get here, don't worry about it now. OK, bye.' Beth hangs up, sighs, rolls her eyes at me. 'She wants me to let you know that you shouldn't have gone to sleep so long because that's just going to make your jetlag worse.'

We laugh, I agree and we have a quick embrace. I want to hug for longer, but Beth is too practical a person for that. I follow her into the kitchen and soon enough she carries on wiping down the countertops, filling the dishwasher, tidying away.

Beth looks good and always impresses me. She's just turned fifty-four, and made a pact with herself to lose weight when she was diagnosed with type 2 diabetes. After finalising the divorce it was like she saw some kind of spiritual light that told her she could sing another song, compose an entirely new arrangement going forwards. I was envious but I wasn't quite ready to get rid of my husband for inspiration. She soon became like one of those before and after women you read about in Weight Watchers' success stories. She started waking up around 5.30am, walked the dog for around thirty minutes, working up to a speedy pace, then when back home would do a pilates workout DVD for another thirty minutes. Soon she progressed into a jogging routine, starting slow but worked up to full running in hour-long stretches. By this time old Bailey was finding it hard to keep up with her. Before long she was signing up for 5K, then 10K races, then half-marathons, yes, thirteen miles, each time picking up the pace. Now's she's a lean machine. I've warned her not to lose any more weight or she'll risk having that big-head-on-a-skeletal-frame look.

Beth's mother Jean arrives, striding into the kitchen with a radiance to her clear, Mediterranean-blue eyes, her well-managed waistline showing only a hint of love for a cupcake or two. She's the picture of health, the kind of attractive senior woman you might see in an American commercial with her WASP-ish husband enjoying a glass of wine on a terrace overlooking a sandy beach. She holds out a small bunch of white peonies. 'No, they're not for you, Beth, they're for Jo. I'm so, so sorry, Jo, about your mother. She was something special.' She gives me a squeeze, rubs my back, and we both clear a few tears from our eyes.

Danielle's right behind her. I can't seem to take my eyes off her face, flawless in her plumped youth, that little brush of eye-liner with its simple feathered wing-tip at the ends. I thank her once again for giving up her room for me.

'You've all gone beyond the call of duty,' I say, feeling the releasing effect of that second glass of wine, which prompts more tears and then more offers of kindness from them.

For a moment I sit quietly with my glass, catch a waft of the peonies now and then, watch, smile, listen to the Connelly women some more, and think to myself, *Oh, this is what a nice family life is like.*

Beth's way of forgetting about work and relaxing before bed is to watch TV. It's all fast-moving, this channel-hopping – will it be *The Good Wife* or *Modern Family*? – along with those long commercial breaks promoting the profit-seeking potential of the pharmaceutical industry. All you need is a friendly chat with your healthcare provider, not to mention a damn good insurance package, and the choices are endless, along with the long list of side-effects, including death.

'Ooh, this looks like a good one. Tom Cruise. We like Tom Cruise, don't we, Jo?' says Beth, eyes steady on the screen. 'Yes we do,' she confirms for me.

It's the more recent version of the actor, playing the role of a bandana-wearing rock star. We catch it from the middle of a scene in which he's in a room with a pool table. He's moving with serious intent towards an attractive woman who wears her long blonde hair in a big 1980's style. Suddenly Cruise breaks into the classic Foreigner anthem 'I Want to Know What Love Is' that we recognise straightaway from our younger days.

'What? What the hell's going on?' Beth shouts.

'Oh my God, is that really Tom Cruise singing?'

Soon enough, they're tearing their clothes off in high comic fashion while serenading each other.

Beth jumps from her cosy spot on the couch, grabs the remote and sings into it, stroking her hair, moving her hands down along her hips and to the top of her leg suggestively. I sing back and try to mimic the sexy actress's moves and carry on until the end of the number when the blonde falls off the table and there's a commercial break.

We look at each other and start laughing. We laugh so much I'm left with a stiffness around my jaw and the realisation I've actually lost some bladder control. I race to the bathroom, returning as Danielle enters the room wondering what's going on. We calm down, enough to convince her to watch the scene with us on playback.

'It's this amazing scene with Tom Cruise who looks like he's really singing,' says Beth.

'But he is really singing!'

We fall about. Danielle just stares at us.

'Anyway it's one of the most amazing things you'll ever witness in your whole entire life!' squawks Beth.

Danielle joins us with some willing curiosity and sits quietly through the scene, witnessing more of our wonder and hysterics. When it's over she offers her verdict. 'This is crap. I'm going to bed,' she says, and leaves the room.

As the night continues we drink more wine than Beth has allowed herself in a long time.

'I'd like to say I'll hate you in the morning for doing this to me, Jo, but I could never hate you for anything. I'll just hate myself instead.'

We laugh more, we laugh harder. My mouth aches. It's a welcome release after all the built-up sadness I've been holding.

'This is like old times, Beth. Remember all those nights we dreamed about our future? Did you ever think it would end up like this?'

'Married, a kid, divorced, over-worked, constantly counting calories. You leaving me to live in England. No, I didn't imagine this. But it could be worse, I can't complain. And going to London…that was the best thing you could have done for yourself. How was I going to try and stop you? And by that time I got myself married. Hah, look where that got me.'

As teenagers Beth and I were inseparable. That was before she met Gary, her first serious boyfriend in high school. I was still in the picture, often as the best friend who had to get fixed up with one of his friends so we could go out on double-dates. But in truth I was always jealous. Not because Beth had a boyfriend and I didn't, but because I wanted her all to myself. We use to fantasise about the future when we had good jobs and could afford to get a nice place together. Sometimes we'd joke about living together as lesbians, adopting kids to make our family, spending our old age together. I'll never know how Beth really felt about the lesbian thing, beyond it being a shared joke, but at the time I pondered it secretly. I knew for sure that when Beth became serious about boyfriends, my emotions would take over; bursts of anger at my mother, sudden nasty turns at someone else in class, snide remarks to Beth about Gary, urges to find ways to break them up.

During one of the many nights I stayed overnight at Beth's, I remember waking from an intense dream. It felt as though the dream's events had just happened in real time. In it I was lying with Beth in her bed, just as we were that night after we came home from a party. We were both drunk and silly, nudging up to each other closer until we interlocked our legs and swung a free arm around each other. Through laughter and tears we said how much we loved each other as best friends and we began to kiss, slowly and carefully. I took the lead and covered her body with kisses and more touching. I didn't remember anything else except that I woke up in the early hours when it was still dark and felt wet in my groin, Beth asleep next to me, still wearing the nightie she wore to bed, the same one I remember lifting in the dream.

I never mentioned what I thought must have been a dream to her and it never happened again. I assumed it was my unconscious taking me to a place I wasn't brave enough to visit in my waking world.

I've often asked myself what kinds of struggles we would have been up against if we did decide to try this out for real, declaring our love to our families, our friends. Or maybe we could have escaped somewhere else, some happy-hippy town out in California and done things our way. That was where people could be free, wasn't it? But making realities out of fantasies is not so simple.

Our excessive wine-drinking and retro-music extravaganza send me to sleep fast. At around 2am I wake up from a dream where I'm roaming around in my old high school's quiet, grey hallways in search of a classroom. I'm scheduled to teach an art lesson, but I'm late and know I'll get into trouble with the principal, the same horrible man who had the job years ago when I was a student there. I start running as fast as I can, conscious I have no cane to slow me down, but my new speed frightens me. After I make my way to the top of a steep staircase I begin to fall, pinging sensation at the chest.

I wake up gasping for breath with my usual nagging leg pain. Sleep doesn't return fast enough. I take a pill for the pain, take another 10mg of the melatonin Beth offered me earlier to help with the jetlag. Still an hour and a half later, I lie in bed staring at the ceiling, ruminating.

High school. In my last two years there vivid dreams, mostly nightmares, took over many nights, waking me frequently and leading to long periods of insomnia. For some time I feared the idea of sleep altogether. The fright around what might be waiting for me when I lost conscious control was overwhelming. Could someone break into the house? Did I remember to lock the door? Was my mother coming home that night? Was I alone again?

Dozing in class was a common occurrence. I could get away with it sometimes with sympathetic or otherwise uncaring teachers, but on other occasions I had to pay for my inattention when I was made to stand for the rest of the lesson, given detentions or extra work. Never once did any teacher question my tired eyes, the persistent under-eye bags or why I suffered somnolence at such a young age.

My nightmares showed a clear pattern. I sometimes suffered from sleep paralysis in which I was frozen in a vulnerable position, unable to cry out. In my dreams I was often at risk of physical attack by some faceless man. Variations of scenes would play like the conventions of a thriller or horror film. In the dream I would be lying in my own bed. I'd be woken by the sound of an intruder entering the house or coming up the stairs to my room. In the dream I would sometimes sit up and struggle to focus my eyes on something but couldn't because the room was completely black. The sound of footsteps and heavy breathing would close in. I'd try my hardest to scream but no sound would emerge, until the shadow of an overwhelming male figure with no facial features hovered over me, ready to pounce.

Nightmares continued in the years after high school when I was working full-time, going out with Mike and sharing an apartment with two other young working women, one a lonely cat lover and the other a cool, wise one in her late twenties who worked at a bank in Boston. Unfortunately for him, Mike was frequent witness to my night terrors.

'This shit's a bit weird, Jo. Maybe you should see someone about it.'

When my nights and days became too difficult to manage I agreed with Mike that it was time I took some control, so I did the only thing I thought was right at the time; I joined the growing number of Americans in therapy. I searched the telephone books for a local shrink that my health insurance would cover and hoped to get some pills to help me sleep.

Location and convenience were my main priorities. Man, woman, it didn't matter. I pretty much picked the first name that fitted the bill. My first session with the suited, pasty-complexioned, white-haired man, who appeared to be in his sixties and whose name I don't remember, started with a summary of why I was there.

'Can sleeping pills help maybe to stop the nightmares?' I asked. 'They're getting a bit out of hand.'

Without making any small talk, he took out his notepad. 'Tell me about your family,' he said, not looking at me while making notes already. 'Tell me everything.'

When I started the sessions I had already been enrolled in night classes at community college. Sociology 101 was the course that introduced me to what families like ours must have looked like to an outsider, those professors and writers of all those books on our reading list. I discovered quickly that we were a typical working-class case study. We owned our own unique differences, yes, but basically I began to understand everything that had happened in my life for what it was. I learned also that not all families were like mine, in spite of similar loony-bin cases in the neighbourhood where I grew up. The exclusive mental-health hospital where my brother was lucky enough to stay as a frequent guest on Ma's health insurance, after one of his depressive lows, showed me how different many lives were beyond the confines of our social demographic.

'You wouldn't believe who his father is,' Dave whispered excitedly one day about a fellow patient. When he earned daytime leaving privileges he was invited to their homes on weekends, those patients who became his friends. 'His mother made this wacky dish with chicken and peanut sauce. Can you imagine that? Chicken with fucking peanut sauce.'

With a confidence that surprised me, I listed my life events to the shrink. I started with my parents, my mother's teenage pregnancy, their work in factories, my mother's later start in nursing. I assumed I would get around to telling him about the trouble with Auntie Peggy and Uncle Ron.

I said, 'My parents got married too young, obviously. They're kind of split up at the moment. They don't live together, but seem to end up in bed every now and then, when it suits my father, that is. But he doesn't hang around much. He's proud of that, too. "Everybody knows I ain't much of a family man," he says, like it's something to be proud of.'

'Do you want them to stay together?'

'No. There's no point. But it doesn't really matter what I want. Never has. So.'

Then I gave him the lowdown about my brother. 'OK, so Dave was a juvenile delinquent when he was young, not too surprising, I guess, considering. He was a high-school dropout, has had lots of problems with drugs. Now they say he has manic depression too. Looks like one of his overdoses was more like an attempted suicide.'

He interrupted me to ask, 'How old was he when this first happened, the overdose suicide attempt?'

'Fifteen maybe. I can't remember. Around that time.'

'And you were?'

'Thirteen, I guess.'

He continued taking notes. 'Go on. Continue.' he said, eyes on his notepad.

'The hospital said at the time he had a personality disorder and depression, obviously. But he's off drugs now and on meds for the manic depression, and managed to pass his high-school equivalency. And now he's doing a course in air conditioning, heating and refrigeration. There's supposed to be good money in that.'

'He's spent a long time in the hospital then. I suppose there was a lot of attention on him. Is that right?'

'I guess.' This irritated me. 'That's why I'm here. So I can have my own therapy. Not for him, or them. So I can get rid of these nightmares.'

'The faceless men. Yes, we'll get to that. What about grandparents?'

I offered the shrink a short story about my father's parents. I cried when I told him about my father's mother, Nonna, and the time I saw bruises on her arms that my grandfather had put there.

'You're close to this grandmother then,' the shrink said.

'Yes. She's like a mother to me.'

'In a way that your mother isn't?'

I sat on that one for a quiet moment. 'I don't know,' I said. 'I'm not sure what you mean.'

During the third session I got the feeling the shrink had heard it all before. This insight surfaced after I recalled one of my latest nightmares and then I noticed he had fallen asleep. At first I thought I had it wrong. Of course, he must have been hanging on to every gripping word I uttered about my tragic life. I stopped talking and waited. His head had begun to droop forward, so I could see the thinning circle of hair revealing the shiny-skin scalp. The bifocals resting near his hairline began to slide down. Once they dropped beyond his nose and onto his mouth he woke with a sudden jerk. I waited for him to say something, like, *Oh dear, I'm so sorry, how rude of me.* But he just looked at me as he adjusted his glasses and rubbed his eyes.

'You fell asleep,' I said, pleasantly, in the courteous way my mother had taught me, at the same time trying to practise a new, much-needed level of assertion, which may have been noticeable in my tone. 'Did you know you fell asleep?' I asked, smiling.

The shrink held his accusing eyes on mine with a long stare. 'Are you angry?' he said.

That stumped me.

He coughed and straightened his posture, although not enough to hide his fat stomach. 'You're upset that I can't be who you want me to be,' he declared.

And there it was. My first experience with my very own shrink and I couldn't keep him interested or awake for long enough to offer me any useful advice or to even hand over a prescription for sleeping pills. I hadn't even got on to the nightmares and what he proposed to do about them. I was being tested again. That night I knew I was finished with him. My plan was to walk away from this one and start another search for a new shrink. I could do it, I could have control.

Seven

Constance Rosenfelt. Tall, thin, Jewish. In spite of her full head of shoulder-length silver hair, it was difficult to guess her age. Her complexion was olive without the need for much make-up except for a dab of subtle lipstick and blusher. Her wide, dark-brown eyes sparkled when she smiled, a nice thing she did often, no holding back. She offered clarity, a ticket to a world of sanity that I almost resisted at first. She had admirable posture, something I tried to emulate in my sessions with her. It was rare to see her wearing pants, but they did something for her.

Over time I trusted Constance completely. I was like a long piece of yarn let loose, twisted and torn in places that seemed beyond repair. But Constance knew exactly where to tug and unravel, eventually guiding me to a point where I felt more rounded and secure. I talked about my parents, what it was like growing up with a brother like Dave, and I confronted my inner battles with him. I told Constance every detail I could remember about what happened with Uncle Ron, my aunt's disclaimer, how I gave my mother my blessing. And it was during that session when I was forced to examine the hole inside me that had swelled with helplessness and regret.

'You didn't see him mixing the drinks?' she asked.

'Well, no. I mean, I didn't see how much whisky he added but I knew they were pretty strong and I just went along with it.'

She hesitated, then added, 'Did you ever think he might have drugged you that day? Put something in your drink? It's likely too, Jo, that he may not have mixed any whisky in his Coke if you didn't see him making the drinks.'

As she was talking my stomach began to ache. How could I have not realised it then? My aunt had suffered with insomnia in those days, never as bad as mine, but she always had a prescription of sleeping pills. She wouldn't have noticed if Ron had taken one.

As this sped through my mind another horror descended on me.

'My period was late after that,' I said, then held my hands over my stomach. 'And when my period did come…' I stopped and closed my eyes. 'I remember it was the worst one ever, I had to take a few days off school I felt so awful. I felt awful for weeks. Do you think…do you think I could've been pregnant? Do you think maybe it could have been an early miscarriage? Can that happen?'

She was silent, her expression sympathetic, then nodded. 'I suppose it's a possibility, Jo.'

'Oh, God. Ohhhhh God.' I closed my eyes again, hunched over and wept till I emptied her box of tissues.

It was clear, we acknowledged, there was nothing we could do about this now. Years later, there was no proof of any crime. It was our guesswork, assumptions; it would always be his word against mine, the fifteen-year-old tease, the liar. No, I told Constance, I would not tell my mother, or anyone else. There was no point. *Never, never, never,* I insisted, would any of these revelations leave the walls of her office.

After I'd been seeing Constance a while, she told me she had a husband and children. The daughter was a bit younger than I, the son a bit older. At some point she had offered to see clients at her home in the desirable Lexington area. I expected it would be a worthy abode, but nothing prepared me for the colonial-style house with two white columns in the front framing the entrance. It was set back off the street with a long driveway large enough to accommodate about five cars. I imagined there must have been an in-ground pool in the back.

As she led me through to her office I glanced into a room lined with bookshelves and a white grand piano. It reminded me of stage sets I'd seen in classic Hollywood films. We passed another smaller TV room where her daughter was resting, covered in a blanket, with a box of tissues on her lap. She was home from college with a red nose, flu, and was trying to recover. She offered me a genuine smile. We had a friendly exchange. I felt certain I said the right things, that she wouldn't think I was some weirdo with head issues. I could pass as a young working woman with a few stresses to overcome. *She looked nice, Mom, like she was normal. Not like the other guy who was here yesterday.*

When I left that day – it was a sunny and mild early spring evening, which I remember brightened my mood – I understood that I had reached a new place in life. I had no feelings of envy or resentment towards Constance and her family for what they had in comparison to me. I knew I didn't have to hate them just because I wanted a good life for myself too, a respectable career, a smart, decent husband who would love me, a beautiful home, yes, maybe one with lots of books and a piano. And a pool would be nice. I wasn't so sure about the children.

I am sure about one thing. Constance cared, maybe enough to even love me. I could tell by the way she looked at me. Her patience when I must have been, I don't know…impossible. When I think of her these days I notice a swelling sensation around my nose. I imagine Constance could have died by now, but in reality she may have been only several years older than my mother. She may actually still be alive and well, enjoying a good old life with grandchildren by her poolside. Would her mind ever wander back to our sessions when she's having her morning coffee, when she's shopping in the mall and sees someone who looks so much like her girl, Jo O'Brien? Would she miss me as much as I miss her?

Constance made me work hard. It started right from the beginning when I told her about the shrink who fell asleep.

'Oh, yes, I know him. He's a colleague of mine. Yes, I've known him for years,' she said, the small world of shrinks being what it is, I guess.

Before the end of that first session, she paused, folded her elegant hands together and said, 'Now Jo, I think it's a good idea you see him one last time so you can formally end the therapist/client relationship. You can be as honest as you like but it's important to have closure.'

I resisted. 'You mean you won't see me again if I don't do it?' Why was a woman forcing me to do a thing like this when it was usually stupid men doing the stupid things?

'I would very much like to continue, Jo, but it's important that you do this first. And as I know him professionally it wouldn't be right if I knowingly took a client of his without his knowledge.'

Like it or not, if I wanted to see her again I had to go through this therapy rite of passage.

So I returned to the first shrink's office the next week and told him the news. I was dumping him for someone else, a better prospect. A woman. It felt good to be the dumper and not the one being dumped.

'It's not personal. Her office is more convenient, near work. I'm just trying to be practical,' I lied.

'It looks like you're running away from your issues,' he said, then adjusted his glasses. 'It's a common problem with clients who begin to confront challenges in therapy. They run away when it gets difficult.'

I thought about Constance, pictured her angelic smile, and held my ground. I loathed him. Educated shrink he might have been, but underneath the framed degree awards on the wall, the suit and tie, the bifocals, he was a selfish, greedy, cocksucker out for the one and only, just like the others.

Eight

Around the time I reached puberty, close to age twelve, when I suddenly packed on weight everywhere, grew a girl-moustache and struggled with tampons, my brother taught me how to French kiss. He instructed me carefully on the right ways to move my tongue and lips. He showed me by demonstrating on himself what to do with my hands at the same time.

'Move 'em up and around the guy's chest, his shoulders, through his hair, then later, not straightaway, go for the crotch if you like him enough. Don't do it until you're older and not straightaway or he'll think you're a slut. And you're not the slutty type. Make 'em beg for it.'

At the time I guessed he may have had some experience himself, but it was probably minimal. He was a bit taller than other boys his age, but lanky to a fault, with his knobbly elbows and ostrich knees seeming too bulbous for his limbs. He had the gift of soft, pastel-blue eyes from my mother's side of the family and brown, wavy hair that he had tried to highlight with Sun In hair lightener. The way he did it, instead of adding a subtle, sun-kissed look, he looked like he was wearing a blond hair-piece. To make matters worse, he tried giving himself a haircut. That was when all the fun started. He also had the misfortune of early-teenage acne, made worse from all the picking. This left him with pockmarks that stayed. I caught him one day in the bathroom trying to cover them with our mother's foundation.

'What the fuck are you staring at? Fuck off,' he shouted, after which he quickly washed it all off, only to start applying it again.

He couldn't shake his tendency to fall frequent victim to seemingly harmless jokes, teasing, and the odd gruelling bullying session from the other guys and even some of the girls who joined in. He was a necessary figure in the gang; the one who was always willing to take risks the others wouldn't, the one who could find money to score the booze and drugs they wanted, the one who knew how to party and make everyone laugh, the one who became the most disposable.

Our parents' bedroom was directly below ours, next to the kitchen. The bedroom that Dave and I shared was large enough for two single beds, a chest of drawers each for clothes, and we had a reasonable-sized shared closet. A low wall split the room some of the way down the middle. Dave slept on the side closest to the stairs. He had to walk through my side to get to the shared built-in closet. I wouldn't have described our relationship as ever being close, but we shared sibling escape fantasies that materialised in different ways over our young lives.

When we were younger we would often sleep together in one of our beds and reveal our daydreams about what our lives would be like if we were rich and sent to an expensive boarding school where we could learn how to ride horses, speak a foreign language and have European vacations. To make this fantasy plausible we'd have to be adopted into another family, a wealthy one that was desperate to have us.

'It's weird though,' Dave once whispered. 'Are there really people out there who actually *want* kids that bad that they'd pay to adopt them? Maybe they're just pervs or sickos.'

As we grew older we draped a couple of old sheets over some string to create more privacy. Curtain or no curtain though, this set-up had its obvious limitations as we grew older. David's masturbating habit felt relentless at times, and he took any opportunity he could, whether I was occupying my side of the room or not. It was when it happened in the middle of the hottest, most sweltering summer days that I couldn't quite understand, when he'd crawl into bed facing the wall, cover himself with a blanket, make muffled heavy breathing sounds then fall asleep afterwards – for hours, it seemed. Sometimes I wanted to tap him on the shoulder and say, 'Are you OK Dave? Is everything alright?' But I thought it best to keep my distance.

There was another time that serves as a difficult reminder of the growing anger I harboured towards my brother for being who he was and for my parents for being who they were: too broke to buy a bigger place where I could have my own bedroom. It only happened one time and that was certainly enough. I must have been around thirteen and sleeping heavily one weekend night when my brother came home late after a party, drunk and clearly drugged up. He woke me after he stumbled fast through the door, which banged the chest of drawers. It wasn't unusual for him to make this kind of entrance although most times he fell into his bed and slept through the rest of the night. On this occasion he pulled at the room's divider sheets, causing the string to break, tripped over the fabric and ended up on my side, crawling over to my bed, mumbling my name, asking me if I was awake. I turned away from him, shouted through my blanket for him to go away, but he persisted and climbed in with me.

'Come on JoJo, I want a hug. *Please* JoJo, I need a hug.' He didn't wait for an answer, slid quickly under the sheets and began running his cold hands clumsily along my arm, waist and thigh while I shifted to nudge him away. 'You're so warm… It's nice, yeah, that's nice.' He moved in closer and held my upper body tight. His speech then grew incoherent. 'No, don't do that,' he said when I struggled. 'No, I can't…wait, no, wait,' he said with agitation, his desperate tone mounting.

Soon there was no more talk, but a concentrated effort on his part as he let go of me while he unzipped his jeans. He then grabbed my hand, and placed it inside his underwear. I was able to free myself at some point but was left with the awful memory of the rough texture of his moist pubic hair and the smooth shaft of his hard penis on my hand. His efforts didn't stop there. I fought with him and tried to get out of the bed but he cornered me, gripping my shoulders and neck. He pressed his cold face and wet mouth hard on my back while he pleasured himself with his hand. He started to grunt again senselessly.

'Don't do that. No. Fuck. Fuck you. *Fuck*,' he said.

He mumbled more things I couldn't understand and after it was over he fell back and slept quickly. None of my nudges, whacks, even punches would wake him at that point. I moved downstairs to the couch and tried to sleep again but couldn't. Each time I dozed I'd wake up soon after, startled.

The next afternoon when he dragged himself to the kitchen I glared at him across the table, expecting him to acknowledge what had happened. It was just the two of us in the empty house.

'What the hell were you on last night?' I asked.

'What do you mean? Nothing. I wasn't on nothing.'

I locked my eyes on his while he stared into his coffee.

'What?' he said, looking up.

'You don't remember anything? The sheets coming down. You getting in my bed.' I paused. 'You're an asshole.'

'And you're a fucking bitch. Yeah, I woke up in your bed, saw the sheets. So what, I was fucked up.' He stood and headed towards the medicine drawer.

I watched him fumbling through the bottles and packets of Band Aids. After anticipating naively that he'd offer something more in return, some recognition of what he did, maybe even a tiny apology, I realised that Dave most likely recollected everything, and that he knew, while he'd been sipping his coffee and smoking his Marlboros, that I was aware he was lying. I understood also that he expected me to accept this, to succumb to the idea that it was my job to keep my mouth shut and go along with it. This was the way things were in the O'Brien household.

And yet this was the same brother, my one and only sibling, to whom, when I was around nine, I had planned to hand myself over, every last inch of my being, in trust, when we decided to run away together.

We had talked about it in low voices, almost whispers, across our shared bedroom the night before while our parents watched TV downstairs. We confirmed our plan to pack up and go after an eventful family evening meal. It was Friday. My father was collecting a special McDonald's treat. By the time the food was laid on the table and we started to tuck in, it appeared eleven-year-old Dave felt a bit short-changed with his portion. He'd been expecting something big, the works, something special like a juicy Big Mac with large fries, apple pie and milkshake, all the things my parents had and we weren't allowed. I guess I knew otherwise. His shrivelled single burger with soggy pickle and slab of ketchup on a cold, plain bun and small fries was a let-down. Mine was too, but I knew better. I was keeping quiet.

'Hey, why do you and Ma have the shakes and apple pies?' he shouted. 'What about us? Why can't I have an apple pie? I'm hungry. I want an apple pie too.'

All mouths were busy munching except for Dave's.

He continued, this time louder. 'I want an apple pie.'

Before he could finish the last word the back of my father's hand swung fast across the table and struck Dave's mouth. The force drew blood, a trickle mixed with saliva that crept out of the corner. Dave wailed through his tears as a pool of the red stuff filled up and bubbled in the middle of his bottom lip. His pale complexion next to the blood reminded me of the look of vampires I'd seen in the movies.

I glanced at Ma. At times like this she always managed to hold that same frozen, hollow expression, looking downward.

'I just want apple pie,' Dave cried.

'I don't need this shit. I don't need it after work,' Dad shouted back, stood, leaned over and sent another hard smack his son's way, this time higher up near the cheek and nose.

Dave's crying stopped at some point and he ate what he was given after my mother shared some of her fries. Otherwise she stayed mute. Her reaction never seemed to change much. She would sit at the kitchen table with that look on her face. I told myself there was a reason for this, for her silence, for her inability to shout, *Stop, Jimmy, please, just stop it now, don't hurt my babies.* I knew there was something holding her back, because there were other times, those days and nights when my father wasn't around, when her eyes told us she held something else inside her heart.

'We'll show 'em when we go and don't come back,' Dave muttered that night. I heard his anger but his voice was steady. He'd had enough. I'd had enough. We had to stick together.

'Yeah. They won't even miss us. Probably won't even know we're gone,' I said. 'What will happen if days go by and they don't notice we're gone?'

'All the more reason to go.'

We put a lightweight bag together that I was in charge of carrying. We both had a change of underwear for a couple of days, any kind of snacks we could find – crackers, potato chips, cookies – and as much allowance money and small change as we could pull together. Then we set out, me depending on my big brother to lead the way.

Our light jackets for the fall season seemed enough when we started but it soon grew chillier. An opaque grey sheet smothered the sky, there was a smell of damp cold in the air and I wondered what we would do if it started to rain. Dave led us south on Main Street with the intention of getting us to the centre of Boston eventually. I tried to keep up with his fast walk but tired quickly. He remained quiet, his eyes darting side to side, as if he was checking to see if we were being watched. His lower lip and cheek showed some swelling with a faint dark blue-violet bruise. It was enough to remind us why we were out there.

In total, we must have walked about forty long minutes before I said I needed the bathroom. I worried about this. There was no plan for this sort of thing. 'A number two,' I whispered to confirm the urgency.

We could see a local shopping plaza nearby across the main road and Dave said I could go into the Friendly's restaurant. He waited outside but they wouldn't let me use the facilities. I tried the local department store, then the doughnut place and had no luck there either. I went back to Friendly's and tried to sneak in but was caught and sent away. They kept a special eye out for kids like us.

'Just go behind there.' Dave pointed to the area behind the stores where trucks delivered goods.

'But…but I don't have toilet paper.'

We walked around to the back and saw a row of large trash bins and dumpsters near the fence area where there were lots of trees on the other side. Making sure no one was around I stood behind the bins, unzipped and pulled down my pants, squatted, felt the cold wind on my skin, and relieved myself as fast as I could. I felt sick at the sight of what I had left. The smell, combined with the odour of decomposing food, made me gag. Feeling like a filthy stray animal, I crept away, head down. When I reached Dave I started to weep.

'God, you're so pathetic,' he said with disgust, not looking at me.

'What if we have to go again? And then again?' I cried, trailing behind him.

Dave said nothing. Shortly after that he turned around and led us back in the direction of home.

I forgave my brother for being mean that day, but he never owned up about trying to force himself on me that drug-induced night when I was thirteen, and I never forgave him for that.

Nine

Disappearing is different to escaping. Escape implies that the person will surface again at some point in a clever Houdini-like move. To disappear is to make a claim for permanence. Once you decide on it, there's no turning back.

My attempt to permanently remove myself occurred over a bottle of aspirin. It was another idea Dave and I considered together after my father belted the both of us one night. My mother had caught us smoking. We begged her not to tell him but knew we were wasting our breath. Dave and I made a pact to do it together after school that day, although for some reason, I can't recall why, Dave backed out. I do remember how much that irritated me. It's one of those episodes where a lot of details from that time get murky. What Dave did next, what I did next, what my mother did next, what my father did next. When was the time Dave started to get into trouble with school? When did he first go away then come back, then go again? When did things begin to look like they were getting better before they got bad again?

It is a full bottle of Bayer aspirin from the mirrored-front medicine cabinet in the bathroom. I have it in my hands, look at my reflection, challenge myself to see how long I can hold my gaze without blinking. What will happen? How long will it take before I slip away? No one will know. They'll say she died peacefully, such a nice way to go, in her sleep. *She had such an angelic expression. A pretty young thing, wasn't she, yes a bit pudgy but that was just baby fat. Only the good die young, you know.* It doesn't take much energy to make the final move, after counting around thirty of them. *Yes, that should be enough.* But the uncoated surface of the pills makes them hard to swallow; they keep getting stuck on their way down, leaving a chalky, acidic trace at the back of my throat. I slug lots of water to help ingest more than one at a time. I stare for a long time at the mirror, waiting, close my eyes, open them again in search of something. *Give me a sign, Jo. Do you want to live, or don't you? What do you want, Jo? Tell me. I don't know. Tell me. I have no idea. It's too late now. I'm done.*

I move to the couch, get the cushion all comfy and lie down to prepare for my dreams. Dave comes home before I doze.

I tell him, 'I did it, Dave. Remember we talked about it? I did it. I'm going to sleep now.'

His anger shakes me up. 'You…you stupid girl,' he shouts, hovering over me. 'That's so *stupid*, because once they find out they'll put *you* in the loony bin and want to lock you there for ever.' He won't stop, just keeps screaming louder and louder, on and on and on. His mouth is moving rapidly, trembling, spitting. He doesn't make any sense. How can he breathe? His eyes want to kill me. 'Ma'll be home soon and she can deal with you. You can't let them know about this, ever.'

'I'm just gonna go to sleep. It's OK. It'll be OK, I'll just sleep.'

I try to drift into my much-wanted sleep where I'll be taken away. Where I can float weightlessly, be carried by the clouds into that place the nuns at school and church talk about, that somewhere called heaven where an illuminating, perfect God is waiting to take me into his loving arms. But will he forgive? I've done a bad, very bad thing. I am forever doing terrible, unforgiveable things, but God and Jesus are supposed to forgive us for our misdeeds, especially if we confess and say our penance, those fifty Hail Marys and more. I am a dirty, rotten-to-the-core girl, just like the nuns have accused me of being, especially the third-grade nun who caught me talking again when I shouldn't have. The one who saw me, at the corner of her eye, saw the *brazen and bold as brass*, *Joanna O'Brien*, and another girl, practising a kiss (long before Dave tried to teach me). We were as bold as brass together, leaning across the aisle to meet our faces in the middle and touching each other's noses, then the tips of our tongues, not the lips – what a strange tickling sensation – while the kids behind us giggled. Sister was writing out maths equations with her back turned. But God and nuns see everything at all times. *You disgusting little thing. You are dirtier than dirty and will pay for it.* I know this, they've told me this, but still I can't seem to stop myself. I am willing to pay the price. Punish me, hit me, hurt me. Go on, slam my head against the blackboard again. Still, I pray every night that God will take this evil out of me once and for all. Please let me wake up one day with a purity I have never known. But it doesn't happen. He's not listening. This act, the pills, will kill the devil growing inside me. The jury is still out on whether God will forgive.

Before any sleep comes the stomach suffers, tidal waves of nausea come and go, a piercing ringing sensation cuts through my ears and head. My eyesight blurs and I'm dizzy. My body tingles all over. I am fascinated with the numbness in my fingertips and keep rubbing my thumb across them to see if they are still there.

'You're as white as a ghost, but you don't have a temperature,' my mother says when she comes home from her job at the shoe factory down the road. Her fingers look dry. It's from sorting the different colour shoes and laces. I feel their calluses when she sets her hand on my forehead. 'Do you have any pain? It's probably a bug.'

I go to bed later and puke into a big pot, then wait for sleep, puke again, pray for sleep, puke, puke, puke again till nothing but saliva then dry heaves. At one point I see Dave peering over from his side of the room. He wipes his eyes, stares at me, and walks back to his bed. I pray to dream of heaven that night but it doesn't come, just dehydration and a headache that feels as though my brain has been kicked by a sadistic soldier in metal-toe combat boots. The tingling and buzzing through my ears never ceases. I have visions of a grim, cold purgatory. God is showing me a thing or two. *That'll teach you.*

My mother takes me to the doctor in the morning. As he hovers over to listen to my chest I see a clump of light hairs at the tip of his nostril. The flesh of double chin hangs over the top of his buttoned shirt and tie and wiggles when he moves. For a quick second I wonder how this happens to men when they get old, but my weakness stops me from caring.

'Hmm, you don't look too good. Need fluids.' Wow, he's a genius. 'Give her lots of fluids. Must be flu, something viral. Hard to know with these things. Better stay home from school this week.'

Hard to know. *You can't let them know.* None of you want to know anything.

Ten

The next morning at Beth's is a slow start after my difficulty sleeping. For a long while I stay in bed gazing at the bars of sunlight creeping through the spaces between the window blinds. I count the number of slats, once, twice, three times, till I begin feeling dozy again. At the risk of falling back into dreamland I force myself at 11.30am to get moving when I hear Beth and Danielle in the kitchen.

'Well, hello and good morning,' Beth says, her happy voice too loud for my waking ears, as I step into the room.

A quick reminder of Jon's frequent question pops into my mind: *Why do Americans have to bloody shout so much?*

'I was going to get you up before I went food shopping, but you were really out of it so I just thought I'd let you sleep.'

'You know me with this horrible jetlag. I fell asleep OK at the start but then woke up a little later and that was that. Even after all that wine and an extra melatonin. And now my head's paying the price.'

'Yeah, well, thanks to your bad influence, that wine put a dent in my run this morning. But you know, I always say,' she sighs, extending her arms over her head to begin a stretch, 'some exercise is better than none.'

I envy Beth for her determination and persistence. She's out there no matter what, rain or shine, keeping up the fight without any breaks. There are some times though, like now, in my hungover, fatigued state, when I'd like to take a swing at that bouncy holier-than-thou attitude.

'I think it's time for a good dose of something for this damn leg pain,' I say, searching for some pity. *Poor me.*

'Is it bad today?'

'You know, when it builds up, yeah.'

'How about a little massage?' Beth says.

'Oh my God, my mom gives the best leg rubs,' Danielle says, touching her face in wonder. 'When I've overdone it with training she just finds the aches and does her magic. It's *amazing.*'

Beth's usually been too busy before to give me a massage so I'm a bit taken by surprise.

'Maybe later,' I say.

'No, let's do it now,' says Beth, clapping her hands. 'Come on. I'll get my table. Won't take too long.'

When Beth first lost all the weight she took a massage course and really got into it. She was interested at first in self-massage techniques to help recover after her training runs. Then she offered massages to family and friends, eventually gaining a bit of a reputation and encouragement to take it further. Her hope is to be able to give up the high-flying IT world and take it further into a viable small business. It's something she could pull off, but it's about getting it right and squeezing in a hell of a lot of time, outside of her job, to train and qualify. And that's only the start. The next challenge would be making enough money. She wouldn't want to give up that double garage, would she?

Before I know it I haven't even finished my coffee and my pyjama bottoms are stripped off. Soon I'm face down, peering through a padded opening at the top of the massage table. Beth begins working on my leg carefully, making sure she doesn't make it worse. All is quiet, finally, and I close my eyes, try hard to get myself into the present but away from the presence of the pain. I focus on the temperature of her oily hands and how they feel on my skin, the sensations of her fingers as they knead their way in and around the muscles of my thigh area, down to the shin and the calf. Jon used to try to massage me in the early days to help soothe the stiffness and spasms, but he just didn't have the patience to perfect the technique. His thoughts were always somewhere else. But Danielle was right about Beth. There is a kind of magic in the way she directs her hands, in the way they manage to feel somehow like they've disappeared into my flesh. How does that happen? I'm cherishing the moment, yes, but my mind too quickly takes me to a place of disappointment in knowing it won't last. No matter how good it feels now, I know I'll return right back to the same place afterwards. The despair of being trapped inside this body – nothing can take it away.

After breakfast I find I have six voicemail messages; one from my father, five from my brother, and an email from Jon, assuming I arrived safely, asking how things are going and suggesting when we can try a Skype call.

Jo, yeah, it's me, Dad. I talked to David last night about the money. Ma's surprise. He's not too happy. How about you try talking some sense into him. OK, call me later.

Hi, Jo, it's Dave. Can you call me as soon as you get this? Dad told me about this thing in the will...Did you know anything about this? Well, OK. Call me as soon as you can.

Yeah, hi. It's me again. Dave. I left a message a little while ago. Call me when you get this, please.

Hi, Jo. OK, another message. Where are you? I want to talk about this business with the money. It's not fair. What the hell was she thinking? Can you call me straightaway?

Yeah, hi. Me again. I don't know what's going on with you now. Why aren't you returning my calls?

With each message I can hear the tremble in Dave's voice, a slow rumble working its way up to an explosion. By the last one, he had no hesitation in letting me know how he felt.

What the fuck, Jo? Call me.

Dave did have a point when he asked, 'What was she thinking?' My mother must have assumed that by leaving things this way her wishes would be straightforward, non-negotiable by law. The deal is done. What does he expect me to do about it? I have no legal power to change the terms of Ma's will.

Before calling Dave back, I mull some of this over with Beth to get it off my chest.

'You don't owe your brother anything, Jo. Dave was always out for himself and now he's getting what he deserves.'

It was unfortunate that Beth never got to see much of the good in my brother. I feel shame, too, in knowing that over the years I've probably closed my eyes to his better side. When he was working and making money he always insisted on buying me the nicest birthday present his money, or credit could buy – even a Ralph Lauren jacket one year! He wouldn't blink an eye about taking me out for an expensive meal to celebrate. And yet at the same time this frustrates me. All those times I tried to get closer to him and he pulled away. Never trusted me or anyone else. The times when he had troubles in his marriage or got into debt. He'd clam up, in shame I assume, not want to talk about it, hide from me and my parents for days, weeks even.

'No, let me take that back,' Beth says, her face hard. 'Dave's lucky he's getting anything. He should be grateful.'

'Well, I don't know. He's got mental-health issues. Some of his stuff gets beyond his control.' I notice my habit of biting the inside of my cheek has returned. In the past, I would have reached for a cigarette. 'Anyway, what makes me any more deserving? I left town years ago. Broke my mother's heart. And there was all that stuff about her troubles with my aunt. She wrote about it in her diary, the one my father found. Remember that stuff about Peggy's contract? You know, Beth, things would have been fine between her and Peggy if I'd kept quiet.'

'Oh, I remember, alright. That was messed up. But hey, remember, it wasn't your fault.'

Beth knows many things about me, including Auntie Peggy's husband taking me for ice-cream and being interested

86

in me, but I have never told her everything I remember about that afternoon in the truck all those years ago.

'I can't stop thinking about it, Beth. It's all going round and round again in my head.'

Beth listens in silence, her mouth open, as I recall the events. Her face changes as I get to the bit about the joint, the whisky, his hands on my leg, falling asleep, but I fall short of telling her my suspicions about what really happened that day. It's just too shameful for words.

Now she looks angry.

Beth falls silent, takes a few seconds to respond. 'You know,' she says, shaking her head back and forth. 'I said it at the time. He was a nasty piece of work. I thought he was capable of terrible things.'

Yes, I'm thinking, only Ron and God know the whole truth about what happened.

'But you know what, Jo? Maybe that's just what it took to finally stop him from taking advantage of some other poor fifteen-year-old girl. Telling your mother. Her confronting him. And your mother and Peggy and that stupid contract thing, well, just remember, you were always there for her through all the shit and you know it. She made her own choices.' Beth stops to catch her breath. Pulls her shoulders back. 'But then she wanted you to have a decent chance at life. And in the end going away gave you that. OK, it was at a cost, but that's just the way it had to be. End of story. Don't start the self-tormenting now. Won't get you anywhere.'

Eleven

After a shower I tidy the bed, glance at Shawn Mendes and say, 'What the hell are you looking at?' and decide to give him a five out of ten. I see my mother's diary on the bedside table and fast-forward to the later pages, a dark time in Dave's life, when he overdosed on Zoloft and had to have his stomach pumped.

> Nicole had little Amy with her, my God I can't imagine what that was like. She dropped Amy off at her friends and took David in. He spent the night in the ICU, next day was sent to the hospital's mental health unit and he ended up there for about two weeks. I feel so so drained at times.

I forgot how badly things developed for my brother during that time after he and Nicole split up and the stress of work piled on top of him. Managing finances was never my brother's strength. The potential for those bad periods when his energies were their most heightened and excitable was a frightening reality. When Ma talked about him over the phone I could hear the anxiety in her voice. With her heavy long sighs and pronounced silences I could picture her jaw clenching tighter, only just managing to exhale her cigarette smoke.

'How's he going to take care of himself when he's old? His employment's been on and off for years now,' she said, stopping to take another drag. 'He has no savings, no pension, nothing, and when he is making money it's gone faster than he can put it in his pocket. I can't begin to imagine what might happen to him later, Jo. I just can't.'

Unlike my father who never blinked an eye about how much to splash out when the treat benefitted him, my mother was fiercely conscientious about how she spent her hard-earned salary. She limited her bigger spending to her essential car purchase and annual breaks in the sun. When she had saved enough she bought her own little cottage in a nice Cape Cod town on a street with neighbours, who, for the most part, she said she 'could relate to'. A builder and his family lived across the road. A retired nurse and her husband occupied the other end, a property manager lived next door to the right. They were all 'very, very nice people. So friendly, Jo', but 'that family with all those noisy kids and all kinds coming in and out at all hours' and the 'snooty, yuppie couple in that big new-build place on the corner' weren't worth her time or effort. 'There's something funny about those yuppies. The way they look at us, like they're better. I don't know. It's just a feeling.'

In later years, when it became obvious that I was staying put in London, Ma would make a point of flying over to see me, without my father, of course, although the trips every two years tapered off when she grew bored with the rain and the prospect of me dragging her around on the underground to another museum or shopping on Oxford Street. She hated relying on public transport.

'Aren't there any malls nearby where we can park the car?'

She hated the bustle and hard work of big city life and hoped I would grow tired of it and come back home.

'Jo, I'm amazed at how easily you've adjusted to everything here. The expense of living in London. All these little houses attached to each other. Tiny flats. No built-in closets? Hardly any storage? The rain. *I* couldn't do it, that's for sure. But I'm so glad you're happy. Really. I just want you to be happy.'

Other treats she fitted into her budget were cigarettes and booze, always in full supply. Aside from these basics and occasional meals out, expenses like hair maintenance, clothes, shoes, accessories, stylish house furnishings or any luxury items, didn't get much of a second look. In spite of the healthy stash I now know she was accruing with her biotech investment, she made it her mission to live a frugal life.

The hopes that her children would follow her virtuous ways were fulfilled mainly by me. Unlike Dave, in my younger years I grew up with a sense of my position in the world that was aligned closely with my mother's. I accepted I should never expect any sense of entitlement to anything. I continued to live out the expectations required of the good girl who never fussed. I ate that soggy McDonald's burger without complaining and said thank you very much for the privilege.

Over time I internalised an irrational fear of spending, convinced it would only lead me into poverty where I'd end up living on the streets. I saved every penny I earned from allowances, birthday money from my grandparents, money from all the times I helped look after my younger cousins and later when I did more babysitting. I saved until I acquired a fair amount to spend on something that was important to me; a record, a teen mag, a necklace or bracelet. Whatever I chose had to be worth it.

My savings added up but were easy enough to manage without a bank account, so I continued to stash the money in a special place in the back area of my underwear drawer. One day, Dave found my hiding place. He must have been around sixteen at the time. I only discovered this when I came home from a friend's one Saturday afternoon. I guess it was nothing new that the house was empty except for Dave who was upstairs.

'Oh, hi. Yeah, hi, Jo. What's up? What's goin' on?'

His voice was nervous and hesitant although he was acting nice to me. He was packing a bag of clothes in a rush. That was probably the moment when I sensed something was up.

'Hi. Nothing. Just been at Donna's. What're you doing?' I sat on the corner of his unmade bed. 'You going somewhere? You staying at Dom's tonight?'

'Yeah, I guess,' he said, not looking at me. 'I'm running late though, so I'll talk to you later.'

Off he went jumping down the stairs. My instincts compelled me to wander over to the drawer to look at my money envelope. I used to enjoy counting the notes, feeling the smooth material of the older ones next to the crisper new ones in my hands. By that time I had acquired around fifty dollars, which would have gone a long way in those days. I must have sensed something funny going on with Dave and my instinct was right. When I pulled back my underwear to find the envelope I saw it was gone and in its place was a sloppy, handwritten note on a letter-size sheet of white paper that read, Jo, Sorry I had to borrow your money. Will pay you back. There was no signature.

I screamed a prolonged '*No!*' as I heard the front door slam shut.

I ran as fast as I could and managed to reach him as he was running out of the driveway toward the main road. Coming up from behind I pushed Dave with all the strength I could muster. When he turned around I swung fast and hard, then kicked, aiming near the groin. I thrashed my arms around in a fury and scratched his bare arms and neck. I punched his stomach with everything I had, then pulled at his arms and hand, sending the bag sailing into the street with most of its contents spilling out – a pair of jeans, some T-shirts, underwear, toothbrush and other small items. I headed fast toward the bag scanning with my eyes for the envelope but Dave was taller, bigger and much stronger. He didn't hesitate to throw me down with one quick push. I landed heavily on my wrist and arm. The gravel of the pavement tore through the fabric of my shirt and scraped my arm, which began to bleed. Dave started gathering his things quickly.

'I said I'll pay you back,' he shouted.

'I didn't say you could take it. I want it back. *Now*,' I screamed long enough to create a stir on our quiet street.

By this time some of the neighbours had opened their curtains or their front doors, their glares not showing concern but annoyance. Dave wasn't deterred by them or my tears. When I tried to stand he didn't hesitate to send me back down to the ground, the final brutal climax, with a sudden vicious thump aimed at the middle of my chest as he shouted, 'Fuck off.'

I fell hard again and hit my head. He hesitated only for seconds to see if I could open my eyes. As I wasn't going anywhere at that point he had plenty of time to grab his stuff, run to the corner and disappear.

I was left sobbing on my own in the middle of the road, trying to catch my breath, snot bubbling out of my nose, my head pounding. The neighbour directly across from us, the heavy-set, soft-featured mother of a girl called Barbara who I used to play with, stepped out with rollers in her hair, wearing a white polyester house-dress.

'Come on inside,' she said, and led me through her living room and into the kitchen, shaking her head back and forth in disgust.

'I hate him, I hate him, I hate him,' I mumbled through my tears.

I wondered where Barbara and the two older brothers were. Barbara never said much about their absent father. He left when she was around three, but somehow they always managed just fine without him. I always wanted to know just what their secret was.

Mrs Molina cleaned my arm, bandaged me, gave me a glass of milk with two Oreo cookies. 'Now get yourself home, take two Tylenol and lie down,' she said. 'When's your mother coming home?'

Dave called a couple of days later to let my mother know that he would be away in New Hampshire, something about factory work. All went silent after that for a month or so when

93

he headed back to Massachusetts to stay with friends. I'm not sure now what made me angrier: his vanishing act, how it upset my mother, or that he never paid my money back.

Finally I return Dave's many voicemail messages, starting with a long and feeble apology about how I forgot to turn on my phone. I listen to him holler about how deceitful our Ma was all that time she was hoarding her money from her investment over the years when she could have, at the very least, thought about her only grandchild, his daughter Amy's needs, her future, things like college money.

'You know, if Ma and Dad didn't mess things up so much when we were kids,' he shouts down the phone, 'well, maybe I wouldn't expect any favours, but this is the least she could have done for me. She could have at least treated me with fairness and the same respect she's given her golden girl, Jo.'

'Whoa, hold on there, Dave. Golden girl? That's not exactly fair.'

'And won't Dad already have enough with the cottage in Cape Cod that Ma bought and now the sweet pension and savings she worked so hard for? What's he done to deserve all that when he treated her the way he did? Huh? Tell me.'

'Well, I think...'

Dave's speech grows more rapid as he interrupts me, with short breaks between thoughts to inhale his cigarette, clear his hoarse throat, or cough. 'I'm not trying to lash out at you personally, Jo, but Ma was always "*Jo* this, *Jo* that" and then I'm the one who's painted as the thicko, the lame one. How could she...tell me, how could she be so cold? She must've known I'd feel this way. So now, now she hasn't even given me the chance to grieve for her the right way. All that time she was in that hospice saying her goodbyes and all that and never once did she give any hint of this except to keep saying stuff like, "Make sure you take care of yourself, David. Be happy and focus on the important things, one day at a time," blah blah and the twelve-step Narcs Anonymous shit. I should be in a different state of mind to grieve, but now she's just fucking pissed me off. I didn't ask for this, you know. Of course I loved Ma, you know, she was good to me, but she shouldn't have done this.'

The rant continues. Every now and then I try to interject to defend a mother who lost many nights' sleep over the years worrying about her beloved son. I remind him about the difficult times when he got into trouble with money and drugs, and ever so carefully, I remind him of the time she mentions in her diary when his credit-card charges added up to over $7000.

'You can't hold a person's mistakes against them for ever, Jo. That was a long time ago and things are different now. No, it's not like that now. It's not.'

'Ma wrote to me once about how proud she was that you wanted to apply for an engineering degree. Remember when you wanted to do that? Why don't you read some of the letters she wrote to me?'

'No,' he says, 'I don't need to read the diary or the letters, don't want to know anything about them, thank you. Maybe if she let go of some of that money years ago I could've got through school. Did she ever consider that obvious thing, Huh? Did she?'

I check my reflection in the mirror while Dave continues to offload. I'm definitely looking fifty-four today.

'She only made this arrangement with the money because she wanted to know that if your moods got out of control and if drugs became a problem again that your finances would be safe,' I say. 'And you know Dad's not going to live for ever. When he goes everything else will be split between us. It's not like you're going to be suffering. And having an extra twenty grand a year now is like having another salary, and you don't have a dependent child now.'

'Yeah, well that's all easy for you to say from where you are because you've got this lump sum. And I'm guessing your salary is pretty good doing what you do, and, sorry to say this, but no family responsibilities. I know that's not your choice, Jo, but that's the way it is, you don't have kids and you've been able to keep having your fancy vacations. Well, I've never seen anything close to a Greek beach in my life. I wouldn't mind a real vacation, all I ask is for some of the things other people like you and Jon have.'

I shake my head in the mirror. As I move in closer I'm shocked to spot a couple of chin hairs. Using my fingernails as tweezers I manage to pull one but stop there and return to the conversation. By this time I know I have to control myself, think hard before I say anything that will make things worse.

'Well, I did work hard for our honeymoon and it's not like we have Cape Cod and guaranteed summer on our doorsteps here. Plus, I can't tolerate the heat of those places during the British summer now and on top of that I've had to cut down to part-time and that means less pension.'

'OK, so that's a good point, so why didn't she do your deal in instalments like her plan for me, knowing what your disability is like, huh? Tell me that. So you're not tempted to blow it all on another vacation. Yeah, we're both disabled.'

I cringe at the label, and think, *yes, I'm doomed too.*

At this point I hear his voice cracking just a bit, although I know he's not really crying.

One of the times when we were visiting Ma at the hospice I broke down outside her room. Dave showed some honest compassion in his eyes.

'Oh, Jo. You know I want to cry too,' he said. 'I feel the pain just like you do, there's a lot of pain in here,' he pointed to his heart. 'But it just won't come.'

At the time it felt like a special moment of sharing, enough for me to close my eyes and nod in sympathetic agreement. 'It's not unusual,' I said, pulling myself together, 'for many men who've been conditioned by society to act like impenetrable iron men of steel. Just look at Dad.'

'Yeah,' he agreed, patiently. 'That's kind of true. But it's more to do with my meds. I used to cry a lot on my own when I was young, like a little fucking baby, but since all that time in the hospital, then all the different meds… it's all gone. Dead.'

Now I pause for a moment and hold the phone away from my ear while he continues to complain about his hard lot in life. When it's my turn I have a go with my best shot at squeezing in the last word. 'Well, our disabilities are different, aren't they? Yours is different. All the kind of instability that comes with having moods that go up and go down. I mean, that must have been what Ma was thinking when she did this.'

Long silence.

'Hello? Dave?'

'OK. We all have our demons, don't we? Look, I need to go. I'll see you at dinner later.'

Twelve

The sight of my mother's disabled parking blue badge on the car's dashboard is unsettling. Am I turning into my sick, old mother well before my time, yet without the same fortitude? Waiting in her car to meet Dave for dinner, reading through a draft for a journal article I've been writing, is a frustrating and futile effort. My eyes pass over the same page repeatedly as though the words aren't mine. It's as though an alien power has invaded my brain and is attempting to send a message, written in an unfamiliar language, in the form of incomprehensible drivel. I close my eyes, count to ten, tell myself this isn't the time to attempt scholarly heights. It's also the moment I remember I've forgotten to contact Jon again. And then Dave texts, says he'll be a little late, he's leaving his car behind, catching a cab, and tells me to wait for him at the bar where they make killer margaritas.

Dave's chosen a place he knows well, one that specialises in a grilled menu. My family have always liked their meat and nice and charred it must be. If they could fire up the barbecue on Christmas day they would. I was a bit anxious about driving here, finding parking in Davis Square, Somerville, and having to walk a fair distance, but then remembered Ma's blue badge and thought, *jackpot*. Let's make life easier today. I'll step out with my cane and not feel bad about it. Hey, I've earned the privilege. Today I can call the shots.

While I'm sipping away at my big strawberry margarita at the quiet bar I look out the window and spot three white male teens, maybe fifteen or sixteen, hovering at the nearby bus stop in hoodies and jeans that sit low in a way that annoys older folk. All carry skateboards. One laughs at something, starts to shout. He sets down his board, then positions one hand on his jutted hip, the other under his chin. The others laugh in encouragement. I notice the object of the joke is waiting at the same stop some distance away; another white boy, similar age, fair-skinned and slight, a bag across his body. His purple pants are noticeably tight and his hair is shaved on both sides, the top in a ponytail. His blond locks look bleached with darker roots showing at the base. I can see from here that his eyebrows appear to be pencilled in a darker hue. He's got the kind of pretty face I always wanted when I was that age.

A bus arrives and I'm relieved to see him skirt to the front of the line and get on quickly while the skateboarders stay behind. All three of them are shouting now, their voices screeching like angry crows. Their steps follow the direction of the boy's movement as he heads to the back of the bus where he disappears to the other side.

My fantasy is to get out there and knock a hard-pointed finger, the end of my cane even, into their chests. You should be ashamed at yourselves, I'd say. Who do you think you are? You're nothing, you're worse than nothing. Yeah, you little fuckers, I'll show you a thing or two. I would frighten them with the rumble of my authoritative anger, send them running away in tears. They would relive me in their nightmares. Their parents might feel a bit ashamed too. Yes, that would be a good thing.

Or they would ignore me, dismiss me, laugh at me.

I'm seething but I make an effort to slow down, take small sips of the margarita, savour the taste that the sweet strawberries have absorbed. These killer margaritas could kill me.

The skateboarders jump onto the next bus after rustling their way through the line. They are the future college generation, their parents pushing them to get a degree in something, anything, in the hope that their offspring will have a better chance in life than they did. My current students are their role models, the ones who are sitting in my lectures, in the back rows of a crowded hall wearing headphones plugged into their expensive laptops. They are multi-tasking, apparently, an admired skill in which they will claim great expertise on their CVs. While supposedly listening to me rattle on about postmodernism they're watching YouTube videos of cats walking on their hind legs on tightropes, the latest instalment of *Keeping up with the Kardashians*, or maybe something more intellectually challenging like *Breaking Bad*.

'Hey Jo,' says a voice, and in a moment I've forgotten all about my students.

Dave seems happy enough to see me. He knows the bartender, a cute brunette called Amber who has admirably muscular arms, probably from shaking all those fancy cocktails. 'Hey Amber, this is my sister Jo, from London, the one I told you about. She's a professor, you know. Can you believe it? I

101

got a sister who's a professor.' He play-strikes my shoulder with a bit too much force.

Amber tells me she's heard all about me, yes, only good things, of course, although I notice she locks her eyes into a stare, half smiling, which makes me feel uneasy.

'Don't believe what he tells you. It's not all it's cracked up to be,' I say, feeling the heat of embarrassment. Over here anyone with a PhD who stands in front of a classroom gets called a professor, but across the waters in the UK that title is reserved for the top-flying few. And I'm not one of them.

'Wow,' says Amber. 'I'd love to go to London. See the palace and check out all those pubs. Love the accent. My friend's mother is English and when she comes over she's always saying, cheerio, cheerio. It's so cute. I love it.'

'You get so used to it working and living there.'

'I can hear you got a bit of the accent too. Oh my God, that's *so* cute.'

Dave orders himself a traditional margarita. 'You taste more of the triple sec that way,' he tells me in his serious voice.

He takes our drinks and I lead the way back to the table I found that overlooks the street. There's the usual small talk and then he throws in something about how good he thinks I'm looking. 'Have you lost some weight since last time?'

'Hah. That's funny. No. If anything I've probably gained. Comfort eating and all that.'

'No? Sorry, but you have, you're definitely not as big as you were last time,' says Dave, appraising me.

He was never very good at compliments, and this sort of comment convinces me he has never been sincere with them.

I've always had the sense that there's an agenda behind them, although maybe this is just his weird way of trying his best.

'You know stress can do that. With Ma dying and everything. But your eyes look pretty tired, Jo. Do you use concealer? That might help.'

It hasn't been long since the last visit but there is something different about my brother's appearance and it's not his weight. He always keeps his hair in fashion, not just a standard barber's job, but an expensive styled cut, which is noticeable. In spite of his widening middle-age spread, he's managed to keep a good head of hair, only showing a slight receding line at the front. That's when I notice he now has golden highlights, probably to cover some of the grey. We talk a bit about grooming, the latest celebration of letting yourself go grey at our age, how it works for some but not all. Finally after trying to figure out what else is different with his face, it dawns on me that his teeth are so white it looks as though they're almost popping out of his mouth.

'Had 'em whitened. Totally worth it. Gets rid of all the years of discoloration from smoking, coffee, red wine. Just like new now,' he says, then pauses to offer a wide smile. 'I thought, hey, if I'm going to have it done, make them as white as they can, get my money's worth. Otherwise, why bother, right? You should do it, Jo. You won't regret it.'

We talk more about smoking, how hard it is for Dave to give up completely, although he claims he's cut back loads. He says he only smokes about five a day, but I'm suspicious. He stepped into the restaurant reeking of cigarettes, and by the end of dinner, he's stepped outside twice.

Dave says the same thing about his drinking.

'It's completely under control now, not like in the past. Those days are gone. Long gone with the drugs. I can handle the booze, have a few and be OK, and I stay away from drugs, Jo.'

It's funny how we can talk ourselves into such things; if we repeat the mantra, *everything's fine, I can handle this*, we will believe it. It will become our reality. We hang on to that hope. I, too, have been guilty of this.

'Look, Jo, this thing about Ma's surprise money stash. OK, I've calmed down a bit but, still, you have to admit it isn't fair. This yearly instalment idea isn't going to give me anything close to enough to do anything with. I don't know what she was thinking, that she was going to be doing me some kind of favour.'

Of course I've prepared for this, so after Dave has ordered for both of us I try my best to emphasise the good.

'Well, I'm sure if you combine this year's sum with what you have in savings you can maybe put down a deposit for an apartment or a condo and then you wouldn't have to be spending so much in rent.'

I feel a tiny twinge of guilt for suggesting this as I assume he doesn't have much in savings, if anything at all. OK, I don't actually feel guilty, I want to make a subtle point, maybe throw a little jab, something to get him to think about how important it is that he should have saved something by this time in his life. My mother's voice speaks through me. I can almost feel my jaw clenching. Since Amy turned eighteen he's told himself he's the only one he's had to worry about financially.

'No, buying a condo's not a good investment, no. I'm thinking of something bigger, like business. And I don't have enough. I need a bigger pot. I'm not sure yet, but I know I want to go that way, not the property way.'

We oscillate around buying a place to live, how good, I stress, that would be for his security and stability, the best investment he can make. He rebounds that it takes away his freedom if he wants to leave Boston, no he wouldn't want the headaches of renting it out.

'You know, Jo, I've always wanted to have my own business. What's wrong with that dream, why is Jo's way always the right way, tell me that, go on, tell me?' he says, slapping the table with his open hand.

I notice the couple at the nearby table glancing our way. 'Calm down,' I whisper.

'Oh, come on. Cut the condescending shit.'

'OK. Dave, if you're in business you'll be bound by that too, you wouldn't have the freedom to just leave whenever you want,' I say.

'So I could set up business somewhere else. Like you did. What's wrong with that? You know,' he says, leaning forward. 'I've been going over all this with my therapist, and he agrees this deal with Ma's money is just wrong, worse than all the other family shit. And he thinks you and Dad can show some goodwill by just sharing some of your lump sums now, and I can pay you back when I get the future instalments and we all get the same amount in the end. It would be a way for me to have enough to do something solid. That's the fairer way. And to be honest, Jo, it's not your business what I do with it, I'm not asking you what you do with *your* life.'

By this time my nerves are unsteady. I'm tiptoeing on a narrow bridge with a long drop below.

'Well, that's nice of him to throw that out. At the end of the day this is the way Ma wanted it for you, Dave. To protect you, I'm sorry, from yourself. She was thinking about what's best for you. She only had good intentions.'

'But it's not what's best for me and you know it. It's easy for you and Dad to say that from where you're standing, the ones with all the money and the houses by the way. Dad has the city house, then the cottage to have his fun in and you have your nice place, your nice job, your nice life in London with Jon. And I have shit,' says a sturdier, colder Dave.

'But that's why buying property's a good investment. Property always goes up in value. And by the way, it's not all so wonderful for me. Remember I'm part-time now, so, no, I'm not a high earner, it costs a fortune to live anywhere in London and I have to think about retirement too.'

Dave pauses a minute to order another drink. He continues but the volume of his voice begins to rise again. 'But you have your high-earner hubby and no kids, and you guys will always be fine. OK, so you got this thing with your health and that's not great. I'm sorry you got that, but you're OK at the moment, right? A day at a time with that. Right?'

'Can you just keep your voice down, Dave.'

'I ain't fucking shouting, Jo. If you want to hear me shout, I can shout.' He looks around, pulls his shoulders back and breathes in. 'Look, you work hard, that's fine, but I do too. I work hard in a tough physical job that's not going to ever pay any better, and I'm not so young and strong either. I want to look bigger. Other people do it, right? I can dream, why can't I be allowed to dream? I can have ambition, can't I?'

'It's not that, Dave. It's also about managing your life. I have to manage mine, right? Well, you have to manage all your stuff. You said it before. You wanted to do things before too, back to school, the degree, but all the other shit got in the way. That's what Ma was worried about and I am too. So is Dad.'

'Hah, that's a lie, Dad doesn't worry about anyone but himself and you know it. Look, just think about what I've said and talk to Dad. Plus, what are you going to do with all that money? Are you going to let it just sit in the bank or what? I know what you're like.'

'I don't know, maybe I can pay the mortgage off now,' I lie. We paid off the mortgage five years ago. 'All this talk about Ma's money, it makes me uncomfortable, it's not right. It was her money, we didn't earn it. I wish it didn't happen. We could've just ended up with the inheritance split evenly between us after Dad goes, whenever that will be.'

'Hah,' Dave laughs. 'Don't hold your breath.'

I'm saved by the interruption of Dave's phone, and it's all, 'Oh, hi, honey, sweetie, gorgeous, whatever you say, oh no, not too late, babe.'

It appears there's a new girlfriend now, someone about ten years younger than him, divorced, two older kids still living with her but one's in college in Boston, and she happens to also tend bar here where they make the killer margaritas and she does nails and pedicures at discounted prices from her apartment. He was going to introduce me to her tonight, this Karen person, the one to whom he referred previously as the 'friend with benefits', but her plans changed and she ended up going out with her daughter somewhere.

We order coffee. He has his with a Sambuca shot on the side. It seems he's fallen for this one.

'At first it was just sex,' he says in his noticeably rapid excited speech. 'Oh my God, and what great sex it is. I still have it in me, Jo.' He sits back, taps his extended stomach. 'But, you know, we've gotten to know each other now and she's good. Sensible. No dramas. Keeps me in my place. And she's worked in the restaurant business a long time, really knows the ins and outs. She's got a good head for business. She does good, you know, makes good money.'

I can already see where this is going and feel my heart racing again. He's smiling, telling me how cute she is, how the other day she surprised him with a homemade meal at her place when her kids were out for the night, and then she slipped into this sexy new lingerie she bought just for him.

'And she's in amazing shape, Jo. Works out at the gym, really looks after herself. And she's cut back on smoking too. And her breasts. Oh my God, they're just the right size. They don't sag like other women that age. *So* sexy. And her talent in the bedroom,' he whispers, moving in closer. 'The other night…I didn't think I could still do it, you know, sometimes these meds really do a job on me, it takes me longer. And with my age too.'

This is where I try to stop him, laugh it off, deflect the conversation in the way I've always had to do with him, in such a way that won't trigger an argument.

'OK, enough Dave, I'm happy for you, you don't need to go into the details.'

He stares at me with a half-open mouth. 'You know, there's nothing wrong with talking about sex, Jo. It's only society's taboos around it that hold us back. I'm only trying to share a bit. I'm only trying to be *honest* about being happy. It wouldn't cost you anything to be happy for me.'

We don't say much after that, just eat and drink and glance at the other diners. None of them look like they have a problem.

Later, we walk to Ma's car in silence. He lights up again and I shock him into sharing his cigarette, throw in a cough here and there in between drags. I feel an odd sense of release. After the margarita, the whole challenge of the evening, I can't hold back my temptation. Maybe I can stop there and remain intact. Those itty-bitty-triumphs.

'So, JoJo,' he says, avoiding my eyes. 'I'm only asking you to seriously think about the money. It's about doing the right thing.'

'I'm still trying to get my head around Ma dying, you know. Anyway, do want a lift home?'

'No, thanks. The night's still young. Got people to see, things to do.'

On these final words he extends a quick hug, his body stiffening upon contact, and a sadness fills me. He taps the hood twice with the palm of his hand, looks away with a tight smile. And it's in this quick succession of movements that he becomes Dad. In spite of their physical differences, he is a younger version of the old man – a buffed-up option with silky hair and glow-in-the-dark teeth. All he needs is the toothpick.

When Dad was feeling particularly generous, he would take Beth and me, and Dave, when he was around, for a day out fishing and sunbathing on the deck.

Dave developed a passion for fishing after being lucky enough to be the one to catch the most: flounders, blue fish, even cod. After a while Beth and I turned in our poles, enjoyed working on our tans and plunging to cool ourselves in the deep dark waters. With Dave taking the role of master fisherman, I assumed my father would resent him and make excuses to not take him out, but I was wrong. The sea seemed to be the place where they both found peace. They were happy in silence together; the boat, fishing rods and equipment, the beers, providing them with points of connection. When the prize took the bait, the excitement and pure pleasure shared between father and son was like witnessing an unimaginable feat of nature. Like ball lightning or fish falling from the sky, it was the once-in-a-lifetime occurrence you may never see again, so when you do, you make sure you give it your full attention and awe. These were the only times I witnessed my father offer his son any praise.

Yeah, you got it, that's right, hold it steady, you're doing just fine. Just be patient. No, no, no, not like that. It's OK, don't worry, you still got it, OK, take her in easy, that's it. That's it. Your brother, did you see that? He's the best. One of the best fishermen I've ever seen.

Back to shore and into the land of traffic jams, nagging wives, humid kitchens, the impending start of another long, hard week of labour, mean bosses shouting, *Get your ass in on time, or else*, or, *You wanna raise? Fuckin' raise, my ass.* All that was enough to undo the ocean's magic. Business as usual.

Shooting and hunting were my father's other pleasures and he would take my brother out, not me, to teach him how to fire a gun. He showed him how to aim properly at the target, how to handle any recoil, how to rid himself of fear. The realm of men, rifles and journeys into the wilderness of New Hampshire, sometimes New Jersey, in search of non-suspecting innocent deer for a later feast dressed up in the name venison, were saved for the colder months. But this idyllic father-son dream was short-lived after young Dave fell, then rolled into a rocky ditch, ending up with a broken arm. The group had planned a full weekend away and weren't happy at all when it looked like Dave messed up their schedule. They moved him along for a while, tried to convince him it was only a scratch, but the pain was so bad he cried he couldn't continue. I heard my bone snap, Jo, that's how bad it was.

Dad drove him back home to Massachusetts that same afternoon, but left Dave with my mother to take him to the ER. I remember that Dad swore, 'Never again. I tried and look where it got me.'

He had a quick sandwich, then drove back up north that same evening to rejoin his friends at their lodge. That was the first and last of Dave's manly father-son hunting adventures.

Thirteen

Late Sunday morning, I'm alone in the quiet of Beth's kitchen with my first cup of coffee. Beth is out, if not on her usual run then maybe at Whole Foods grocery shopping again or driving Danielle somewhere. There's another voice message from my father asking if I've seen my brother: *Call me. I wanna know what's happening. We need to set a time to see the lawyer and sign those papers.*

I call Dad and tell him Dave's idea about the money and he's against it, interrupting me straightaway, as if he guessed this was coming.

'No, no, no, no. No. He can't use your share. No, the deal's done. It's what Ma wanted, he can't change that. It's what the will says, you can't mess around with a will, Jo. I'm the executor for Christ's sake. It's tough if he don't like it, it's the way it is. And I told him when I talked to him. I said, "Why are you being like this? You and Jo get everything when I'm gone." And then he says to me, "But Dad, that ain't gonna happen for a while and I need it now." What a thing to say.'

By this point I can hear his speech slurring.

'I can't talk about it no more,' he says.

We look at Tuesday, late afternoon, early evening as a possible time to sign the papers, give the lawyer our bank details and so on, so I need to check if Dave is available. I also want to look through my mother's photos to see if I can put an album together to display after the memorial service at the restaurant where we'll have the buffet.

'Whatever you want,' he says. 'You know what to do.'

I tell him I've been reading her diary. When I ask if he wants to read it, he says no.

'I don't want to know what she said about me, I told you. It's the past, I don't need to know. It's your thing, you have it.'

'Do you want anything in the eulogy, any little bits, special things about her or you together that I can say?'

'Nope. Say what you want.'

We agree that I'll head over the next day sometime when he'll probably be out. We both wish for this silently and acknowledge it's for the best.

Then I check emails and see a new one from Jon.

OK, you must be busy. I'll be working a bit from home tomorrow, we can try to speak then. By the way, looks like you forgot to pay your last credit card bill. Now you've got a red notice.

For Jon, keeping in touch regularly when we're apart is all he asks. 'Just let me worry,' he says. 'Let me worry about you. Let me be the one who wants to hear your voice. What's so wrong with that?'

If it wasn't for Constance Rosenfelt I never would have met Jon. It was through Constance that I found the courage to apply to the fancy pants Ivy League where I later took up a study abroad year in London. It was late in that first term when I spotted him in the student bar one night, ready and waiting. Willing, it seemed. I couldn't believe my luck. Over the years I've seen that the happier things in my life have come my way from being in the right place at the right time. But I also know there's a fair bit of effort in the trial and error needed to orchestrate the right conditions for good fortune; it all takes a lot of time before any rewards are handed out. I guess you could say that's how things happened over the course of my college days before I met Jon. After that, life seemed to come a lot easier.

After doing well at community college, an excitable student advisor called Benji sought me out to talk about my future. Benji had a lot of hair and a beard and a cuddly puppy look.

'You know, with your grades here you should consider applying to the Ivy League universities,' Benji told me. 'Some of them have entry programmes for older students like you.' He shuffled through his paperwork and circled a few items in red pen. 'Oh, yeah. You're looking very good on paper. Just the type they want,' he said, smiling up at me, adjusting his glasses.

I laughed at the thought. Yes, I had worked hard, actually discovered that I did have some kind of academic knack for which my teachers patted me on the back every now and then, but so what? I was under no illusion I was anything special, so he kind of took me by surprise.

'But my high-school grades were average. You can see they weren't so great, really.'

'Doesn't matter. Forget about the high-school stuff. They don't care about that. They want to see your grades here and your potential. You're twenty-four, right?' He looked through his papers again and made a note. 'That fits.'

'But I have no *potential* for Ivy League,' I laughed. 'Plus, there's no money. None.'

I could barely get by then, having already taken loans for those classes, and I was working loads of hours to pay the rent, bills, and squeezing in study time. I lived on a limited menu of baked potatoes with grated cheese for supper when I was my healthiest. I alternated this with packet macaroni and cheese and visits home to my mother where I filled up on animal protein every now and then. In spite of my meagre diet, I never seemed to reduce in size.

'Financial aid. Scholarship. I'd highly advise you to look into it. What can you lose? Just apply.'

I went along with the idea and was offered an interview. Before the big day I had a look around the campus and noted a high volume of rich-looking, attractive students wearing designer jeans and smiles that conveyed their ease and sense of entitlement. When passing one group with tanned faces accented against their impeccable teeth, I caught fragments of conversation about how great spring break was in Acapulco. *So much better than Florida last year. Way better.*

My interview was with the dean of the mature students' programme and a student. The dean was an older-hippy soul who wore a flowing skirt and had long greying hair. The student was male, white, around thirty-five, with a buzz-cut. He wore thick glasses that made his eyes look tiny, like a rat's, and a shirt and tie that made him appear more serious than the dean.

I could feel the sweat in my armpit beginning to trickle down my right arm, but I was determined to hold my shit together and do my best to act like a smart person. 'I've developed a very big love of the arts over the years,' I said, sitting tall and smiling, just as I had practised in the mirror that morning. 'I guess I showed some talent when I was younger for drawing but now I like to see art and learn about the history and all that sort of thing. I see you have a fine programme here for the arts, the liberal arts and fine arts and all other kinds of art stuff.'

She nodded, smiled for a few seconds, and asked if I'd been to any exhibitions recently.

'Exhibitions?' I hesitated. 'Oh yeah, I've seen Norman Rockwell's work at the Norman Rockwell Museum in the Berkshires,' I said, with as much enthusiasm as I could muster. 'On the way home from a weekend away.'

It wasn't exactly recent, but I had dragged my mother there on our way home from a day trip to western Massachusetts. The outing was Dave's idea, his attempt, he said, to bring him, our mother and me together for the day. He had spent a weekend in the Berkshires once with a girlfriend he'd met during one of his stints in the hospital. I was always sceptical about these relationships of his. Weren't these addicts just bound to encourage each other and fall off the wagon? Dave bragged that his girlfriend's parents were academics. They had a big second home in the Berkshires near Amherst. Apparently they were from old money, a preferable option, Dave indicated, to new money types.

'To look at them you'd never know it, you wouldn't ever guess they were loaded. They don't wear fancy clothes or drive nice cars. It's all *understated*. But they have big houses, lots of money in the bank, and trust funds for their kids. That's what Sally is,' he said. 'She's a trust fund baby.'

The rest of us who didn't have the luck of being born into old money would be forever stuck in narrow, crevice-like places. But if they had trust funds and future inheritances, which meant they'd never have to worry about where their next meal came from, why were they just as messed up as we were? What excuse did they have? Wasn't spring break in Acapulco enough to snap them out of their misery?

'When I was young I always dreamed of becoming an illustrator and Rockwell's been a favourite of mine,' I told the dean. 'I like Monet paintings too. I've been to the Museum of Fine Arts in Boston.'

The dean liked that. Then the subject changed to my impressive community college grades.

'Well, we can see you've really worked hard in every subject. Looks like you're a great all-rounder,' she said with genuine interest.

Rat-eyes decided to interject. 'Why in the world did you take Intro to Physics if you might want to major in art history? And what kind of things do you expect from doing a degree here?' He narrowed his eyes even more in anticipation.

I wouldn't have taken the stupid physics class if someone at the college hadn't said something ridiculous like, oh, it can't hurt, you know, for a liberal arts degree, and you'll definitely be able to transfer the credits, but I didn't tell him this. Somehow I walked through the cauldron of his cross-examination and reached the other side intact. 'Well, I've been so, so excited about just learning as much as I can about everything and anything in the world. Nothing's ever wasted on me. Nope.' I was quick on my feet, picking up on what the dean had said about being an all-rounder. I worked hard to sound natural and relaxed. 'I want to be as well-rounded a human being as possible and try to understand the world in its entirety. Physics was tough and I got stuck sometimes but I saw my professor for lots of help and I felt so rewarded afterwards. And you know, I think art is a reflection of the world and everything in it, like physics and science and all sorts of other things. Politics. Philosophy. Yeah, I just want to learn everything.'

'That's really great. It's so great. We like our students to be well-rounded and inquisitive,' the nice dean said.

'Yes, I can really see that. The atmosphere here just kind of gives that impression.' I smiled, trying to imagine what Acapulco was like at spring break.

The student continued to stare me down, sensing, I'm sure, that I was bullshitting. At that point I thought I was doomed. A feeling of failure loomed over me, but the dean extended a friendly handshake and quiet chuckle.

'Thank you so, so much for taking the time to come and see us. It's been so, so nice to meet you.'

I liked this woman very much, although afterwards, when I retraced all that was said, I wondered, seriously, if her overly warm style was a form of sarcasm I hadn't spotted earlier.

Or maybe that was just my paranoia.

A few weeks later I was shocked to receive a letter from the university telling me I was in, in spite of the student who hated me. I was accepted to the state University of Massachusetts, Amherst, also, around the same time, although they didn't seem bothered about wanting to interview me and I didn't care about visiting them. I'd looked through the brochure, been that way to see some of the Berkshires on that day trip I brought up during my fancy pants Ivy League interview. The University of Massachusetts, or UMass, was miles away in the green hills and mountainous western part of the state, a world apart from everything that was home and too familiar; parents, brother, mental hospital, weird aunts and uncles, a family combination that most sensible people want to avoid. A new start, that's what I wanted. In my mind I constructed an image of myself as someone who worked a quiet job in a second-hand bookshop with a relaxed, contented smile on my face as I read all the books on offer. I thought, hey, maybe I could even try to pass myself off as one of those understated trust fund baby types.

Constance asked me to call her straightaway with my news when the letter arrived from the Ivy League. I could hardly get the words out for tears when I tried to tell her the news. Maybe I was scared shitless. 'I can't go there. It's for rich kids, not townies like me. I can blend in with the rest of them at UMass, that's where I belong.'

She didn't reply right away. 'Jo,' she said, then hesitated. 'If you don't take this up you might regret it. It's really simple. It's just a better institution, better reputation. And there are others like you there, you'll see. And look, they wouldn't have accepted you if they didn't want you.'

So I told my mother my news, told my friends, convinced myself I should go to a fancy Ivy League university after all and that it was cause for a small celebration.

My parents and I had beers in the back yard at the house. The temperature was mild, the evening May sun warm, a reasonable enough time for a barbecue. Dave was going to try to stop by later.

At this point my brother had been married to Nicole for a few months. He was on a good path then, was clean and seemed happier than he had ever been in his life. Nicole and I had our differences, but at the time she was sweet enough in her own way. Her personality came across as a bit flat, a straight, boring surface with no challenging undulations or exciting views at any point. But her immutability seemed to work wonders for my brother and for that we were all grateful. Like a faithful canine companion, she appeared, without much effort, to steady his unpredictable ups and downs. They lived in a one-bedroom apartment in Chelsea, Massachusetts, although Dave was looking at exciting air-conditioning contract possibilities in Florida. That all meant he'd have to leave the homestead and his pretty new wife for a little while to stock up some earnings.

'Jimmy, isn't it great?' Ma said. 'Your daughter got into an Ivy League. Oh, Jo, that's so great, it's so… *so* great. I'm *so* happy for you.'

She came over to my chair to offer a hug, tears in her eyes. My mother's attention and excitement kind of made me happy and annoyed at the same time. Meanwhile my father was quiet, as usual, puffing away at a big cigar. At that time he'd grown a moustache, a goatee, and sported a stud earring. His expression showed a kind of fullness before he'd even eaten. It was the kind of look you might see on a fat cat.

'Yeah, tell me something though,' he laughed. 'What kind of strings did you pull to manage that one?'

'Oh, Jimmy, stop.' My mother laughed, looking at me to see if I was laughing too, then slapped his arm. I chuckled along, *hah, what a hoot, oh, what a riot, that was hilarious.*

Good question, yes, what kind of tricks did I play to gain entry into that ivory tower, that squeaky-clean place that reserves its seats only for those young, pert asses, the offspring of the distinguished, and, of course, did I mention already, the financially comfortable? I realised my dear old dad's sting didn't veer too far from the truth on this occasion. My average high-school grades wouldn't have gotten a look in. This was when my good luck kicked in: I just happened to be around when the university admissions office was trying to do something to enhance the diversity of its student body. Not fair, really, having all these privileged trust fund babies all in one place, have to mix it up a bit, someone thought, get in some other types. I know, let's contact those community colleges and see what kind of specimens they have. That's why they included older townies like me who did OK at the local community college, where, let's face it, there weren't too many future Nobel Prize winners.

As I guzzled my beers and took another one of my mother's cigarettes (I couldn't fight the longing during these visits home), I mused on the prospect of someone like me studying at a place where I knew I didn't belong. In my head I began to add up the money from the loans I would need. I had already taken out loans to get me through community college, and I began to lose count of how many years I would be paying them all back. OK, so maybe I would borrow less, I thought, and just work as many evening shifts as I could at the printing company where I did casual work. Hah, who said I needed lots of sleep or food? It would be a long road, but then on the other hand, wouldn't I land a dream job and have a dream life with an Ivy League degree?

I took my beer to the front by the driveway and had a good look at the house. For years the brown paint on the window frames had been peeling away. A soiled off-cut from an old carpet was slung over the railing near the front door. The white door was stained with grimy fingerprints, particularly around the knob. Why hadn't I noticed all of this before? The mess of what my father called his 'car-repair business' occupied the space at the side of the house where he had put up a corrugated lean-to roof. Dark oil spots permeated the tarmac; in the peak of summer heat they steamed up and created a stifling smell. Dirty rags, barrels full of spare parts, cans overflowing with cigarette butts, and tools filled every corner.

Not far from all the filth was my father's shiny Ford pick-up truck. Every few years he bought himself a new one to replace the old. The truck was needed, he claimed, to pull the six-person-capacity motorboat that sat behind it, the newer one he just purchased, which allowed him to treat his love of deep-sea fishing. Priorities were important, after all. Parked on the street was his red two-door sports car, just washed and waxed, that was 'better on gas, my everyday car,' he had told me with a proud twinkle.

My father's cigar had left a thick scent in the air, even here. I had started to feel the dizzying effect of the alcohol and sat down on the front steps. After a few minutes my mind began to wander up and down: education, books, intellectual conversations – would I have them, would I not, could I fake them – work, jobs, money, more money, Acapulco, no money, never enough money, food, hunger, desire, understated clothes, trust fund babies, boats, shiny cars, more money, men, men's smelly cigars, cool men's earrings, booze, lies, strings, oh, and all those strings, the many strings being pushed and pulled, spun and weaved together into Jimmy O'Brien's universe.

Fourteen

On the kitchen table during a fine and sunny Monday morning my father has left a list of instructions:

> Call the numbers Ma wrote down and tell them about the memorial
> Call this place and tell them not to send any more stuff for Ma
> Cancel this policy I dont even no what it is
> Go through Ma's stuff upstairs ~~kepe~~ keep what you want get rid of everything else
> Theres more in the bedroom closet

I start with the phone numbers of my mother's friends and acquaintances, the one my mother titled, People to call when I'm gone. When they answer, some of their voices sound suspicious at first, like I'm about to try to sell them something.

When I call to cancel my mother's death by car accident insurance policy the salesperson tries to convince me to take one out for myself, in spite of the fact that I reside in the UK.

My mother hated throwing things away or handing stuff over to charity. She was adamant she would find a use for everything again at some point. The upstairs room I shared with my brother became the hoarding place for old items such as the cheap winter coats and scarves my mother wore in the seventies, blankets eaten through in the middle by moths, extra sets of 100 per cent non-iron polyester bedding. Thrown into a laundry basket are at least ten pairs of shoes my mother bought for her nursing footwear. I remember watching her slapping on white shoe-polish some afternoons before rushing out for her evening shifts.

'Why do you bother with that?' I'd ask. 'They look fine.'

'No, no,' she insisted. 'They need to be spotless. There. Perfect.'

LPs my brother and I bought, a strange mix ranging from *The Sound of Music*, *Saturday Night Fever* and Carole King, to the likes of Peter Frampton, Queen, David Bowie and Bob Seger, are all stacked in a pile next to a cheap record player and speakers. In the closet are old bathrobes and towels, more worn shoes, more old nursing journals, a few formal dresses with padded shoulders my mother would have worn to weddings or anniversary parties. Next to them are two men's formal polyester shirts. One white, one light-blue, also yellowed, a cheap red tie slung around the top of the hanger, waiting for my father to wear for a special night out.

But it's the boxes and crates full of photos and photo albums that dominate everything else in the room. My mother was always the keeper of our family's visual archive. She framed our life events the way she wanted to remember them, neat and tidy with no signs of cracking. Aside from the displays on some of the walls downstairs, in the living room, and on a small kitchen unit that also holds my father's collection of cheap model classic cars, all the rest of the photos are here, stacked and stored in some fifteen or so containers.

I find my 1979 high-school yearbook, complete with my old friends' signatures and farewell messages of good luck. There are a few images of me with Beth. We sit close together, hugging, inseparable, ready to take on the world. Beth's note to me next to her graduation photo is brief. To Jo, You are the most beautiful, strong girl I have ever known. Don't ever change OK? You're the best. Best friends always. Will always love ya, Beth. A boy called Chuck, who ended up with a gold front tooth after suffering a drunken fall on his face one night, writes, Knock em dead Jo. The world aint gonna know what hit them when you get out there. Johnny Hartman, a long-haired mechanic with a motorbike with whom I was desperately in love, but would never have, because his long-term girlfriend, Colleen Miller, a cosmetology chick, was tinier and prettier than I, and never let him out of her sight, wrote the most profound note: To JoJo, Don't ever give up on your dreams you are so talented. Don't ever stop being a dreamweaver. Don't let anything stop you from getting what you want and from getting out of this shit hole. Johnny. The quote I supplied for my own photo read: The best days are yet to come, can't wait to see what's out there. I owe everything to my best friend Beth, I couldn't have done it without you. I laugh at our teenage profundity.

The same box holds photos taken throughout my junior and high-school years. Dave and his old neighbourhood friend, Dom Santori, the best man at his wedding, huddle together in our front yard comparing their flexed-arm muscles. Each one eyes the other as though preparing for combat. I'm posing on my own in our backyard in black and white, gazing off into the distance with overdone eye make-up, mascara so thick it weighs down my eyelids like a row of black crows. It was the year I experimented with plucking my brows which resulted in the expected fine-lined arch. Boy, I thought I was something. Now I'm standing near our front door with Barbara, the girl from across the street, both of us puckering our lips, one hand on a hip, the other holding up our long hair, heads tilted back. I find Beth, both of us proud of our bikini bodies on the beach. Beth and I posing in our prom dresses. Beth and I with our prom dates donning matching corsages. We are waiting in hope, anticipating something remarkable around the corner. I'm in awe at the sight of our youthful beauty, over-plucked brows and all, how flawless the smiles of our teen years *appear* from this distance of years with the fuzzy magic of the lens. What a downright shame I couldn't have enjoyed it more then. We were told by adults and teachers it was supposed to be the best time of our lives. But they were all liars. Who were they trying to kid? Our smiles masked everything.

I find a few photos of my graduation day from fancy pants Ivy League when my mother was snapping away, ordering me to smile. 'Oh, you can manage a bigger smile than that, Jo.' No wonder I was pouting. It appeared as though I may have tried to trim my own hair in my effort to save a few bucks. I wore the expected gown over a sleeveless A-line sundress. I looked awfully wide in the thing but I remember buying it especially for the occasion. The things we choose not to see when we spot a bargain. I finished off the look with the cap and tassel, but the garb was enough ammunition to provoke my father into making a full-blown ground strike. He agreed to join in a couple of photos only, and was reluctant to attend the ceremony as the second guest-ticket holder.

'We'll see. Maybe,' was his response, his most overused phrase throughout my childhood and beyond.

His evasiveness over the years generated the expected effect. By the time my brother and I were old enough to know better, we stopped asking him for anything, material or otherwise, but my mother, in her persistence, in her endless desire for some kind of marital and family order, still clung onto hope that he'd change.

By the time Dad had sat through the first half of the speech from the honoured guest speaker, the world-famous physicist Stephen Hawking, Dad's patience had ran out. He had more important stuff to do, it seemed, the details of which we would never know. It was all top-secret, hush-hush. Who knows, maybe over the years he was concocting a challenge to Stephen Hawking's theory of cosmology and couldn't stand to listen to the little man basking in celebrity stardom from his wheelchair. Oh yes, our old man, Jimmy O'Brien, was a mystery.

When he'd had enough, he stopped fidgeting, stood up, stepped over the long line of other crossed legs in that crowded row of seats, the ones that belonged to those proud, suited middle-class parents who looked on with pride, wiping away tears from their eyes, and he left as fast as he could. Dad wouldn't waste any more of his precious time on the canapé spread, the small talk with other parents or faculty who didn't mind schmoozing in the hope that they would generate some charitable donations over the summer. Many guests, of course, would have been wealthy alumni who'd want to give something back, especially if their younger ones were waiting in line.

During my time at the Ivy League I hovered between two opposing worlds. While my mother cheered me on for my academic curiosity, my tenacity – how she loved to see me work hard, sweating every last droplet till there was nothing left – it was obvious that she thought a more practical vocation for a woman, like nursing, made more sense. When one day she asked me out of genuine interest and concern, 'What kind of job will you do with an art history degree, you know, when you have to pay back your loans?' I struggled to respond. She had a good point. At that stage I had no idea what I would do after my degree.

'Well, I want to be a well-rounded, educated person. It's for the love of learning about the world,' I said. That was the sort of thing I liked the sound of when I studied at the community college, alien as it was to some of the others there, and what I tried to articulate in my fancy pants interview. 'What's wrong with that? Maybe I'll get a job at a museum.'

She waited before responding. 'I guess it's good you got the printing company to fall back on.'

My grandmother, Nonna, wondered why I was wasting my time when I was the perfect age for having children with my great child-bearing hips. She was already planning to sabotage my aspirations. 'I told my friend Carmella all about you, Jo, that you're single and we were thinking you should meet her son, Marlon. Ooh, he's a handsome one. And he's got a good job. Does maintenance over at MIT. Good benefits over there.'

Dave vacillated between encouragement and siding with Nonna. He was thrilled at the prospect of me meeting the children of the rich and famous yet warned me of the inevitable. 'Yeah, there's a biological clock ticking away. If you're not careful, it'll be too late. Tick, tick.'

My father didn't bother adding much of his two cents, except to say this: 'I was good at drawing. You know you got that talent from me, right? But that was like a kid's pipe dream,' he laughed. 'Anyway, I didn't have to finish school, and look, I've done alright.'

To him I was a traitor to the labouring working class, the people doing the real work. To my family I was a vacant dreamer, the one who had some cocky nerve to voice a ridiculous whim about living a different life, one in which I imagined the beauty in impractical things. I guess I always knew the arts were a luxury only the middle- and upper-classes could afford, but I wanted to feel what it was like to have some of that luxury too, just a little taste, in spite of my family.

When on campus I was never just a typical student like the other younger, wealthier ones around me. I became the flexible undergraduate always available to help out at the printing company during school breaks. And yes, OK, maybe some of my talk about all those books I had to read, all those essays I had to write, kind of got on my co-workers' nerves.

By this time, Mike and I decided to go our separate ways. He had no interest in my studies, felt hard done by when I couldn't spend time with him, and he wanted to settle down and have kids as soon as possible. 'Time's ticking on, Jo. Got to get on with it.' In the end it was clear that he wasn't going to be the one to help get me that new money I'd need for the grand white house, books and piano. Not to mention the swimming pool. Mike still worked at the printing company and that was alright. It wasn't long before he found himself another girlfriend, a younger new employee from the Philippines. She was a cousin of one of the supervisors who worked in the delivery area. He fell madly for this little thing and it wasn't long before they planned to get married. I was happy for him, really I was, and wanted to stay friends. Sometimes after I'd had a few too many drinks when I was alone late at night in my shared student apartment, I would call him and reminisce about all the good times we had. The last time I did this, he told me politely it would be a good idea if I didn't call anymore.

I'm not sure if it was him I missed so much as his family and their frequent parties, especially the family reunions where they all seemed genuinely interested in each other. I enjoyed bumping into his mom, Sheila, who worked in the accounts department. We arranged to have coffee now and then and the conversation would take us to the subject of Mike and his new life, how thoughtful his girlfriend was, how generous her family were. 'They're like that, the Filipinos. Very loyal people, you know.'

I managed to find some consolation through the small group of older students. The university worked hard to support us and organise social events for us and I learned to appreciate them. Some women in the group were middle-class, in their thirties and over. They had families but never had the chance to go on to higher education or their degree was interrupted, probably when they had children. In my book that was another good reason not to have kids. Some of these women became wise big-sister figures. They looked after us younger ones, yet shared our anxieties too.

Early on it was easy to spot the others who were like me. I could pick out the ones who had emotional wounds that hadn't healed. They tried to cover them up with smiles, layers of surface bandage, but the minute they were nearby I could almost smell it; the aftermath of suffering. In the first year I became close friends with thirty-three-year-old Michelle, who was in her second year of mathematics. She confided in me about her family history that consisted of continued sexual abuse by her father. Throughout the unbearable heat and humidity of the Boston summer, she wore long sleeves to cover her self-harm scars. There must have been at least twenty light tone marks of different lengths and thicknesses, like rickety steps of a ladder, all the way from her wrist to the upper half of her left arm. I had a sympathetic but uncomfortable laugh with her when she joked about it.

'I like to call them my laugh lines,' she told me one night over a drink. 'I did it when I was drunk or stoned. It was a good way to laugh through it all.' I was always surprised that she could smile and look radiant when she explained such things.

I admitted to Michelle that I had tried it too, in my teens. And I agreed that drunk or doped up was the best way, sometimes with a friend for a bit of encouragement. I remembered the time one of the gang, her name was Donna, an obese, pimply girl who had a mean father, deliberately smashed the bottle of beer the two of us were drinking one night in a dark corner of the local park. 'OK,' she said. 'We'll take turns.'

As she pressed the sharp glass into her skin, she screamed hard and fast. 'Fucking bastard, fucking bastard.' She stopped at two small scrapes, just enough to draw a bit of blood and cause lots of redness around the cut, then handed it to me.

'Fucking bastard, fucking bastard,' I repeated, copying her intentions, ending up with nothing more than a mere scrape, then we both cried, drunk after two beers, holding each other and swearing we'd stay best friends for ever, a pact we broke that same year when we went off to different high schools.

What did it all mean?

Frustration in times of helplessness, self-hatred, and maybe even boredom. Yes, simple boredom. Not knowing what else to do with ourselves when there were no other options.

Michelle and I connected instantly, shared an apartment the following year with a quiet history student called Leah, and I looked forward to our regular conversations about art, literature, philosophy, politics, feminism, and messed-up families. But Michelle's lows came on fast. She would disappear suddenly into the dark corners of the library, come home, not eat and lock herself in her bedroom, or go astray somewhere else for days.

I found it difficult not to take it personally. Michelle had no problem achieving the highest marks on all her assessments and exams. Later on when she graduated, a year or so before I did, she finished with *summa cum laude* honours and was offered a full scholarship and expenses on a PhD course. We lost touch after I graduated but I discovered through a mutual friend that she gave up on academic life about midway through her PhD. After returning from a big trip to the East she settled down in a quiet California town, unmarried, where she began her new life teaching yoga.

Somehow Michelle smiled through the dark shadow of her past, and spoke with a confident tone that meant all around her would stop and listen. When she wasn't saying something worthwhile or pondering something important, she made it clear, even in silence, that she just didn't give a shit, she didn't need people. This is what I most envied about her. The approach drew even more people, men in particular. Male students, young undergrads and the older postgrads, flocked around her, wanted her opinion, were desperate to sleep with her, ached to devote themselves to her. And all she had to do was smile occasionally, offer a slight bit of encouragement, yet somehow manage at the same time to convey that she could survive without them all quite easily.

Unfortunately, I couldn't work the same kind of miracles. In the first term I attended the introduction party for new mature students and set my sights on getting to know an attractive guy called Brendan. He was a dark-skinned black man from Michigan, twenty-seven years old, and studying engineering. The army paid all his tuition and expenses. He had a gripping shy smile that transformed his face. When I first engaged him in small talk he seemed wary and disinterested, but at some point I got him to hook his eyes on mine and that smile appeared.

After a bit of persistence, I was successful in setting up a first date. Later we became an item for a while that semester, which made me feel pretty damn pleased with myself. I was attracted to our obvious differences, yet I convinced myself we had more in common. His mother worked as a mid-level manager in the field of social work. A caring profession, I thought, like my mother's. His father left them years ago when he and his brother were young, and that made him angry, but his mother stayed strong on her own and got by with the love of family. Of course he was angry, I understood that, for sure. *I was angry*. What could be better than to be angry together? Although I could only dream of Ma leaving Dad for good, staying strong for her children. We were a good, natural match, I thought, like blues and oranges, purples and greens. Mix them all up and you get a perfect complimentary kaleidoscope. I stopped myself at whimsical imaginings of what our mixed-race kids might have looked like. But while I daydreamed about growing old with Brendan it soon became clear that even though he admitted to *liking* me a lot, he wasn't sure how far we should take our relationship.

'You're white, Irish and Italian-American, working-class from Boston. That combination kind of spells disaster,' he joked one night when we were in bed together. It didn't matter what Ivy League I was attending, I couldn't get past those things. 'It won't exactly sit well with my mother and the others back home, and family is family, after all.'

When he uttered those words I sensed they had been well-rehearsed. It was only a matter of time, I realised, before he'd get rid of me. By some horrendous coincidence, his best friend and roommate at college, another army scholarship guy, just so happened to have been the buzz-cut student from my interview. Well, it was no surprise to find that this guy, Sam, had taken an obvious dislike to me, as I first suspected at the interview. He could see my desperation through all of the bullshit and good posture. Not having Sam on my side wasn't going to fare well for my future prospects with Brendan.

Sam displayed openly his distaste for me whenever I hung out at their apartment, when I talked too much, laughed too loud, or supposedly, in his view, phoned Brendan too much. When they had others over for meals and parties it was clear I was the odd one out who hadn't learned the right things to say or not to say. I came across as the laughable side-kick. One evening someone brought up the subject of eighteenth-century English poets.

'Oh, Alexander Pope. I know him. And you know that big Wordsworth book store in Harvard Square. That's probably named after William Wordsworth. Yup. Bet that's named after him,' I made the mistake of saying.

I couldn't quite understand why they were all so hung up on Tom Waits' music and I only realised afterwards how naive I had been in admitting this openly.

'But he's pure classic stuff,' Sam insisted. 'Exactly how is it that you don't *get* Tom Waits?'

Sam's treatment and Brendan's diminishing interest made me feel like I was the outcast of all outcasts, a tedious person, an embarrassment. I went to record shops on my own and listened to Tom Waits and still didn't warm to him. What was I missing? Over time I learned it was best to keep my mouth shut, always trying to find only the right occasion to speak, but after a while it felt as though I was taking my chances by just choosing to be present. By just breathing. At some point I turned into a speechless, non-existent nobody. Not much of a turn on.

Brendan threw strong hints my way when the time came to say adios.

'Not tonight. No, I'm busy tomorrow night too. Let's just have some space, OK?'

He later agreed to have a meal together at a cheap, local Mexican place, during which he said, through that tender smile of his, that we should call it a day. He meandered through all the nice-guy gentle ways of doing it. *Oh, how sad, you're such a nice person, you're special, you'll find someone else,* blah blah, and then the sobs started (mine). One margarita followed another, then another. By the time we were both tearful, giddy, and not so steady on our feet, we headed to my place and made our way into the sack without hesitation.

That night I had to confess to Brendan, finally, after some time, that I suspected he had never quite known where the spot was, the all-important female pleasure organ. He was baffled, and admitted to guessing. All the time we'd been sleeping together I hadn't mentioned it, well, because of fear of embarrassing him. How could I hurt the poor guy's feelings? He was just too nice. And didn't we have something special? He'd come around, I thought. But his breaking up with me was the turning point. I had to say something. *No, you didn't know, did you, at your age and with all the girlfriends you say you've had. They were all faking it. So now who's the idiot?*

Brendan was eager at once to get things right, to discover this new unknown territory, and he insisted I show him the way. He was amazed at this new enlightenment and the night carried on. It was the most passionate time we'd had together. I woke in the morning with a bad hangover, told myself it was the last time I would drink so much, maybe I would even stop, that would be something, wouldn't it, but in spite of my pounding head, I looked forward to the day with a newfound hope. Surely Brendan would have second thoughts now.

As he was getting ready to leave, after little sleep, a quick breakfast, and still wearing that grin of his, his last words to me were, 'Let's be friends, OK?'

We had a long kiss and embrace, but what I really wanted to do was rip that stupid expression from his face. *You're welcome for the anatomy lesson, all future girlfriends will benefit from my sisterly kindness. Stop smiling. Please. Stop.*

Fifteen

Through the window I watched Brendan unlock his bike, stretch his arms over his head, and gaze up cheerfully at the sky. It was the start of a clear but cold day. I waited till he rode off, feeling the last grains of energy leave my body before the tears started.

Slumped over in a chair at the kitchen table wearing only a long T-shirt and underwear, I focused my eyes on the cockroach traps I had set out in the dusty corners. My bare feet felt cold, but I couldn't muster the strength to move. My low-level sniffling built up and I tried to control my breathing. Soon I let go of a guttural grunt that I wasn't expecting, a surprising sound resembling the cry of a wounded animal on its last leg, one that still clung on to a final hope that someone would come to the rescue.

I allowed myself to scream as loud as I could. I carried on like that, rocking back and forth in that same chair, howling like a lunatic, like someone who needed to be dragged away and strapped in restraints. I cried out as hard as I could manage until my throat was rubbed raw and there was nothing left. In the silence and through foggy eyes I spotted a cockroach. Surprisingly, in the midst of the sunny kitchen, it scurried across the room, ignoring the traps, only to disappear again.

For most of that morning I cried on and off, my eyes ending up bloodshot, swollen slits. By 4pm, after a sleep, I felt an unexpected lightness in my body. It was as though all the waterworks had flushed out a heavy lethal toxin and I was ready to start anew. I pulled my tired ass out of bed, made a sandwich, coffee, opened a book, took out my notes, and began my return to studying for my end of semester exams. By the time I sat down in the exam hall for the first one two days later I was ready to fly through it, a soaring eagle in charge of its destiny.

The other exams came and went successfully. I discovered later my results were close to 100 per cent. Over the college break I increased my hours at the printing company, ate as much stodgy, holiday food as I could stomach, and looked forward to the next semester. In spite of spotting Brendan arm in arm with a new girlfriend early on, a pale, blue-eyed blonde one at that, he became a comical figure of the past. Although I did think that maybe, just maybe, I should have let him continue assuming he knew his way around women's anatomy, then I'd be the one smiling, wouldn't I?

But I stopped laughing when I realised, around seven weeks since that last night we slept together, that my usual reliable period was still not forthcoming. My hunch that I was pregnant was confirmed soon enough with a test kit. I had been taking the pill for a few years by then, but fell into that unlucky minute percentage of women who still manage to conceive. Looking back I think maybe I could have missed a pill, that stupid seven-day break after the twenty-one day cycle could have thrown me off. Recurring thoughts of a cruel God entered my psyche and wouldn't leave. *That'll show you. Don't mess with me, girl.* Whatever direction I decided to take at that point, I knew I would feel the consequences of my decision for a long time.

When I phoned Beth and told her, without hesitation she said, 'Just let me know when you want me. I'm there,' and offered some of her savings to cover the abortion. I had never asked anyone for financial help before, but Beth's charity didn't worry me or send me into my usual guilt. I contemplated briefly telling Brendan, asking him for some cash, if for no other reason but to make *him* suffer some guilt, but concluded I didn't want any of it. I wanted to rid myself of him, erase those unrealistic fantasies.

Beth thought otherwise. 'Why should these guys always be allowed to walk away? Why can't they feel some pain for a change?'

I've learned that when life speeds along in a frenzy it takes no mercy on the weak. There was no time to feel sorry for myself. Following the termination, to my great surprise I returned to my studies with an intensity I didn't know I possessed. My emotional tragedies were nasty inducements for kicking me into action. It was like a sharp, fast rocket was shoved up my ass and the only way I would feel any relief from the discomfort was to continue moving at full force. Between obsessive reading, keeping up with my schedule of classes, museum and gallery visits on the weekend and working in the evenings, there was little time left for fun. But that didn't matter. The only thing that interested me then was the reward of intellectual stimulation, those exquisite occasions of discovery after hours of study when a difficult text finally offered a special turn of phrase – the boom when everything made sense. And I could claim these epiphanies as my own – I earned them, after all, didn't I? No one was going to take that away from me, damn it, not if I could help it.

I lost interest in men completely but some months later, with encouragement from Constance, more of those young college guys started to jump in and out of my life, fast and furious like hot popcorn kernels. At some point when my finances shrunk to their lowest again, making it a strain to pay for therapy sessions (by that time I only had basic student health insurance) I agreed with Constance that I was stronger, that things were well enough for me to have a therapy break. She urged me to phone her if I needed, and especially in case of any emergency. In my mind I pictured my student apartment in flames with me hanging outside my bedroom window, telephone in hand, screaming to Constance, 'Help, I'm trapped!' and her, minutes later, climbing a ladder. 'I'm here, Jo. I'm here to save you. Don't worry. It's all going to be fine.'

My academic performance continued to improve and my confidence grew. In contrast to the early days when the fear of embarrassment stunted most of my attempts to voice my opinions in lectures, I later built up the nerve to take chances, to engage in debates, but only after I'd done the reading, considered the potential arguments. At worst, I developed impressive bluffing strategies. In spite of some of my new bookish self-assurance, on the dating scene I attracted all sorts of losers.

I met one guy through a mutual college friend. Rob Segal was a nice Jewish student from the Boston area who was in some of my art history classes. We became friendly after taking part in group work which involved weekend outings to city museums and galleries, and he'd sometimes offer to treat me to coffee or even lunch afterwards. Rob was a kind, quiet-spoken, intelligent soul. I was touched when he seemed to encourage my ideas and input over the others in our group. We shared notes, books, had serious discussions in the library about important things like Picasso's Guernica and the power of politicised art. Rob enjoyed wearing tweed blazers over T-shirts, with jeans and sneakers. My brother would have described his look as understated, upper-middle-class. There was no mistaking that Rob was loaded, one of those single-child, trust fund babies. The way he spoke and dressed signalled that he was no townie. But the biggest giveaway about his background was the Beacon Hill, Boston apartment where he lived alone and had parties. Later he confessed in a whispery tone, 'Mom and Dad bought it as a gift for me. Something to do with managing their taxes. They use it too, and extended family and friends from out of town stay here a lot when they come to visit.'

In my efforts to be polite – my mother always said, 'Whatever you do you should at least try to be polite, even if you don't like someone' – I tried to maintain my act of being in the know about such things.

'Oh, yes,' I said. 'Well, that makes sense. Very sensible idea. Such a convenient location. I mean you can't go wrong with that. And what an amazing view. You can see for ever from here.'

Even though 'for ever' felt like a far-off place indeed, I thought I sounded convincing. But inside me, way down in that hollow vessel where I fought with my loneliness, I couldn't find a way to make sense of my reaction. The tears flowed later that afternoon on the train home when I realised I might never know the reasons why some things in life happened the way they did.

Loaded or not, it turned out that sweet Rob was the one I really had my eye on, but I was learning, I guess, that such unlikely matches were just not meant to be. In spite of his encouraging smiles over our pleasant post-museum encounters, he showed no romantic interest in me, whatsoever. I first wondered if he was gay, but found out he preferred another Jewish student at the university. She was an English major from Manhattan who was stuck with the unfortunate name Mindy, although this didn't appear to bother him. This detail was another sign that I was not the right one for him. He revealed his Mindy interest to me one afternoon over coffee when he told me he was invited as her date to her cousin's Bar Mitzvah in New York City. It was meant to be the Manhattan party of the year, he said, with all sorts of important people attending, and he rattled off some names I didn't recognise but should have. Then he filled me in on where he was with this Manhattan Mindy character.

'She's got a birthday coming up and I want to get her something really special, like a nice piece of jewellery. I need a woman's careful eye on this, Jo, to make sure I get it right. Will you help me out here?' he asked.

I knew then I was out of my depth and declined his offer to go shopping on Newbury Street when I remembered that the most expensive gift I ever received from my ex-boyfriend, Mike, was a Timex digital watch.

I had the feeling he sensed I was trying to close in on him after I made the mistake of leaving a few too many messages that week to confirm our meeting. That was the same afternoon he said he wanted to fix me up with his friend, Edward. (Yes, it was Edward, not Ted, Ed, or Eddie.) Edward came across as nice enough, I guess, but he was dull, suppressed of any possibility of light or colour, a bit like those overcast skies across Britain that threaten us every season. He was eager from the start to get me into bed, but I held off. Ultimately, I was uninterested in any college student under the age of twenty-five who wore office shirts and ties for a night out on the town and was destined for a career as a banker. A solid financial future was certainly attractive to me, but I wasn't that desperate.

Other prospects around that time stood me up, didn't call after the first date, or were so over-the-top enthusiastic, little over-excited puppies wagging their tails and salivating at the first offer of any tiny morsel, that I ran away as fast as I could. For some reason I hung onto the hope that something promising awaited me.

It was that absurd thinking that led me to one guy at the printing company who managed to hook me into a whirlwind romance before I called it quits on the boyfriend business. Like me, he also worked evening shifts. He was a trained paramedic and told me, and everyone else at work, that he was studying at Harvard as a pre-med student. Like my fancy pants Ivy League, he claimed they accepted older students on a special entry programme at Harvard and they offered flexibility for part-time studies. He recalled exciting stories of his paramedic days, told me all about his Harvard lectures and the professors, spoke in impressive medical terms, took me around the campus, gave me little tours of the libraries, treated me to some expensive meals in Harvard Square – he certainly knew how to choose those places – even took me one weekend to meet his family in Vermont in their nice but simple abode where they lit fires in the winter and joined each other for cross-country skiing outings. One time he presented me with a nice bouquet of flowers for no reason at all except to write on the card, You don't really know how special you are, do you?

It dawned on me that we may have been meant for each other when he admitted, like me, he had no interest in having children, not even one day.

'Why should women be expected to bear the children? Some people just don't want them, shouldn't have them and there's nothing wrong with admitting that. Like you, I have other plans. Bigger plans,' he said that day, with those piercing blue eyes, when we shared our ambitions about the future.

And what a future it was going to be. I could see the skies opening to clear a path for us to flap our eager wings anywhere we damn well wanted. We giggled, joy emanating a bright, promising, almost blinding light from our dreamy eyes. Like me, he was so busy he didn't have much extra time for seeing friends, he could just about squeeze in our dates. Like me, he worked all sorts of hours to finance his studies, but, I thought, he'll get there, he'll be a big success one day. It'll all be worth it. All our suffering, the delayed gratification, will pay off, I told myself. The realities of the world, however, are not at all as perfectly sweet and ripe as we'd like them to be when we bite into them. Rarely does anything that presents itself so tenderly turn out to be the authentic peach for which we are hoping.

I should have known something was a bit strange when Doug always found an excuse not to take me to his apartment. It was being renovated after a plumbing leak from the apartment upstairs. Or an old friend was camping out there for a bit on a surprise visit and it wasn't the right time to see it. Or the place was stinking and needed a good cleaning, and so on. A few months after we'd been seeing each other the truth about Doug was revealed when someone at work tipped me off.

'OK, sorry, Jo, I'm going to be straight with you. Doug ain't no pre-med student at Harvard,' the evening print production supervisor revealed to me one night when Doug called in sick.

This was Pete Soames talking, the guy who'd been trying to get into my pants for years, but Pete insisted his story was legit, then called for some back-up. Three women I always enjoyed sharing small talk and a laugh with from the negative stripping room came to see me during the coffee break with sincerity in their eyes. Joanie, the wise chain-smoker with yellowing teeth who left her abusive husband years before and never remarried, placed her hand sympathetically on mine.

'Last night we saw him with the other girlfriend who caught him in his lies. So sorry, Jo. It's best you find out now.'

Pam and Patty, twin sisters who went on double dates with guys from packaging and deliveries, confirmed everything. 'We can't wait to give him a piece of our mind, Jo. He was pretty convincing. Son of a bitch.'

Doug was a pathological liar, found out after one of his girlfriends, someone he'd been seeing while dating me, caught him in the middle of his many lies and made a surprise visit to the printing company to challenge him. He might have worked as a paramedic once in his day, but there was no pre-med, no studying in those nice science and medical libraries at Harvard, no studio apartment near Cambridge. No future. Yes, I did meet his real family in Vermont; a mother, a father, a younger brother even, whom I remember had a lazy eye, and we all had a real meal together eating a real, overcooked roasted chicken with all the trimmings at a solid-pine dining-room table in a small, slightly stuffy, but real, welcoming kitchen. I touched the day, breathed in the inviting scent – yes, it was a bit dry, but made with motherly love, and the gravy was pretty good too. Hell, it was *home-made*. I had taken it all in, remembered the quality of the sunlight as it shone through the lace curtains that created a floral pattern on the table. I had washed my hands in the bathroom with the rose-scented soap, felt the rough texture of the towel when I dried them. I kept telling myself, yes, it must have been real. I couldn't have just imagined it all, could I? But maybe there was something odd about the way the brother had looked at him sternly with the one focused eye, the other going off in the opposite direction and then at his parents after Doug said, 'Yup, this girl here is the real thing. Gonna get her to marry me, I am. Isn't she something?'

There was a girlfriend he had been living with, I was told later. She had a young child, a daughter. Then there was another girlfriend, a hairdresser. Did he take them to meet the family? Before the liar disappeared from the printing company for good, I had the chance to confront him on the phone. I tried to remain rational and sane. 'Why? That's all I ask. Why did you do it?'

His voice sounded calm, revealing no signs of emotion, and he said very little, which made me think he certainly had the potential to make it big in the American medical profession one day. 'I told you what you wanted to hear,' he said. 'I offered myself to you as someone else, someone you wanted me to be.'

Constance came to my rescue and she was kind enough to offer me a nice discount. I was, after all, one of her most loyal customers.

I was just about hanging on with work and school, exams around the corner, but I couldn't sleep and the nightmares I'd had as a teenager returned. I spent some time with sympathetic Beth, but she was busy working, planning her wedding, getting cosy with Paul, seeing her family. I was lined up for a bridesmaid role, but she knew I couldn't cope even with tedious bridesmaid demands at that point and, without holding a grudge, Beth let me pull out. I breathed a weighty sigh of relief. I felt I was in her way, dragging down the mood of what was meant to be her special time. I made excuses when she phoned to invite me over. I lost my appetite, the pounds began to drop off and my energy decreased. I showed up to classes but found it impossible to concentrate.

I'd admitted to Constance I was drinking too much, spending what little money I had on a cheap bottle of wine that I would I finish in one sitting on my own. I'd soak in a hot bath full of bubbles after work, gulp my way through to the last drop, fall asleep and wake up drunk with the glass in my hand submerged in cold water, the skin on my fingers and feet shrivelled like raisins. My room-mates were either in bed or out, sleeping at their boyfriends' places, living their lives, I imagined, while I was there, alone. Again. Did they try to warn me about the liar, tell me that things didn't quite sound the way they should? Maybe. The shock of the fall was too unbearable. Humiliation took over any urges to retrace my steps.

I didn't exactly fit into any simplistic alcoholic category. Downing a bottle of wine alone wasn't common for me, only occasional when I hit a low point. Yes, I had binge nights too before that point, but didn't everyone?

'My drinking habits overall are considered pretty normal by others' standards,' I reminded Constance. 'I'm no different from my friends and the amount they drink. And my family, well, they can drink me under the table.'

The problem was the lows were creeping up more frequently and I knew if I didn't control myself – well, let's just say, I didn't trust myself anymore. Constance encouraged me to try Alcoholics Anonymous, even though I didn't consider myself to be one.

I went along with a fair amount of scepticism, but after a couple of meetings I found I enjoyed it, maybe a bit too much. What a voyeuristic pleasure it was to hear the minutiae of others' telltale rock-bottom stories. The stay-at-home middle-class mom with too much time on her hands for liquid lunches, facials, and hosting dinner parties. Oh, the stories she told: 'I didn't remember what happened after I had sex with that workman and I didn't know if I wanted to remember.' The ex-homeless park-bencher who never quite got the break he needed: 'Going OK for now, but that half-way house…it ain't so good for me. Too many others there just gonna drag me down again.' My bath-time boozy aftermath of falling for a liar wasn't as interesting as any of their rock-bottom stories. I worried that if I continued to attend these sessions, I might find ways to land myself into even scarier situations in my attempt to keep up with the others, to experience the severity of their agony. How could I otherwise empathise? It dawned on me in one of my sessions with Constance that maybe that was the danger I fell into as a twelve-year-old when I dared to swallow that bottle of aspirin. Was I trying to keep up with my brother?

When Constance asked, 'Did you feel certain at the time you could have died from that overdose?' I had to think hard about my answer. There was probably something at the back of my young mind telling me I wouldn't die, I admitted, although I had no way of knowing for sure. I thought longer and revisited the question at our following session.

'Maybe it was the thrill of the risk-taking, getting so close to the danger zone that must have attracted me. Maybe I wanted to know what it would feel like,' I told Constance.

'And what did it feel like?'

'Scary. Thrilling, maybe. Like I was in suspense, wondering what was going to happen next. But when nothing much happened except for feeling really sick I was just disappointed. And lonely again.'

I stopped drinking for a while, replacing alcohol with smoking and excessive coffee drinking. After much weight loss and a continual lack of sleep, Constance said, 'Jo, I'm worried now. In my opinion you've become clinically depressed and I'm thinking you need something more than just talking. What do you think about trying antidepressants?' She advised me to look into getting approval for extensions on my upcoming exams and essays for medical reasons. I lived in hope the pills would fix me.

My mother stepped in fast. 'You just come right over and I'll take care of you, Jo. I don't want you worrying about anything, do you hear me? Nothing.' She offered to do my laundry and feed me. She had never cared much for wasting her time in the kitchen preparing home-cooked food, but she made a sincere effort by serving me endless cups of instant coffee and tea, eggs on toast, tuna or egg salad sandwiches, spaghetti with a lovingly opened jar of ragu sauce. Cigarettes on demand. She braced herself for the times when I broke down, held me close with firm, decisive arms, told me she loved me. If she could, she said, she would never let anything bad ever happen to me again. I fell into her, felt her soul, forgave her for past wrongs, and wanted to believe that she could protect me.

Nonna visited one afternoon bringing with her a box of Italian cannoli from her local bakery, which I tried to eat but couldn't manage. Months later, when I returned to the routines of life that irritate and at the same time make us feel grateful, she said, 'Jo, I knew things must have been bad when you couldn't eat that cannoli. Very bad.'

On that 'bad' afternoon when we sat together on the old, worn couch, I let my emotions loose. Nonna held my hand and said, 'Oh, Jo. I know you're going to meet a nice, honest fellow one day. I know you will. You just got to make sure of one thing.'

'What's that, Nonna?'

'Just make sure he ain't a drinker.'

Sixteen

I reassembled most of the scattered bits that were left of me after Doug and filled the gaps in-between – well, the pieces didn't fit back together exactly as before – with the bonding power of some newly acquired wisdom. I completed my exams and essays after a short, helpful extension and was preparing for two summer classes, feeling worn, but compelling myself to continue. It seemed I had developed an unexpected talent for producing strong work when under pressure. I was surprised I reached an impressive 3.8 grade point average at that stage, higher than the 3.5 needed for the study abroad programme. The dean who first interviewed me and who continued to look after us – us older students who still felt the urge to hang on and suckle until forced to release our airtight grip – held a meeting about late applications as there were still spaces in London in their autumn term. I didn't say much, didn't ask any questions. Up until the moment when the dean pulled me aside, I hadn't even considered applying. My mind was preoccupied with more practical things. There was summer school, more paid-work hours to schedule. Life's bills to pay.

'You know, Jo,' the nice dean said. This time she wasn't smiling. The look in her eyes was resolute and in that flash of a second or two I knew she wasn't playing around. 'You might be apprehensive, but if you don't do something like this now while you're not tied down with family and all that…well, you could really regret it later on. And I bet you'd love all those great museums.'

On my way into work that evening and later that night in bed I thought about the dean's approach. She had been quick with her advice and gave the impression she wasn't going to waste her breath trying to convince me. I remembered Constance's earlier warnings about regrets, thought about how sick they could make you feel, how they could fester and escalate, eventually erupting into something dangerous. I didn't want to live with that hovering over me. But I knew I had my future work cut out.

It was during the third year of my four-year degree when the university awarded me with extra living expenses money on top of my full-tuition scholarship. I was over the moon; things were looking up for me. I scrambled around in a manic mess studying and working that summer, moving things out of my apartment to my old bedroom and my parents' damp-cellar storage area before my London departure. The hardest thing, when the time came near to leave, was saying goodbye to Constance.

'You've come such a long way, Jo, all through your very hard work. You should be proud,' she said, all the time her smile warming the room with its honey-like luminosity. I appreciated her gesture, but knew very well that without her I would have been nothing. I wouldn't have been flying off thousands of miles away for a year, that much was certain. I knew also, in spite of what might have been suggested by my marks, that I still had a long way to go before I would evolve into a more concrete *something* on my own. I thanked her for everything and sobbed on her shoulder when we hugged at her front door. I started to move away but her hand remained on my arm for a few seconds. I took her hand and we stood there for a moment, both of us wet-eyed, until we embraced again and said our goodbyes.

Alice, an art history student from Somerset, introduced me to Jon in the latter part of that first term. Alice loved wearing wide-leg pants, along with floppy velvet hats and neck-chokers. Her accent sounded a bit like Princess Diana's, but then so did many others there, I thought. She was less pretty than the princess but she had a flawless, milky complexion and carried her petite figure with a chest that seemed too large for her frame, with catwalk conviction. She made it her mission to take me to expensive London restaurants with grand chandeliers that served traditional afternoon teas, complete with odd, tasteless cucumber and butter sandwiches, scones and miniature cakes. I was shocked to discover these arrangements were so expensive, but Alice insisted it was all worth it and wouldn't say no to paying after I said I couldn't afford it.

'No, no, no, my love, you can't come to London and not have tea. I won't have it. It's my treat and I won't take no for an answer.'

It was Alice who showed me how to prepare and drink tea, and for this I am forever grateful. I can't imagine how ignorant I must have appeared before knowing all the ins and outs of it.

'The proper way is to pour the milk first *then* add the tea from the pot after it's had plenty of time to brew. *Always, always,* make your tea in a pot. And always hold the saucer with your cup as you are drinking. Like this,' she said, demonstrating in her princess-like way, sipping, pinky-finger extended.

Alice was a bit of an enigma. Well-mannered and polite, always careful with her words, she wasn't an emotive type, but after she had a few drinks she didn't hesitate to show her other side.

She became one of my closest, most loyal friends for many years before she headed out of the city, had three children, and adopted a more restrained existence along the London commuter belt. But that's another story. She was always willing to lend a padded shoulder for me to cry on when I needed it and for that too I'll always be indebted. Her past was undramatic, her life secure with a good stock of that old family money that would make her life easier until the day she died, but none of that stopped her from working hard, seeing the world through the eyes of others and treating her new poor American friend to generous meals out.

Jon was a grad student studying for a master's degree in Social Science Research Methods when I met him that night in the student bar. He was sitting at a table with a small group of other guys including Alice's cousin Owen who played guitar in the student jazz band in which Jon was the keyboard player. The five of them looked as if they were in deep debate when Alice waved to Owen from the entrance. While the others appeared conservative to some degree with their tidy, short haircuts and Oxford-style shirts, it was Jon who stood out with his Mediterranean looks and wavy jet-black hair, long enough to be tied back into a ponytail. Hmm, rebel type, I thought, with a twinge of excitement.

Jon emanated a kind of cool, the authentic kind that some people are fortunate enough to acquire without effort. But that easy cool also intimidated me. My instinct was to turn away when I saw his eyes looking in my direction, so I turned to Owen when he initiated a conversation. I noticed soon enough though, after Owen smiled a bit, that he had a set of obviously discoloured and crooked teeth, the kind my American friends joked about when they criticised the diabolical state of British dental care. Later that night I saw Owen sucking on sugar-cubes when we were all having coffee.

In the end I was subjected to Jon's cool gravitational force, good teeth a bonus, and I allowed myself to talk to him. It turned out his surname was Weinstein. Throughout the night Jon's hair kept slipping out of its band and after a while he gave up and left it down and unkempt, which I preferred. This revealed a funny habit of his, one he still keeps to this day, of twisting the front wavy ends with his index finger when in serious thought or discussion about something. It was endearing.

Jon happened to be the quieter one out of the gang, not exactly shy, but more contemplative. But once he started on a topic that interested him he had no problem keeping the conversation lively. Politics and social justice were his passions as well as music and the arts.

'Art history?' he said, his dark eyes widening, leaning forward to listen. 'What aspects are you interested in? Tell me more.'

It wasn't long after I mentioned Frida Kahlo when I saw I had hit the jackpot. Jon took the cue and showed off his knowledge of her communist history, about Trotsky, their affair and much of what was happening in the political context at that time.

'And I love her painting with the feet in the bath. All those pieces of her world surrounding them. Beautiful.' He paused, his eyebrows turned up slightly as if asking me to offer him a sign, something to let him know he was on the right track.

'I love that painting too. I *love* Frida Kahlo. I just love her *so* much,' I said, with excitement. 'Where did you say you were from in the States?' he said.

Other female students that night, friends of Alice and the others, came and went. Some were much prettier and sounded a lot smarter, but Jon stuck it out with me – yes, *me* – the whole night. All of us moved on to a wine bar where we listened to live modern jazz for free, where we stayed on later drinking coffee, laughing our silly young hearts out and watched Owen sucking happily, like a baby with a pacifier, on those sugar-cubes.

Afterwards Jon pulled his bike along as he walked me to the nearest underground station. 'Have you been to The Photographer's Gallery yet?' he asked. 'They've got great exhibitions and there are some nice little places to eat around there. I could give you a tour. How about tomorrow?'

We tried a first nervous peck of a kiss on the cheek, our lips just brushing past each other. When our skin touched I felt a light buzzing sensation pass through me. We said an awkward goodbye. As I sat on the tube I noticed a couple of other passengers looking at me then realised, when I caught a glimpse of my reflection in the glass opposite, that I couldn't stop myself from beaming. It's these fragments of memory – the musicians in the wine bar, those laughing faces, the sugar-cubes, his kiss, my face grinning back at me – that have stayed with me.

Jon and I spent several hours together on that first date roaming through galleries, bookshops, covering the streets of Soho, drinking coffee, walking through St James's Park, stopping for a pub drink and testing what he described as quality British ale. After a cheap meal at a small, crowded falafel joint called Gaby's, we ended up settling for the night at his place.

Jon lived in a Victorian converted two-bedroom flat in Battersea that was owned by a friend of his, a PhD student at the university. It turned out that Martin's parents bought it so their son could rent out the second bedroom. Somehow I wasn't too surprised. Meeting all these understated trust fund types had become the norm. I couldn't seem to escape them. I wondered how financially solvent Jon's family was, but it turned out he came from a humbler background.

His father was a small-business family photographer specialising in weddings and bar and bat mitzvahs, hence Jon's interest in photography. His mother was an administrator for a solicitor's office. He had to be careful about his spending, he said, as his grad school grant didn't offer that much. He was using some savings from the time he'd been working at the Institute for Public Policy Research, a London think-tank where he worked first as an intern and then as a researcher before applying to do a postgraduate course. He was lucky enough to secure some paid research work when the opportunity arose.

It was then I discovered that all British undergraduate degrees and some master's programmes were government-subsidised. My rich friend Alice and other students I met didn't have to worry about tuition; it was all taken care of, whether they needed financial help or not. I almost cried when Jon explained this to me, but I held back as I listened to his overview of the history of British education. Looking back now it seemed it was a Golden Age, this no university fees thing and grants for those who needed them. But it was weird too, I thought, with all these posh types taking the free ride and still enjoying the good life, as Alice's taste for extravagant high-tea outings showed. Yes, their parents paid taxes, with some of them, let's not forget, managing their taxes, as Rob Segal had explained to me, by 'gifting' expensive apartments to their kids. But what about all the working-class, tax-paying folk? I noticed there weren't so many of them at the university.

When we arrived at Jon's flat we stopped in the kitchen first for a drink. It was bigger than I expected and unusually clean for two young men, although Jon mentioned Martin wasn't so great at tidying up after himself. After hearing Jon's story about British education and government spending it was a quick move to the bedroom. There I saw two walls covered with a colourful combination of tightly stacked bookshelves and musical equipment. I was impressed that his books and music were labelled like a library, in alphabetical order. After I selected several books to scan, one on public health, another on sociology, another on photography and art, Jon made sure he set them all back in their right places afterwards. To my relief, he took hold of the situation by dimming the lights and

161

playing the mesmeric and, I have to admit, sexy, Miles Davis record, 'So What'.

When I saw him undressed that night for the first time, that touch of low lighting from the bedside lamp casting a golden shadow across his skin, it was a revelation to see all his strength captured in his long legs, particularly his well-defined thighs, calves, and surprisingly, his narrow torso. I found this sudden physicality appealing but somewhat overwhelming. But it was the combination of those two things – what a turn-on.

We continued seeing each other, sleeping together, and soon enough were at it like rabbits to the point of amorous exhaustion. He made sure we managed our time together around the demands of our courses, his music, cycling, and any paid work commitments. It was hard to imagine he ever found time to sleep with all he had going on.

I was excited I'd met a clever one who took such pride in his organisation skills, but could also work magic with his fingers on the keyboard and in the bedroom without me having to guide him. On top of that he was what my mother and Nonna would have called *a handsome fellow* who happened to not be too aware of his good looks, and, well, he just so happened to show a genuine interest in me. There was one other major plus: he wasn't a psychopath. It was hard for me to believe, but there was nothing difficult about our relationship. One thing, though, always lurked around in the back of my mind in those early days.

I couldn't quite get the likes of Rob Segal out of my mind. Was my thing with this Jon Weinstein serious or just a fling? Did the fact that I wasn't Jewish matter at all to Jon in the same way I assumed it mattered to Rob, whose Manhattan-Mindy girlfriend could offer him everything his Jewish heart, and, let's be honest, his Jewish family, desired? But then, who cared if we were just a fling? I told myself I would be OK with that too. After all, I reminded myself, it was the sexy, woman-on-top, late 1980s, with Madonna starting that underwear-as-outerwear trend, although I never quite built up the courage to buy myself a corset. I still felt the urge to confront this fling or no fling issue one night after seeing a late-night film when we waited at a bus stop near Marble Arch.

'So, have you dated lots of non-Jewish women before me or am I the first?'

He didn't seem put out by the direct question, but was thoughtfully silent before answering. 'Yeah, I have. And I also had a Jewish girlfriend when I was an undergrad but it didn't last long, maybe four months or so.'

'But would you ideally want to marry a Jewish woman? You know, keep the tradition and all that, have Jewish kids.'

I was nervous about how far to go, but I knew I had to face up to the truth at some point. I knew that any talk about marriage and kids with someone you haven't known a long time is the kiss of death. I was treading on dangerous territory, but what the hell, I thought, what do I have to lose now after everything that's been? I prepared myself for the end with some sense that if that was the case, at least, feeling the force of Madonna behind me, I would be the one in control this time.

He was quiet again in his usual, thoughtful way before answering. 'Well, I guess I want to live my life in a way that's not dictated by all that stuff, all those boundaries. It's too constraining. If I consciously try to seek out a Jewish woman for that reason then I might miss out on something else. Plus, marrying a Jew wouldn't guarantee happiness, better mothering or happier kids for that matter. Kids can grow up rejecting their religion and not wanting anything to do with it. And anyway, this Jewish girlfriend I had once was a bit of a nutter, a total control freak. She was the last person I wanted to settle down with.'

I said nothing, not wanting to risk revealing my own nutter tendencies, although I had been proud of my ability, at that stage during my time in London, for at least managing to pull off the impression that I was as normal as everyone else. This was helped, I'm sure, by the mask of my respectable academic study in art history. When it seemed things were going my way, so much so that I felt the same rare sensation in my being that others would have defined as contentment, I began to worry less about what bad things might be lurking around the corner.

Although there were pedestrians a fair distance away at the other end of the street, our bus stop had gone quiet after a busy time of people catching night buses or taxis. A minute or so passed with silence between us as we were both gazing outward to the road, pondering what to say next. But our thoughts were broken when suddenly we witnessed a dreadful thing. A car sped past us on the opposite side of the road and hit a person who was walking across at the same time. The impact was enough to send his body into flight over the car then with a thump onto the street.

I screamed at the same time that Jon shouted, 'Oh my God, did you see that? Did you see that?'

The car didn't stop and the person was left there, unmoving. We started to cross quickly, noticing a couple of other cars were approaching. We saw that he was young, maybe around twenty-five, with short dark hair, a couple of days unshaven, with features that suggested he could have been Middle Eastern. I remember he wore a black leather bomber jacket that felt softer than a rose petal when I touched his shoulder. He was breathing but remained completely still. His eyes widened when he saw us, not turning his head but moving his gaze in my direction, then Jon's, then back at me again. His lips quivered but he couldn't speak. The first person we saw was a waiter at a nearby restaurant who had only just stepped out to light a cigarette. Jon shouted at him for help.

'This guy's been knocked by a hit and run. Call an ambulance,' he shouted, trying to keep his floppy hair out of his eyes. I steered a couple of potentially oncoming cars away from us. When the street went quiet again I crouched low and held the man's cold, motionless hand.

'It's OK, everything's going to be OK. You're going to be OK,' I said, knowing I had no idea how things would turn out. The waiter moved a bit closer, still staring at us, now smoking.

'What are you waiting for?' Jon shouted again. 'He's been hit by car. A hit and run. Call an ambulance.'

With that, the waiter seemed to realise finally what was happening and ran inside.

After that, the restaurant staff and customers came over, and passers-by appeared asking us what had happened. They'd seen nothing, they said, and stayed with us until the ambulance and police arrived. I squeezed the man's hand and just before the ambulance took him away I noticed one of his eyes shed a tear that trickled down into his ear.

The police took us to the station with them to record our statement. The car was dark blue, we thought, or was it black? A smallish model, maybe, older, but we weren't too sure, we told them. No, we had no idea what make it was, who was driving – man or woman, never saw the licence plate. It was dark. It was gone as fast as it came.

'How could someone do this?' I asked, not expecting an answer. 'How?'

'You wouldn't believe what some people are capable of, love. The things we see around here,' the young female officer said, chewing gum. 'I could tell you some stories, I could.' The smell of spearmint mixed with stale cigarette smoke surrounded her. She was pretty in a no-need-for-make-up kind of way.

Jon's composure held up, although I noticed he closed his eyes every now and then and took deep, slow breaths as we waited. But I was a wreck.

'It was his eyes, Jon. He was so scared. What if he didn't have any ID on him? What if he doesn't make it? What if his family end up wondering what's happened to him?' I tried hard not to, but kept repeating the words, 'It was his eyes. He was scared he was going to die.'

Jon said little but held my hand in a grip, then wrapped his arms around me.

When we made it back to his flat we lay in bed, Jon making efforts to keep me calm. 'The guy was in a state of shock,' he said, 'but it's amazing how strong a young body can be. If he's lucky he can recover from his injuries. But then again,'

Jon admitted, 'he was knocked high up in the air and came smashing down. And he wasn't moving. It could be his neck.'

After that we said nothing but held each other, Jon keeping my hand in his, stroking my arm, kissing my cheek every now and then. I cried for the hit and run guy at different times that night, prayed he would survive and be able to walk away.

The next morning was a Sunday and we phoned the police station hoping they could tell us any news. We were kept on hold for a long time and almost gave up until an officer returned to inform us that the man had died a few hours before in the hospital. He didn't tell us anything about the extent of his injuries, didn't know any details, just that they would be in touch if they found the driver. We never heard from them again.

Our shared witnessing of the hit and run that night, our look into the eyes of another human being near to our own age who was so close to death, created a special bond between us. Over the following months Jon and I spent many nights together awake in bed, surrendering ourselves to the inward space that was created from our memory of that night. We stayed close, wrapped in each other, legs and arms intertwined. His mouth quivering. That tear rolling into his ear. How precious, we thought, to feel the heat from our bodies, to taste each other's kiss again, both of us imagining in our own different ways that if he hadn't crossed the street at that very second he'd still be breathing, would maybe at that moment be lying in bed and taking in the scent of his own lover. I had a picture in my mind of his mother crying for her baby.

Jon and I didn't bother ourselves with the usual anxieties or questioning about the future of our relationship. None of those tedious things mattered to us, the stuff that made up the worries I had brought up that deadly night about Jewish girlfriends, long-term commitments.

'I want us to just be, Jo…just as things are. But for a long time,' Jon whispered to me one morning after bringing me coffee in bed.

'Me too. But I'm going to have to go back home. Soon. I'll need to go back.'

It was all decided in simple, straightforward terms, so easily that I'm reminded again how luck can work its way into the most mundane circumstances.

Final exams of the year approached and my plans were to fly back to Boston and take a summer class again to make up the credits I needed to graduate the following academic year in May.

'You know I was talking about you today to someone I know in the department, an Irish PhD student,' Jon said when we met at the arts library. His mood was unusually light and cheerful in spite of the stress of course deadlines. 'I mentioned your grandmother was from Ireland and he was telling me that people like you, children, grandchildren, can get an Irish passport. And the thing is, Jo, if you have an Irish passport you can live and work here because the UK and Ireland have some kind of common area agreement thing, and are both part of the European Union. Yeah, can you believe it? Looks like Ireland is looking for its people to come back home.'

'Really? That can't be right. Is he sure? No, that sounds too easy,' I laughed. I felt a surge of excitement, mixed with fear. Could this happen for real? Could I have the freedom to pick up and leave Boston without anything stopping me, with Jon behind me the whole way? Was Jon serious? But his smile was wide and sincere.

'Let's call the Irish Embassy and find out, but Jo, he wouldn't have said that if he didn't know for sure.'

And so it was. How funny fate is. How different things could have been.

We hugged long and hard at the security gate at Heathrow on the morning of my departure. As we stood there I took in Jon's sweat, absorbed by his T-shirt, the one he had worn the day before when cycling to the student halls to stay with me. I welcomed the smell of a body embracing the challenges of life. But then I was going back to the overly hygienic, God-fearing USA and I was going to have to make the best of it, at least until my Irish passport application came through.

'This is only the beginning, Jo,' Jon said with a hopeful tone, his voice cracking slightly. 'You'll finish your degree, get your passport, and then, hey, the world's your lobster, as they say. What's there to worry about? I'll still be here if you come back. If you want me.'

By that point I couldn't hold back the tears or speak.

'Don't forget to call me when you get there,' he said. 'So I know you're OK, that you arrived safely.'

It was the first time ever in my life that anyone, family or friend, had asked that of me. A little phone call was all it was, to let him know I was still alive.

Seventeen

After looking through photos I fall asleep for a couple of hours and wake up disoriented when I hear movements downstairs; the fridge door closing, the tap turning on and off, cupboards opening then slamming shut. I make my way into the kitchen and see my father sitting alone at the table, hat and jacket still on, staring at a can of Budweiser Light and a shot glass filled with brown liquid. It's never clear when he'll be home. I glance at the clock: 1pm.

'I finished work a bit early,' he says, looking into his glass.

I dig a bit more. 'Oh, but you said you'd be working till around five.'

With his eyes still lowered, he says, 'It's always like this, changes on the day, the job, when they tell you to go. They move people around at the last minute. You never know. It's good I ain't got money worries,' he says with a chuckle. 'Driving trucks keeps me busy.'

He ends with a heavy shrug, raises the shot glass to his lips and swigs after taking away the toothpick. His usual negative disposition seems different today; more pronounced. Bleaker. His shoulders and torso are slumped. His face doesn't just register as blank, the furrow in his brow communicates something else; it's as if the firing squad has prepared him. The offer's up for any last words, but he's too tired. *Just get it over with.*

'Well, maybe as Ma just died it's not a bad idea to not go to work, you know, spend time with the grieving.'

He shakes his head. 'Nope,' he says. 'Can't sit around. No point. Good to stay busy. No, I don't sit around.' But he continues to do just that, sitting and staring into his glass.

I bring out some photos of my father and mother together when they were young in an effort to inspire him to tell a story or two. Maybe he'll even manage a smile.

One of them appears to be the only picture from their wedding day, my mother wearing a simple white dress. My scrawny-looking young dad with chiselled cheekbones, slicked-back shiny-black hair, wears a basic dark suit and tie. My grandmother, Deirdre, is leaning toward Terry on one side and her husband, my grandfather, is on the other side of the frame standing next to my father. My grandfather's younger face is close to what he looked like in his miserable older years, but the skin looks tight and rigid. His mouth appears locked with only a suggestion of a slight upturn at the corners. In fact, none of them are smiling. Their stolid faces reveal an odd kind of acceptance. *Here we are then. There's nothing else we can do about it now so let's make some attempt at having a half-decent party.*

My mother is pregnant with Dave on the day of their early September wedding. She would have been sixteen when she and my father both lost their senses, if they ever had any then, when they let their young bodies take over before thinking of any consequences. Would that have been the same night my grandfather packed the brutal punch that sent Ma down those stairs? She'd stayed out all night and didn't tell her parents where she was and when she returned the next morning, there he stood, waiting.

'He punched me right in the face. On the nose, actually. I thought it was broken for a while, but it was OK, just hurt like hell.' The blow knocked her backwards down the flight of stairs – 'Oh, no, there weren't too many stairs, I don't think' – and when she hit the bottom he moved fast after her, pulled her up and threw her a couple of other punches for good measure, one to the jaw, the other to the side of her head. 'Wow, did I end up black and blue after that one. That's when I got this little chip in my front tooth. See? Right there.' This was not the first time her father would strike her, she told us on multiple occasions, each time with an odd sense of pride, perhaps in recognising her own robust nature. 'Well, he knew what he had to do when we got out of line. I guess I deserved it. He let me know I wasn't going to get away with that kind of thing.'

My mother sometimes pined for the decisive quality a good parental smack would convey. 'Kids can use a bit of discipline these days,' she said when Dave's daughter, Amy, acted up in her teen years. 'They're walking all over parents nowadays.'

I count back nine months from my brother's birthday at the end of March and work out that Ma's night of passion with Jimmy O'Brien, the guy every other girl in the neighbourhood wanted, the guy with the fast car, would have happened sometime in June. The perfect season for romance. I imagine the young Theresa Doherty with her firm teenage body, with the curves she hates because they dare to bulge to extremes in those places where older and younger men's eyes lingered. Yet at the same time, she loves her physical power, the way

172

it controls Jimmy, drives him crazy when she flaunts herself from a distance. She's just waiting for the right time to hand herself over in the name of love to her older nineteen-year-old boyfriend. If she had been any younger and if it happened today, Jimmy O'Brien just might have been thrown in jail. He should count his lucky stars that all he had to do was plead guilty to the parents about his role in the crime, the deed that was discovered only when there was talk of a baby, and take the punishment of marriage.

'Look at you, Dad, you were so young there. Just a kid,' I say, trying to find something, a little space where we can begin to talk about Ma, the captivating young Terry.

He says nothing but holds the photo in his hands and stares. Releasing a bit of a sigh, finally, he says, 'Yup. That was a long time ago.'

He's still steadying his gaze on the image when suddenly he makes a surprising sound as he gasps for breath, and starts weeping. For a second I think it could be the start of a heart attack, then it builds quickly to a loud whimper until he finds a break. 'Shit… I thought I was done with all this.'

Then the wailing starts. It's the first time he's let himself go in front of me over the whole time Ma was dying and is now gone. So many tears suddenly. And the nose, how all that watery mucus runs into his mouth. He wipes it fast with his jacket sleeve, leaving its trace there, wet and bubbly.

'It's OK,' I say. 'It's normal, Dad, you need to let it out.' Someone needs to say such things at times like this.

And he continues to bawl. He can't stop himself and while I'm encouraging him I'm feeling a sense of helplessness when he struggles for air as though it's his last breath. What will I do if he can't stop? What will I do if he collapses? What will I do if he wants me to embrace him? There were only two times in my life when I'd witnessed my father crying. The first time was during my childhood when my mother caught him entwined in a lengthy string of lies about where he'd been, why he didn't come home some nights and even full weekends. He'd been seeing another woman, spending time at her place. We found out she was divorced, had her own children whom, oddly enough, he didn't seem to mind being around. I may have been twelve at the time, the same year I downed all those aspirins. Where Dave was on the day I found my father in tears, I have no recollection. Where my mother was, I don't remember either, but their bedroom door was open and he was packing clothes into a duffle bag.

I said, 'Hi. Where's Ma? What's going on?'

No reply. Then, as I stood at the doorway, he stopped what he was doing, although he still didn't look my way. His hands and arms were shaking, and he started to sob.

'What's wrong, Dad? Is it Grandpa? Did something happen to Grandpa?' Then I thought the worst and cried, 'Is it Nonna? Is Nonna dead?'

He turned, looking straight at me this time, still crying, sniffling. 'No. Nobody's dead... I'm sorry... I'm sorry.' Sob, sob and more sob.

It was hard to understand. He left, my mother explained afterwards, because he wanted to be with them and not us, but I had seen him in the bedroom, falling apart. How could it be that he didn't care about what happened to us, and yet he stood there shedding tears? It was the first and the last time ever I would actually hear him utter the words, *I'm sorry*.

Dave and I told our mother that we three didn't need him, we would survive better on our own without him. We huddled together on the couch, me on one side, Dave on the other, and hugged our mother as she cried.

'We don't need that bastard,' Dave finally said, wiping her tears away, to which my mother replied sternly, 'Don't you go talking about your father that way. He's still your father.'

Dad returned a couple of months later. That evening I heard voices from their bedroom, the soft noise of muffled weeping that belonged to my father. I moved closer to their door, but quietly so they couldn't hear me and saw them through the gap where the door was left ajar. He sat on the side of the bed holding his head in his hands, rocking back and forth in a frenetic kind of way I had never witnessed before. I wondered if his head was in pain. Every now and then he'd begin to wail and she'd shush, shush him like a baby, holding him in a tight grip as if trying to prevent him from exploding.

'It will pass. You've got through this before, Jimmy, you'll get through it again,' she said.

I remember questioning if the thing he'd get through again was some kind of problem with money or work. Maybe, I thought, he was in trouble with the police again and he was getting ready for them to take him away, but that never happened. Maybe it was the Irish mafia.

That night at dinner he was quiet as usual at the table, but his eyes were glassy and vacant, as if he was stoned, and there was a sadness, not anger, in them. For days afterwards he was home more than ever, sleeping throughout the day, taking some kind of medicine, and going to bed early.

'What's wrong with Dad?' I asked Ma.

'Just tired,' she said. 'Getting over the flu, that's all.'

'Doesn't look like the flu to me.'

It wasn't too long before he returned to work, coming home for food, leaving again in the evening, with my mother never able to explain where he was, claiming, 'He had to see someone about something.' And it didn't take long before I stopped asking or caring. His persistent absence and her passive acceptance was their habitual way of life that continued for years. He left again and lived across town with another girlfriend when I was a teenager for a length of time that is no longer clear or even significant in my memory. It would happen again; in and out he was, back and forth, never with any firm reason. An impressive yoyo act.

And here he sits now, the man whose wife forgave him for all his wrongs; the woman whose earnings gave him a far better life than he ever would have known on his truck driver's salary or his hustling backhand deals. He has her savings, her pension, the dusty little house, the cottage, her car, and now her investment earnings, but he no longer has her, the regular figure that kept his life in order, the thing that gave him constancy when all else collapsed. Now with both foundation and structure gone, he's going to have to find a way to carry it all on his own. It might be easier if I wasn't here making things worse.

'It's going to be hard for a while, Dad, but time will help. It'll get better.' These are the things you say.

Here and there he swears through his tears. 'Fuck…fucking shit.' He stands, swipes his runny nose with the end of his sleeve again and says, 'Gotta go to the bathroom.'

He returns some time later, eyes bloodshot and dry. 'Look, this guy down the road wants to talk to me about buying this car and he wants my advice and I told him I'd see him this afternoon. There's some stuff in the fridge for a sandwich, whatever. Have what you want. OK?'

Is he telling me, maybe, in his Jimmy O'Brien way, the only way he knows, that he doesn't really need to see his friend? Because, in fact, he should have been working until 5pm and wouldn't have arranged to see anyone now, but with all this crying he's just done, he can't cope with any more talking. *Please*, he's begging me in silence, *don't show me any more photos. Please let me go.*

I say it's all fine, yes, not to worry, I will take care of myself, *of course, I will take care of myself, just set me down in a fucking corner and leave me there.* I remind him, in the nicest, possible voice I can muster, that we talked about meeting tomorrow with Dave to sign the papers, that Dave wants to talk to us about the alternatives.

'We should probably think about what Dave wants, Dad,' I say.

Dad turns away fast towards the door. 'Can talk all he wants but it's done already. What Ma did. It's done.'

I know it all makes sense on paper. But now there's something else stirring in the back of my mind, a sense of something irrational that I can't quite pin down. What would happen, I'm wondering, if maybe, just maybe, *I* was the one who agreed to help Dave? What is going on in my head that makes me think this might be a good plan?

I move to the living room with the half-baked notion that I might find something to watch on TV as I have no energy for anything else, and I see that pic of the young Dave, then his little girl, Amy, posing and all cutesy, then grown up, smiling and proud in her white wedding dress. Now she's a young mother with her own baby in tow, a little girl, and I want to feel happy for her, I honestly do.

Eighteen

What does it mean to settle into a new country where you don't have a history? You start with basics, I guess. Speak the same language – that helps. Find work, make money, build friendships, find love, get married like all those other law-abiding, conventional heterosexual couples. After the wedding you continue to work hard, save money, buy a flat, have a baby, save more money then sell the flat to buy a house that will fit the two of you plus baby and hoards of baby stuff. Often another baby will arrive at some point. This is expected too. Some people are even crazy enough to have more. Later you have grandchildren. *You've been blessed*, people say. You retire. You downsize. Money will go to your children. You die, then it all goes to them. There you have it. You settled. You created a new history, one your kids will look back on with teary eyes and happy bank accounts when they're trudging through your old photos, asking who's who and trying to remember at what exact point in your life you began to look and act old.

I graduated from fancy pants Ivy League with *magna cum laude*. Such a grand Latin way of distinguishing between American university students. I was fortunate enough to gain the middle *magna* one, meaning that I had graduated *with great honour*. In spite of some of the pain that accompanied those college days – I could compare my undergraduate education to the process of having all my bad teeth removed over time so they could be replaced with stronger, straighter and more respectable expensive white ones – coming out at the other end still in one piece felt pretty good. I made it, and London, Jon, and even Alice, with her offer of a tiny, walk-in closet-size room in her south London flat share, were ready to have me with open arms. Me and my ticket to my exciting new life; my Irish passport.

On the afternoon of my London flight my parents took me out to lunch. My mother cried but was happy for me. 'I know you're going to be OK, Jo. You've got good friends there now. And Jon sounds like a decent guy. I've got a good feeling about him. And who knows, you might both find jobs here in Boston in the future, maybe? That could work, right?' she said. 'But I'll come visit you in London.'

My mother had spoken to Jon several times on the phone when I was visiting her at the house and she offered to pay for the long-distance calls. During the second call she told him straight that she was worried about me and wanted assurance from him that I'd be OK.

'Now Jon,' she said. 'My daughter's something special and I don't want to hear about her getting hurt.'

In the background I waved my arms trying to stop her, at the same time mouthing 'Stop. Shut up, Ma!' then grabbing the receiver before any more was said.

After I apologised, Jon said, 'You tell her she has nothing to worry about. Just come. Everything's going to be just fine.'

At the airport my father said, 'I hear they drink warm beer over there. And I hear the food sucks. Better eat good now 'cause you're gonna miss our restaurants. And don't forget to call your mother.'

Jon collected me at Heathrow in the old Ford estate his father had passed on to him. My head was filled with a combination of exhilaration and jetlag, which made me feel like I'd been high on drugs for days.

'I can't believe you're finally here,' Jon said. I could see a tiny welling of tears in his eyes which he managed to hold back after we hugged.

We stopped first for a coffee in the airport where he presented me with a copy of James Joyce's *Dubliners*. Inside he wrote, You can't move to London with an Irish passport and not visit Dublin. This is your homework before we go. Love Jon.

'And start practising a Dublin accent before you order your first Guinness,' he said.

When still in Boston, I contacted top London recruitment agencies, spoke to people over the phone, set up interviews, found temp work, then permanent work in the up-and-coming field of desktop publishing. My experience with the early technology at the printing company, my new fancy pants degree, and, I told myself, my highfalutin' *magna cum laude* status, must have impressed them all. New, confident smile practised and ready to go, I found well-paid work and pretended I was in charge of my universe.

Success continued. My salary increased. I was considered valuable.

'Are you happy here, Jo?' My well-groomed boss, who prided himself in looking busy in his glass-fronted office after

5.30pm every evening, asked me at my three-month review meeting. 'Because we think you're doing a smashing job. Really smashing. And we think you should be rewarded for that.'

My generous salary and my penchant for penny-pinching allowed me to save money; every few months I sent my mother £1,500 instalment cheques for her to deposit and change to dollars so she could pay off my old student loans. I had a future to plan. I was in this perfect, easy-love thing with Jon, the kind that made me feel as though a light wind was lifting then tossing me into the air where I floated around weightlessly, bouncing gently from cloud to cloud.

After that first year in London I moved out of Alice's flat share and Jon and I decided to rent a one-bedroom place in Clapham. We shared the bills. Went food shopping together. Shared the cooking, although it was clear his repertoire was more palatable than my basic, pasta-sauce variations. I returned to drawing and painting in evening classes at a local art college, activities I enjoyed when taking my undergraduate art options. I continued to impress Jon with my creative impulses and even astounded him, and myself, when I took up a part-time Art History MA and finished three years later with a distinction and a thesis on feminist art practice that my supervisor encouraged me to edit into an article and publish.

Sometime that year my dissertation supervisor, Nancy Harvey, a well-respected academic, model feminist, single forty-something mother of two, whose only real vices were chain-smoking and fingernail-biting, put me in touch with a contact who offered me the chance to teach. It was a two-term slot to cover Art History A-level at an all girls' private secondary school.

'Jo, you've really got something and this is a good way to get started,' Nancy said when we met. 'You've got to grab the damn bull by its balls when you can. Wait, I know that sounds kind of sexist, talking about bulls and balls. But you get the gist. *You have to do this.*'

I didn't have the same self-belief as Nancy, but agreed to take a risk and gave up the security of my growing corporate salary, with the assumption that I could pick up work as a freelancer if needed.

Events followed in fast motion. My article was accepted for publication in a high-profile, academic peer-reviewed journal. Seeing my name in print for the first time sent a funny chill through my arms and legs which made me quiver. And hell yeah, it felt good. With a push that made me initially suspicious, Nancy continued to mentor me in her free time, helping me to develop my ideas which I could turn into a PhD project, supervised by her. She showed me where to look for funding, took me through the process in a way that reminded me of the care Constance had offered. Oh, how I missed Constance. Nancy pushed without breaking me. I relished her attention, indulged in as much reading as I could. I fought through my fears of not belonging in British academia. There was too much I wanted to do, too much I needed to do, Nancy reminded me, and nothing was going to stop me. Yes, I wanted to grab any fucking bull that stood in my way and not just tug at his balls. I wanted to crush them.

I was accepted onto a fully funded PhD programme and by the latter part of that first year was teaching some year one undergrad classes. From that point on I didn't look back.

My days in the corporate world had ended. Hurrah, hurrah! I, Joanna O'Brien, was on my way towards becoming a fancy pants academic.

By that time Jon had finished his PhD and secured a full-time lecturer's job straightaway, eventually publishing multiple papers and later a book. Well, what a neat and tidy academic pair we were, indeed. We married later that year at a stylish registry office in Chelsea Town Hall, south-west London. It was an understated occasion celebrated afterwards at our favourite little Italian osteria, probably the smallest wedding I had ever attended myself, squeezing in about sixty people, but we wanted it that way, deciding that our money and energy was better spent on our honeymoon to the Greek island of Rhodes.

My parents flew over, Dad pumped up with drugs to relieve his plane-flying anxiety, but my brother stayed behind. He never spoke to me directly, but told my mother to tell me it was a difficult time, he had no money, couldn't get away from work and had family responsibilities.

'I told your brother he has to come,' my mother said over the phone. 'You're his sister, his only sister after all. I'm not happy about this. Not one bit. But, Jo, I can't pay his way this time, if that's what he's waiting for, then, sorry, I can't do it.'

At the time I thought, OK, this is Dave's way of getting back at me for my inebriated episode at his wedding rehearsal party and my determination to display my alcohol-infused badge of honour, my sourpuss face, throughout their wedding day. (Well, I never asked to be a bridesmaid.) For a second I considered offering to pay for his flight, but decided against it without much of a second thought. I accepted it was probably for the best. I was getting pretty good at dodging uncomfortable encounters. Beth had no problems paying her own way. ('Are you kidding? There's no way I'm going to miss your wedding. You bet I'll be there.') My mother's cousin, Dan, and his wife, Sinead, from Dublin agreed to come. That gave my mother some satisfaction after I confessed I just couldn't bring myself to invite her sister Peggy and by extension Josie. Uncle Tom I wouldn't have to worry about, he'd be too busy tending to the poor, and Uncle Ken, my mother's younger brother, like Dave, wouldn't have the money. I wanted Nonna to come but knew the only kind of long-haul travel she could afford was her annual bus-package deal for seniors' gambling weekends to Atlantic City, New Jersey. A year later I lost Nonna for ever when she died of a heart attack. When she visited me in a dream soon afterwards, she tried to console me.

'It was for the best JoJo,' she said, smiling.

I cried and said, 'I'm so happy to see you, Nonna. Please don't go. Don't leave me. *Please.*' I reached out and tried to touch her. I wanted to feel her flesh.

'Oh, I'll be back, honey. Don't you worry,' she said before she faded away.

And she kept her promise, pops by every now and then in my dreams, hugs me and says how nice it is to see me.

'Well, if Peggy can't come then it won't look good having Josie, so, why don't we just tell them the wedding is going to be too small to invite all the American family,' said Ma on the long-distance line. 'You and Jon can come home afterwards, in another few months when you get a break, and we'll have a party for you here. Yes, let's do that. That'll be nice.'

I agreed at the time as I often did, but we never made it for a visit so my mother's other wedding party never happened.

In addition to our own list of friends, Jon's parents, Marion and Henry, invited his uncle and aunt and cousins. Marion's brother came with his wife and family. Jon's brother Max and sister Yvonne were there with their spouses and toddlers and everyone appeared cheery, overall. My father even managed to behave himself, smiled a few times, ubiquitous toothpick and all (couldn't get him to agree to take out the earring) and pretended to enjoy the meal when he met Marion and Henry. The next day at the restaurant he laughed with cousin Dan while they drank whisky shots and beer.

Henry knew just how much to socialise and when to step back. Another drink handed to Ma and Dad, a compliment to my mother about her dress, a comment about the beauty of her daughter, the bride who was so photogenic.

Marion was another matter.

Having to bear the embarrassment of inviting the Jewish relatives to her son's non-Jewish wedding to witness him hitching up with a gentile, a Catholic-born one, to make matters worse, Marion displayed a controlled uneasiness throughout the day. The first thing that struck me as odd was that she appeared to hold on to her handbag most of the time at the restaurant, even kept it on her lap while eating the main course, which she only finished partially. I wondered if she was unwell and was preparing herself for a fast exit if necessary. Her strained face looked as if she might have been suffering from a stomach upset or maybe a bad case of trapped wind.

Our formal union hit Marion hard. She'd been expecting it, yes, like the prospect of her unavoidable mortality one day, but she hung on to slim hopes that the Grim Reaper would allow her another fifty years or so of contentment before he came knocking. Our marriage was the end of the line, for Marion, of her Jewish history. While I was more than happy to give up my past and the Catholic brutality that went with it, she didn't want Jon to give up his, no matter how hard he tried.

I don't think I can ever forget Marion's fully embodied suffering of pure grief that day. Her mourning was accentuated by the long black and grey dress she chose. While the rest of the family smiled on demand, her expression was blank in the photos. Still attractive with her professionally coloured chestnut shoulder-length hair and careful make-up, Marion's eyes looked tired, her shoulders rounded when they were usually held back. There was one shot of her and my mother standing together, Marion's face a bit stunned by the demands of the camera, her hand grasping that handbag. One of my mother's hands was squeezing Marion's shoulder, the other held a glass of rosé as if to make a toast, her tipsy smile working hard to lighten things up. My mother was unwavering in her desire to have fun that day. For this, I was most grateful and proud.

I didn't resent Marion. In fact, I wished I could have taken her to the side and apologised for everything. For breaking that precious crystal wine-glass the first night we met (part of their twenty-fifth anniversary present, she said) when I must have had a tad too much of that nice bottle of Shiraz. For talking and laughing too loud. For not knowing enough about her world, for not being what she wanted me to be for her and her son. I wanted to be able to offer them all another version of me, but there was only so far I could go to conceal what had been before, the things that made me. By that time I had learned this much.

Over the years Marion accepted I was there to stay, like a permanent fixture that comes with a new house purchase you know you'll have to learn to live with. Eventually it dissolves into the surroundings so much that it ceases to irritate. After a while you realise you might even miss them if they were gone. After much time passed, I was beginning to look like a gem in disguise compared to what Jon's siblings married.

The family witnessed Jon's brother, Max, go through a messy divorce with his Jewish wife, Jill, who decided to take time off from her high-powered law career to raise their two children. In her misery with her plight she proceeded to torture him regularly with accusations that he was a terrible father and a neglectful husband who spent more time at the office or with women with whom he was having affairs.

'I'll tell you Jo,' she said to me one evening after a meal when we were washing up. Over the earlier years Jill had put on weight, not a little, but a lot, and she hated herself for it. 'He thinks I don't know, that I'm a fool. But let me tell you, I may be a fat cow now, but I don't deserve this. He comes home and I can smell her on him. I know these things.'

Max pleaded with her, swore those stories were not true, he'd never dream of cheating on her. His children, those future messiahs in the family, were his life, as was his beautiful wife, extra post-baby pounds and all, of course, his only reason for waking up and breathing every day. He would stab himself fifty times, no, one hundred, two hundred times in the heart before turning his back on them. Max had my sympathies; her constant shouting at him and the little ones was enough to drive anyone out the door to spend more time at a boring office job or into the arms of another. This seemed to me evidence of what could happen to some women who gave up their souls, and their designer wardrobes, for their children.

Jon's sister, Yvonne, also ended up divorced from her Jewish husband, Nathan, whom she'd met when she was at nursing school as he was just finishing his medical degree. He was the ideal catch, a promising young surgeon, every Jewish mother's dream. But it wasn't long after their two children were both in primary school when Yvonne discovered bits of evidence here and there, a bank statement showing large amounts of cash withdrawals, unexplained absences, and, finally, a packet of condoms in the bottom of his briefcase.

Jon was right once again. Landing a Jewish partner, a high-flying doctor or a lawyer at that, offered no guarantee for life-long happiness or stability.

Marion had a habit of internalising pain when watching her children suffer through their divorces. 'He fooled us all, that charmer,' she said of Nathan. 'I couldn't sleep at night when I heard, I was so upset. I am still upset, I don't know what to do, it makes me so sick. I can't sleep at night, not a wink.' She placed her hand on her heart and sighed. 'He came across as so sincere and from that family of his. Who would have known? Who knows how long he would have carried on before she found out? It's the children who suffer most. They're the innocents. Oh, I feel a pain in my heart.'

I agreed the children didn't deserve all the shit that came their way, but somehow they would get over it, I told her. It's incredible how resilient kids can be. What I really wanted to do was take hold of her tense shoulders in my hands, shake and rattle her, make her understand that this break-up stuff was peanuts compared to bigger problems. Far worse things could happen in families. After all, I thought, didn't they have a pretty good life? Yvonne would do well out of the deal financially and her little angelic Lily, who loved her dancing lessons, and her older brother Benny, who had picked up a keen interest in chess and piano, would never be short of money, or attention for that matter from their doting mother and grandparents on both sides. Jon and I were also around to help pick up the pieces when they were working their way through the early rubble of it all. We were always there for those kids when they were growing up. Endless tiring trips to central London through the crowds at the Natural History Museum, Science Museum, London Transport Museum, British Museum and whatever other bloody museums could be found. I never would have imagined there were so many of those places, so many of those tired screaming kids.

And we witnessed all four of Jon's nephews and niece throughout their spotty-faced, grumpy, hormonal teen years, develop into decent, educated young adults facing the world the best way they could. Messiah material they were not, but they all managed to buckle down, get their degrees, find work and earn their own crust. No drug addicts. No jail time. No psychos.

Marion never brought up the subject of children, perhaps because any future grandchildren that resulted wouldn't technically be Jewish. I was never really sure why my views changed and I felt the urge to have my own child. I can assume now it was most likely an internalisation of what society expected of me. I told myself I'd better put my hesitations aside and just get on with the task, as so many other so-called normal, functioning women do. I guess some of the time Jon and I spent with his niece and nephews also helped me to see that having our own family might not be all that bad. Jon was caring and patient with them in a gentle, paternal way I had never noticed before with the men in my family. And in spite of some of the usual irritations (why is it that children just can't stop interrupting all the time?), they did manage to elicit a smile on my face every now and then.

Dear Jo. We had so much fun at the zoo the other day seeing the monkeys and eating ice cream. You are the best aunt in the whole wide world. Will you and Jon take us to the cinema next weekend? Or maybe the zoo again. I love you so much. Lily.

Although it was still relatively early days in my PhD studies, I became pregnant almost a year after our wedding. Even early on in the pregnancy, although I did feel more tired than usual, I felt better physically overall and was relieved from the usual aches and emotional lows that always arrived before my periods. I didn't get hit hard with morning sickness and Jon was convinced that my complexion had a special healthy sheen.

When alone in the flat I would stand for some time in front of our full-length bedroom mirror gazing with pride at my belly, wondering when a more definitive bump would appear.

It was around week ten or so when we both talked about the potential sex of the child, what it would look like, whose traits it would adopt. Jon enjoyed imagining the fun of teaching the child how to read, how to ride a bike, wrapping up together under a blanket in front of the television on a rainy day. But it wasn't long after week eleven when I experienced bad cramps, then the start of bleeding. It happened at work not long after a teaching session, a workshop I held on art and political activism that had gone fairly well, in spite of feeling nausea midway. Ah, I thought, of course, this is the morning sickness everyone talks about. I welcomed it. *This is what we mothers must go through.*

And later – the terrible pain.

We both cried at the disappointment, at nature's cruelty, the way it had pulled us along, the way it allowed us to indulge in ourselves. We wept, inwardly, when we saw couples with babies.

'Just look away. Don't look,' Jon would whisper. And then he would close his eyes and sigh.

'I can't believe how many there are,' I said one evening after dinner that week. 'Suddenly. Out of nowhere, all these pregnant women. All looking so happy. People offering them seats on the tube.'

Jon said, 'Yeah. We just heard in the office today that the department secretary is pregnant, now planning maternity leave. Oh well. Best not to tell anyone in the early days. All the excitement and then you have to turn around and tell them the bad news.'

I hadn't told anyone our secret, but that week when I spoke to my mother on the phone, I spilled the beans and cried. You still end up facing it, one way or another. At first I thought I heard her gasp for breath and I imagined she must have moved her hand over her mouth.

'Oh. Oh, Jo.' She was sorry, of course, so, so sorry, and after offering the usual platitudes, she said, 'It's so common, more common than you might realise. You still have time. And I'm always willing to be a grandmother again whenever God wills it. If only you were here.'

Jon's rational disposition kicked in to remind us also how common miscarriages were and convinced us we should try again. Six months later I was pregnant again, only to have to live through another miscarriage around week twelve.

My consultant, Professor Michael Houghton, said while there could be a small risk that the cervix may have been 'compromised' by my earlier abortion after Brendan left me, which I had to confess to Jon in my first pregnancy, cases of cervical incompetency, when the cervix is weak and can cause miscarriage, usually occurred in the second trimester.

'And from what I've seen it looks like you've got a healthy, strong cervix there,' he said with a tone of light optimism, as though commending me for sticking to a great exercise regime. 'Unfortunately early miscarriages can happen, but we're not entirely sure why they recur. In most cases many future pregnancies will come to full term. You've probably just been unlucky.'

While he tried to reassure me it was in good working condition, I imagined my cervix sitting back, taking it easy, having one too many cigarette breaks, then getting fired, with me paying the dues for its lazy-ass incompetency, its failure to do the basic satisfactory work for which it was designed.

'We've got plenty of time, Jo, there's no rush,' sensible Jon said the following week. 'To be honest, I'm feeling like maybe we've rushed things a bit too much. There's so much going on this year at work and you still have the PhD to finish. Maybe this was a sign we need to slow down.'

I poured my energies into the PhD, which I was relieved to pass with no corrections. Soon after I was lucky enough to be offered a permanent, full-time tenure-track lecturer's job. My first newly designed second year undergraduate programme was a great success and I invested my research time into turning my PhD thesis into a book. Deciding to put the baby business on hold for a while, Jon and I moved fast forward with our academic ambitions and didn't let anything stand in our way.

We got a thrill out of those busy periods when we worked in the flat simultaneously, rat-tat-tat, tapping away at our keyboards, like two content hummingbirds in sync in the evenings and weekends, and treated ourselves with walking breaks in the park, expensive evening meals out and jazz nights with friends. We would chat away excitedly about our next research plans, or we'd gripe about others at work who weren't pulling their weight, those colleagues with families who always seemed to take too much time off. Jon got a promotion and we managed to find a bargain small, three-bedroom house across the city in north London in need of lots of work, but a worthwhile investment.

We devoted any extra time we had to studying interior design magazines, trying out paint samples, hunting down the right builders, carpenters, and bargain furnishings. If I was an outsider observing us I would have hated the sight of our smug faces and run a mile to avoid us at parties.

When I reached my late thirties we talked about trying to conceive again, that big now or never question. By the time we hit the bedroom the passion we used to have had been usurped by our endless discussions about the pros and cons of producing a baby, if indeed, we said, with caution, we made it past the twelve-week mark next time. Pros: Someone else to look after and love and make us less selfish. Someone to put a smile on our faces when we played with it, like a puppy. Someone to look after us when we grew old. Someone to pass on our assets to. Someone to replace us when we die, to maintain healthy population numbers. Cons: Giving birth hurts like hell. Too many sleepless nights. You get fatter, then miserable, look at what happened to Jill. *Well, she was kind of miserable anyway.* Too much worry over him/her. No guarantee he/she will be healthy or happy. What if the child hates us or turns into a psychopath? What if we hate him or her? Too expensive. The cons were adding up.

In spite of our concerns we conceived again. I took extra care of myself, adhered closely to an even more tedious, expensive, organic-diet regime before the word organic became a middle-class necessity. I made sure I got more sleep with no late nights, made sure I didn't stand on my feet for lengthy periods of time, which wasn't too much of a problem. Like air pollution-paranoid urban travellers in China and Japan, I resorted to covering my mouth and nose with a surgical mask when I travelled on the underground to avoid breathing in the airborne soot particles I was convinced were going to kill my baby. I took a week off work when I didn't have to teach so I could join a meditation for pregnant women's workshop and contemplate a peaceful future.

Despite all these efforts, I was unlucky and miscarried near the end of the first trimester.

I guess it was no surprise to me that the same degree of disappointment I experienced the previous two times hadn't returned. I had grown accustomed to bad news. I convinced myself there was a good reason why I would never bear a child, that I was never meant to have responsibility for another life. In fact, it all felt pretty simple. God and the Catholic Church, I believed, were having their last laugh for my earlier dirty sins. I didn't want to think about any future pregnancies, the possibility of IVF, or adoption. I made it clear to Jon I wanted it to end there. I learned to appreciate that I'd probably been spared from making what might have been the biggest mistake of our lives and I began to feel some relief for not presenting Jon with a dark, cursed future.

Although I shed fewer tears that third time around, I caught Jon sobbing quietly on our bed, sitting not far from the bloodstain I had left on the sheet before rushing to the bathroom. It was two-thirty in the morning and he had just returned from the kitchen with some ibuprofen and a hot water bottle. We said nothing for a long time before we talked about calling the hospital at the start of the day to confirm what we knew already.

'Maybe I'm a little relieved, I admit, but...' Then, still looking down, still crying, he said, 'I guess it's hit me now.' He stopped and drew a deep breath. 'It's hit me that we're never going to...we're never going to have the chance to see some of ourselves, our resemblances, all that stuff, in our child. It all feels so final.'

Nineteen

Returning to the house to rummage through my mother's belongings feels like a chore, yet one that might offer some relief at the finish. It's as though my insides have been bunged up for too long and I'm hoping I'll feel flushed and cleansed afterwards.

We've finally agreed, Dave, my father and I, to meet later and talk about the money before going to the lawyer's office. Guilt has been drilling away at me, a repetitive and tortuous pecking action, ever since my dinner with Dave. Yes, it was my mother's decision to arrange things this way, all for Dave's benefit, and yet my father and I are allowed a large sum to do whatever we want, whenever we want. Who's to say Jimmy O'Brien won't do something crazy with his portion? Who's to say I won't fall apart after all these years of playing nice? *Good girl JoJo goes wild. Loses her marbles. It was only a matter of time.*

But what happens if I remain rational Jo? Do I really have any idea what I'll do with my share? Stock investments? Payment towards a flat that Jon and I could rent out? It would be so much simpler to do nothing. Dave was probably right when he assumed I'd 'let it just sit in the bank'.

If I don't support Dave on this it might be the end of whatever is left of us, brother, sister, father. If we agree to distribute the money the way Dave wants it will be perceived by Dave as an investment in him, a symbolic gesture. We are willing, this offer would say, to trust you. We are willing to believe you will now go ahead and honour your dead mother by doing the right thing, the thing she would have wanted you to do. *She just couldn't convince herself you were ready, so OK, now you need to prove her wrong. And maybe you can prove something to me, Dave, prove you're worthy of some of my share. If Dad doesn't budge, the decision, to share or not to share, is all mine. I'll be the one calling the shots.*

I get through my mother's possessions much faster than anticipated. My energy, at least at this point in the early part of the day, feels unlimited, even with the nagging pain in the leg, the spasms that cause it to jerk when I least expect them. But I've given up worrying about what others think.

I fill five large trash bags with her clothes, old and new, a donation for the nearby Salvation Army store. There are a few items of jewellery, none of them worth much in monetary value. She didn't adorn herself with bracelets or earrings, didn't wear make-up. There are only two necklaces and a chain with a gold-plated watch she wore in her early nursing years, a graduation gift given to her by her best friend. I clear the old nursing magazines, throw away the disintegrating shoes and other unusable items. Then I begin to spring-clean the place – I'm on a mission to scrub away any residual evidence of my dying mother. I spot fingernail clippings on the carpet and on top of her bedside table.

Hidden behind her side of the bed against the wall is a small, white plastic cup, which made me wonder why she didn't just drink out of a glass, although glasses do break after you drop them on a tiled floor when you're drunk. It is filled with three cigarette butts in mouldy water. She'd found a place to cover the habit of a lifetime that ended up killing her. She knew there was no point in giving them up with the end in sight, but she still tried her best to hide the mucky remnants. She certainly liked keeping her secrets. I find another cup behind the living room couch in the corner, the regular spot where she watched TV. Where the hell was my father all this time? All this time when she was alone. Smoking. Dying.

During one of my last visits at the hospice I dug a bit and asked her if she had any regrets.

'What do you mean?' she asked, with a look of confusion.

'Well, you know, have you ever regretted not doing something in your life or did you do something you wish you hadn't?'

I kind of knew where I was going with this, but was probably naive in my expectations. But she was near the end so I thought anything might be possible.

'No, not really,' she said, then looked up and paused. 'I had David, then you, when I was really young, and maybe if I didn't I could have been a nurse earlier than I was. That would have helped us with money, that's for sure.' She hesitated again, as though she was searching deep down. Here it comes, I thought, her big revelation, what I've been waiting for all these years. *I never should have let Peggy bully me the way she did.* But instead, she said, 'I might regret not having a cigarette or two, you know, before I go. Don't tell your father though. Please, don't tell him.' She reached for my arm. 'Do you think you can find me one, Jo? I could really die for one now. Hah, that's funny, isn't it? Die for one.'

Hilarious. My mother finding her new vocation as a comedian on her death-bed.

After several hours I stagger to the car, my energy now waning, fill the trunk with the bags and head off to the nearest Salvation Army. The second I walk through the door, my nose is hit with that unique odour you get in these places. It's not coming from the well-groomed elderly man who steps out from the storage room.

'It's all in the trunk, just out front,' I say. 'The car with the blue badge.' The sprightly old guy is keen to help. I imagine he's the kind of gentleman in his late seventies who probably practises gentle tai chi and works here three days a week while fitting his hours around other good deeds.

'I'm so sorry for your loss. No matter how old we are when we lose a parent it's the hardest thing ever. God bless, God bless you.'

The God thing again.

He's in the business of sorting through the leftover items of dead people's lives. Someone else will walk in my mother's shoes. Is this part of what life after death means? How do we make the best use of what the dead have left us? Ma's investment money was another part of her life after death. What we do with it matters. She would have wanted the three of us to stay together as a family, the new trio. She wouldn't have thought that her decision about Dave's money would pull us apart even more. Or maybe she put it out there to test us. Another fucking maze.

On my way back to the house I take a detour to Whole Foods supermarket, sit down in the café for a drink and soup, then decide to fill my father's empty but now spotlessly clean fridge. I do this out of a sudden desire to make a difference to the old man's life, like a little spirit overhead sprinkling magical happiness crystals that will settle and sprout into blades of pure, contagious goodness in my father's weakened heart. While I'm there I stock up on some basics and additional treats for Beth too, although I put my foot down at organic toilet paper.

Arriving back at the house, just around thirty minutes before Dad and I are supposed to meet with Dave, I pick up a voice message from Dad, which I must have missed when shopping. He has to cancel, he says, because his driving route got extended.

I gotta make some more stops in Maine and it's gonna take a long time. I won't be back in time. I called your brother. No surprise he ain't happy, but that's life.

Slightly relieved, although I know it's only a short delay of the inevitable confrontation, I spread my worn body on the couch, close my eyes just for a minute – only a quick minute, I tell myself – after taking a pill for the pain in my leg and eating most of the chocolate-covered raisins.

I wake up much later to a muffled sound, the echo of a door closing. I struggle to focus my eyes on my watch and discover it's close to 7.30pm. When I look up I'm startled to see my brother standing over me. Dave hovers, slightly open mouth, eyeing me with a look of genuine concern.

'Sorry. Didn't mean to scare you like that.'

'Christ. My heart skipped a beat there.' I rub my eyes, lean over to the side table and put on my glasses. 'I must have been dead to the world.'

'Well, you were looking a bit dead. It kind of worried me for a minute, like you weren't breathing.'

What would happen if I was the one to go? Would Dave miss me at all? How much difference would it make to his life?

'Deep sleep. You got Dad's message?'

'Oh, yeah. I'm guessing he doesn't want to face me just yet.'

'Maybe,' I say, still feeling heavy. 'He doesn't usually work late, does he?'

'Who knows what he does. You know what he's like,' he laughs, and heads into the kitchen. 'Anyway, I was in the neighbourhood and thought I'd stop in and pick up the jacket I left here last week. And then I see Ma's car and here you are all crashed out.'

From the couch I see Dave open the fridge door, move in closer to survey the contents.

I shout, 'I've been at it pretty much all day here. Cleaning. Clearing stuff out. Dropped stuff at the Salvation Army then some shopping and thought, oh, I'll just put my feet up, and before I knew it I was out.'

Dave says, 'Looks like someone stocked up at Whole Paycheck. And it sure as hell wasn't Jimmy O'Brien. Nice one, Jo, but I think you might have wasted your efforts on him.' He grabs a can of Bud Light, takes a few gulps. 'What do you say I take you for a drive to the beach? Weather's nice tonight. They still got Kelly's there, all done up now. There's about five of them in the state, but they still do good roast-beef sandwiches and lobster rolls. I don't know about you but I'm starving.'

Much of Dave's Boston accent has softened over the years, but every now and then he exaggerates it for comic effect. And it's that sudden shrill sound of the hometown when he says 'stahvin' that does something to me. It's inside my being. I see my eager teenage self lining up outside Kelly's with friends on hot summer nights. I can almost smell the fried seafood.

'Good ol' Kelly's. I used to love that place. Well, I had a little bit earlier but I guess I could eat.'

Dave decides to take a tour first through some of the neighbourhood streets 'for a little trip down memory lane,' he says. While some of the area seems unchanged, run-down three-storey houses in need of renovation, others are dressed up with colourful flower beds, newly paved driveways, expensive-looking cars. I look for familiar faces, naively imagining characters from my youth sitting on porches, hanging out at the park or the street corner. They'll appear just as they did before, without any evidence that four decades have passed. Without any knowledge of the nation's recessions, the rise of the internet, the global financial bank crisis, climate change. *We're sorry, Jo*, that girl who bullied me at school would say, *for being so mean. For hating you for no good reason.*

We continue on to another few side roads with Dave pausing here and there to remind me of his childhood antics. Crashing parties, getting drunk at this house, skipping school and smoking dope at that house, over in the corner at the park.

He drives over to the nicer part of town. 'I always wanted to live in one of these houses,' he says when we approach a tree-lined row of big colonial-style homes. 'Beautiful. Remember we used to call them mansions? They must have at least six bedrooms and a few bathrooms. There were always doctors and lawyers, all those types living around here. We just never would have crossed each other's paths. They definitely didn't send their kids to school with the likes of us.'

He parks up in front of one with a huge surrounding lawn. 'This was the one me and my friends used to throw rocks at when we skipped school,' he says. 'It was a challenge to see if we could throw them high enough up to the top window and one day I got my aim right and broke the glass. We ran off so fast that day, were scared shitless we'd get caught.' He leans forward, wraps his hands around his face and grunts, 'Christ, was I a little shit.'

'We all did stupid stuff back then, Dave.'

'Yeah, but now, I think, how would *I* feel if some little shit broke a window in my nice house that I worked hard for?'

'I know. Kids do stupid things though. And later we regret it.'

Dave releases a long sigh, and says, 'We sure do.'

We get to Kelly's Roast Beef with its new flashy sign overhead. A digital clock showing the time and current temperature – essential for any respectable beach stop. A set of decent, clean outdoor tables with parasols sit nearby with a large, colourful planter in the centre to add the finishing touch. I lose count of the impressive amount of Kelly's branded trash cans that surround the area and think, *Isn't this wonderful. Such progress.* By now my stomach is grumbling loud and clear.

We sit and I order fried clams, large onion rings, fries and a chocolate frappe. 'Whoa. Good appetite,' Dave says. 'Think I'll stick to the roast beef and a Diet Coke.'

'No seafood? Since we're here at the beach and all that?'

'Haven't had the beef sandwich for ages. But you'll enjoy the clams, Jo. And this one's on me.'

I have no trouble wolfing it all down while I take in the sounds and urban-beach surrounds, with its airy mixture of washed-up seaweed, rubbish, cigarettes and fast food. I watch young women flirt and get groped by young men where they stand at a nearby parked car. *Was I her once?* I ask myself. Did I want to be the big-busted white girl with the dip-dyed ends? She's the one with the empty look in her eyes, gazing at nothing in particular while nestling up to the muscular Haitian guy in the white T-shirt. Every now and then he shouts something in French to his friend across the street who shouts back. Two older couples and a father and young son, both wearing Boston Red Sox baseball caps, observe their exchange.

Dave shifts uncomfortably in his seat. 'Let's get away from this shit. Let's walk on the beach.'

We stand to go. As we begin to walk past them, Dave dares to stare into the eyes of the Haitian who glares back, then rebounds in a threatening tone, 'What you want, man? What you want?'

Dave stares back with an unflinching hostility that sends a chill through me. 'I'm good, thanks. I'm good,' he says, finally.

'That's fine, you want nothing, you're good, so move on, man. Move on.'

'Yup. I'm good,' Dave says, nodding his head, still staring.

'Come on,' I whisper. We cross the road and walk onto the beach, the Haitian's eyes following us, Dave's finally looking elsewhere. 'What was that all about?'

'Nothing at all. Guys like that just like throwing their dicks around. He's a fucking dealer.' he says, stopping to light a cigarette. 'Seen him around town before.' He kicks the sand hard, once, twice, three times. 'Fucking gets me.'

I hesitate, then ask, 'Did you score drugs from him? How do you know he's a dealer?'

'Come on, Jo, give me a bit more credit than that. No, I didn't *score* drugs. Just seen him, heard him around the bars. They get around, these guys. And they'll sell all kinds of shit to anyone. High-school kids. Junior-high kids. And they lace it with all kinds of dangerous shit to make it go further. Wasn't like that in our day. We knew what we were buying.'

'Well, I'm not so sure about that, but best you keep out of his way if you know what's good for you.'

Dave walks too fast and I struggle on the soft surface even with the cane. He stops, waits for me. He looks out towards the water, purses his lips, turns to me with a fake smile and says, 'It's fucked up.' He sweeps his hand across his mouth. 'You're right. I shouldn't let guys like that get to me.'

We don't walk too far before Dave suggests we sit down on the sand and I wonder if I'll ever be able to get up again.

'Revere Beach. Not what it used to be, Jo.' He passes the cigarette in my direction.

'Oh, what the hell,' I say, and take it. I close my eyes and let the quiet settle through a few puffs and hand it back. The sound of soft waves, along with the smell of damp seaweed that gets stronger with every breeze, offer some hope of a peaceful nostalgia, but it passes. 'I wouldn't say it feels that much different, Dave. Except for a much nicer Kelly's. There was always a lot of noise and trouble around here. Remember all those motorbike gangs. Fast cars, drunk kids up and down the boulevard. Drugs.'

'Oh, yeah. That's true.'

'And the beach was never really that clean either. Was always a bit trashy.' I look around and notice cigarette butts in the sand, straws, plastic cups, a broken bottle.

'I was just thinking,' Dave says, 'of when we were kids here with Ma and Auntie Josie and our cousins. All those long summer days. We'd even stay late after the sun went down. Eat pizza. Sometimes Auntie Peggy would come on her days off. '

'Auntie Peggy. She was nice before all the shit hit the fan.'

He looks at me, caresses my arm awkwardly and says, 'Lots of shit happened back then, Jo. But there were good times too.'

My mother's diary entry about Uncle Ron comes to mind. I've been having some counselling with Wendy the therapist (Ron). This stuff with Peggy and the whole business with that husband of hers and Jo is hard. Dave only found out about Uncle Ron when everyone started talking about me. We might have shared a bedroom when he wasn't spending time in the hospital or running off somewhere, but we totally lived our own lives. Maybe it's about time the record was set straight.

I'm just about to share all of this with Dave before he interrupts with, 'I'll tell you though, you can't beat the beaches in Florida. God, I missed those Fort Lauderdale beaches when I left. Soft white sand. Warm clear water. You could swim, way out and still see right to the bottom. Christ, I miss those days.'

As I think about the jump from Peggy to Dave's preoccupations with sandy beaches, it dawns on me how relative our notions of bad and good have been. They depend on one's perspective. For Dave, Auntie Peggy and the 'shit' that happened couldn't quite compare with the grand significance of his time in Fort Lauderdale.

'I remember you liked it there,' I say. 'I was envious. Why didn't you want to make a go of things and stay? You and Nicole, before you had Amy?'

'It was Nicole,' he says, pausing to finish the cigarette. 'She was the problem. She came to visit a few times when I got those contracts but said she'd never leave Mass. Family and all that. I would have made it work, Jo. I wanted it so bad, to stay, get away from these crazy winters. All the shit. Used to go to the beach after work and swim. And the money was good there too. Could've got more work there if I wanted it. But I didn't want to lose her, and we were only just married, I don't know, a few months, I think. Even though I did screw around a little. But hey,' he says, knocking my arm with his, 'I'm not proud of the cheating and she never found out, but, you know, I got into a bit of partying and she wasn't around and one thing led to another. So, maybe that part of it wasn't great but things would've been different if she was there. Anyway, then one of the jobs I had finished and she said, "You're coming home, Dave." And here I am now. Divorced. Amy's done OK, but I know I made a lot of mistakes that she hasn't forgiven me for.'

I can't say I'm surprised by Dave's confession, but it gives me a headache. Like father, like son.

'Who knows what would have happened, Dave,' I say, massaging my temples. 'And it's never too late to try to make things better. Now that Amy's older with her own child she probably realises how hard it was for you. I mean marriage is no ballpark and once you bring kids into the picture...' I shake my head, thinking about our parents, my mother's heartache. The mistakes she couldn't fix. Her inability to walk away. 'I'm sure she loves you.'

He closes his eyes, nods in agreement. I wonder what other right things I should be saying.

'I miss Ma,' Dave says.

I look to see if that fleeting moment with Dave's quivering voice will lead to any tears, but it doesn't.

'Oh, God,' I sigh. 'Me too.'

And it's true. We hardened ourselves over the course of a year or so in preparation for her death, her colluding with us with all her talk about hospice plans and what kind of memorial she wanted. We convinced ourselves we could take it, but the body, with or without the outlet of tears, has no memory at all of that kind of rationalisation.

'She was a good mother, Jo. Not perfect, but you know, I put her through so much hell. You see,' his voice rises, 'Amy was always a good kid, overall, not too much trouble, really, but I didn't do enough for her, wasn't really there for her.'

I touch his shoulder. 'Amy knows you love her, Dave. She knows.'

'But that's not enough, is it? But sometimes, Jo, I just think I can't do it anymore. Can't take anymore. Everything's too much fucking work. I just wake up and want to give up. End it all.' He lights another cigarette. 'Ma kind of gave up later, too, in her own way. With her smoking. And everything else. She knew she was going to get cancer. She always said it was in the genes. What's the point of quitting, right? I'll get it too.'

'Oh, Dave.' I feel a sensation of panic rising. My stomach is beginning to make a loud noise again but this time it's not hunger pains. I move around trying to get into a comfortable position. I undo the first button of my jeans. 'Are you trying to tell me you are seriously depressed?'

'Maybe,' he says.

'Are you having suicidal thoughts?'

His tone changes suddenly from morose to nonchalance. 'Oh yeah. I have those thoughts.'

I try to read his eyes but they're not giving anything away. And although he's making light of it he scares me. Is this what suicidal people do? 'That's serious. Have you told your shrink?'

'Oh sure, we talk about it. I mean I think about it but I'm not ever going to act on it, Jo. It's just shit that flies around in my head, but I wouldn't have the guts to do anything about it,' he laughs, looks at me. 'You don't have to worry about anything like that.'

'Well, that's a relief…I guess. Are you sure?' Those times when he was hospitalised in his adult years, they always happened when he had a manic episode, when his meds needed adjusting. According to Dave the bipolar high was the best feeling he ever experienced, better than any sex or drugs. 'You feel like you can do anything,' he told me then. 'King fucking Kong. You think you can rule the universe. But then you crash and it's the hardest fall you can imagine. There's nothing worse. You feel like there's nothing worth living for.'

'Aw. That's real sweet of you, Jo.' Dave puts his arms around me and pulls me close to him. 'But you don't need to worry about that. I'm a survivor. *You're* a survivor, we're a family of survivors, Jo. Ain't no way we're going down without a fight.'

Twenty

I'm on my way out of town in the Mondeo, heading toward Beth's, when I arrive at a familiar set of traffic lights on the main road near Auntie Peggy's house.

For many years when I travelled in this direction I waited patiently in the car convincing myself not to look at her house, at her car which was often parked in the driveway near the basketball net where the boys would play outside. Tonight as the lights turn green I drive straight on, but at the last second before I have to move into the lane that takes me onto the highway, my commonsense collapses and I give in to my curiosity to turn around at the next opportunity and head back. I meander slowly towards Peggy's house, noting lights on in the front room, and continue to the end of the street. I find a place to turn around and park with enough distance away from the house so I won't be seen.

The place looks the same as when I saw Peggy there before she died. I happened to be in Boston that summer and agreed to join my mother on a visit. At that stage Peggy was strong enough to stay at home, although she needed help walking, couldn't eat very much and used an oxygen canister to aid her breathing. She wore a wig but it was a good quality one that my mother helped her find.

My mother finished her cigarette outside and once in, played her jovial, positive-nurse act to perfection. Oh, Peggy, the wig looks even better today than when you first got it, it's like you've grown into it. You've got a great colour today in your face too. Peggy, look who's here come to say hello.

I had made a point of buying Peggy a goodbye-to-life bon voyage gift, the most expensive Chanel body lotion I could find, no expense spared. Nothing else seemed appropriate, considering she could no longer smoke, eat, drink or be merry, and I didn't want to show up empty-handed. Peggy went along with the façade of playing happy families when I handed it over, all wrapped in its shiny paper and silver ribbon. When she struggled to open the top end of the wrapping I helped her tear it off.

'Oh, that looks nice. You know, I've never used body cream. Never liked that greasy feeling,' she said, taking a sniff after making a sour face.

'But this is different, Auntie. *It's Chanel.*'

'Oh, yes, Chanel. Oh,' she said, putting it down.

'Go on, give it a try, it'll make you feel like a million bucks,' I said. But I think I knew all along that the last thing a dying woman would want is a gift from the niece who once turned her husband into a paedophile with fantasies of having his own teenage Lolita.

'Oh, you know, I think I'll try it later, after a shower. That's what I'll do,' she said, smiling, but I insisted.

'Just try a little bit now. It's a special one. Only the best for you, Auntie Peggy. Just have a little smell. You'll love it. It's *really* special.'

After I helped her open the lid, she squeezed some, with hesitation, onto the tip of her index finger, and tested it on her wrist. 'Oh, no, not too greasy, that's good.'

'No, no, there's no way Chanel's going to be greasy, Auntie.'

'Well, maybe a bit, but not too bad,' she said to my mother. My mother took some, then I smoothed more of it on Peggy's other arm.

'Oh, not too much, please,' Peggy said.

'Just a bit more, Auntie. It's nice and subtle,' I said. I took more and dabbed it on my neck and arms.

'Hmm, I like that,' my mother said. 'But you know what I really loved wearing years ago, Peggy. Oh, what was it called, White something...'

'Oh, that was White Shoulders,' Peggy said. 'Yes, I loved that one too. You know they stopped making it some time ago now. What a shame that was.'

'And Emeraude,' my mother added. 'I wore that one all the time. Why can't they just keep making the good ones? Everyone loved Emeraude and White Shoulders.'

An image popped into my mind of my mother taking the green bottle of Emeraude and spraying it all over herself after a shower, then lighting a long menthol Virginia Slim.

'But nothing beats Chanel, ladies. You can't top Chanel,' I said.

'We all have our favourites, I guess,' my mother said with a nervous smile, looking at Peggy.

Apart from a few bouts of uncontrollable coughing and breathlessness, there was no indication from Peggy about how awful it felt to be withering away with poisoned lungs, especially when she knew her husband was sitting in the back yard puffing on his Lucky Strikes, still faithful to his old brand. The rest of the carton sat on their kitchen countertop, next to Peggy's medications.

I caught a glimpse of the back of Ron's bald head and hunched back, which looked exaggerated when he stood up and wandered around. He appeared to have reduced in size since I was a teenager, but then I wondered if he may have always been that small. His eyes stole a glance inside the house once or twice. He could see my mother and me but kept his distance. Over the hour and a half's time we visited, there was no mention of him.

The kitchen where we talked felt small and cramped, so different to how I remembered it when I was a child. I had spent so much time there having milk and cookies or tea with my aunt, drawing and playing games with her boys. The bigger world of the past, the structures that contained the adults I had no choice but to trust back then, had noticeably shrunk in size and importance. After Peggy's death, I hoped they would eventually all dwindle so much they would turn into motes of insignificance.

By the time I said my final goodbye to Auntie Peggy that afternoon I knew the Chanel lotion and even showing my face was a mistake. Something had compelled me to catch that last sight of Peggy on her way out, with her husband, hopefully, not lagging too far behind. Maybe I had to have evidence of it, see the proof with my own eyes. I left knowing, most likely, that Peggy would never use my present. For a while an insidious bitterness about that swam around inside me. All that money spent on something that would end up in the trash with Peggy's other cheap stuff after she drew her last breath. Still, Peggy had no other choice but to take notice of it. Uncle Ron might have seen it that day too, opened it and said, *Now that one smells good*. She would have remembered the scent when I opened it, when I rubbed it into her skin. She would have remembered I was there in her house.

My reverie is interrupted and I am snapped back to the present when I see the old man emerging from the side of the house near the driveway, with a slow-moving cross-breed mutt. Turns out Ron is still a smoker, one of those people who will take in a pack a day and live to ninety. The world is an unjust place. He moves first to the front of the house where the mutt sniffs then pisses on a tree stump. The dog ambles up the road on his own then stops, looks behind him to see Ron standing still in the same spot with a steady look downwards, puffing away, coughing. Eventually the dog realises he's on his own and continues alone. He stops at the front of a house a few doors up and takes his first big dump. Even from a distance I can see his hind legs shaking.

The dog moves on to the end of the road near the street lights and begins to head back but only after crossing to the other side where he finds another house and leaves his second dump. It's a quicker one this time close to a large bed of yellow tulips. In spite of the dog's wishful nods and whimpers to his master to join him for a walk, Ron remains standing in the same place, only shifting to pace slowly in front of the driveway, towards the front door and back again. When he finishes his cigarette he flicks it into the street and hollers, 'Let's go. Come on, let's go.' The mutt waddles back slowly, disappointed, and they head back inside.

'I don't believe it,' I whisper to myself in the car. 'He's leaving it there. Son of a bitch. Who does he think he is? If he's not capable of walking or even picking up his dog's shit, what else is he not doing? Not feeding him properly, I'll bet. Son of a bitch.'

All lights are soon switched off downstairs, then upstairs, and all is dark, like the other houses. The street is like the corner of a ghost town kept alive only by its proximity to the busier main road. I sit for a long time contemplating the dog-shit that Ron's dog has left behind, imagine picking it up with a bag. I picture myself, quiet with intent, holding the bag in my hands, feeling the warmth of shit through the plastic, then smearing it over the front door of Ron's house.

I remember her expression that evening at home when the truth, or my half-version of the truth, came out about Uncle Ron.

'He's just such an asshole,' my mother had said. 'Bastard.'

As I'm waiting to pull out into the busy street I notice two young white guys, maybe in their mid-twenties, both wearing baseball caps back to front, smoking by a pizza joint. I feel their eyes on me and I try not to look, but when I do one of them grabs himself between the legs with force and shouts, 'Hey, how about some of this lady? Woo hoo!'

Twenty One

'You're back a bit late,' Beth says from the comfort of her usual television watching spot. A clean scent of lemon fills the living room. A can of Pledge sits on the table.

'Did you eat much? I've got some leftovers.'

'Thanks, but we ended up getting something at Kelly's, so, yeah, that was dinner. Fried clams.'

'Clams?' she says, with a look of disgust.

'It is kind of sitting like lead in me right now,' I say. My stomach makes a rumbling sound again.

'Wow. Could hear that all the way from here. You want some Pepto-Bismol?'

I accept the offer, cringe at the chalky taste and try to lighten up the atmosphere. 'So, hey, I stopped in at Whole Foods earlier and picked up a few things for us. Salad, bread, some other stuff. You know, you shouldn't worry about feeding me by the way. You've got enough going on and I can take care of myself when I'm in and out. I also got some more wine, a nice gin for some G&T. You know, we got to keep up our supply, right?'

'Look, Jo,' she says sternly. 'We have to eat anyway so it's no big deal to make for one more person. I mean, it's not going to break the bank. And we've got plenty of alcohol now, thanks.'

I slump into the comfy armchair. My legs and arms feel heavy and I'm trying to visualise regaining the strength needed to put the shopping away.

'How's your brother? He still shooting off about the money business?'

I hold my stomach and close my eyes.

'Hey, are you OK?' Beth says, sitting forward. 'You look a bit off-colour, like really pale.'

I wish she hadn't asked. Driving on the highway I started to feel short waves of nausea. The fresh memory of seeing Uncle Ron, hearing that voice, the thought of my hands smearing shit all over his door (and how good that would feel) raced through my mind, then the words, everything that was said before, all at once flooded my brain. *Keep this between us, OK? No one will understand* …His hand touching my face. My mother's diary… *the rapist (Ron)*.

'Jo? You OK?'

'I don't know.' My eyes water. The taste of clams is rising up with reflux.

Beth turns off the television. 'It's the hardest thing, you know, losing your mother. Even though she was sick for a while, it's still a shock when they're gone.' She releases a sigh, watches me. Waits. 'You were at the house for a long time.'

Beth knows enough about the O'Brien family and that house to recognise their effects. Whenever I've visited in the past it wouldn't take long before I'd descend into a sullen state, all because I'd agreed to stay there in the old bedroom, the birthplace of my nightmares. Eventually when I'm an old woman, if I make it that far, maybe the memories will begin to fade. If I'm lucky maybe some of the things I wish never happened will disappear altogether from my mind with dementia. Only screwed up people like me could look forward to such a thing. What would I feel like then? Would I be happier?

I go to bed soon after having a cup of camomile tea but it doesn't stop the nausea from waking me up later. Then cramping. Soon I'm rushing to the bathroom with just enough time to bring up the clams. And everything else.

The following morning, Beth sits on Danielle's bed with its pink, flowery duvet cover and matching pillow cases. 'There's some broth in the fridge for you, OK?' She's suited up for work, SUV keys in hand, filling the air with a mix of pure cleanliness and Jo Malone perfume; after her morning run, she is a sight of perfection at 7.30am. I am proud of her and envious at the same time. Beth has what I want: feminine grace and self-conviction in middle-age. No excuses. No nonsense.

'Broth?' I say, half awake.

'Chicken soup. My mother just dropped it off. I'll call you later during a break, OK? See how you're doing.'

When her scent dissipates, I'm left with myself and that stale waft of sick in the air. I get up, go to the bathroom and feel relieved to have survived the night. Most of the vomiting occurred in the late night and early morning hours. Beth was by my side through it all, rubbing my back, wiping my mouth, offering water.

'I should have known better,' I cried, in between retching.

After I had thrown up enough to get me to bed, Beth left me to it.

Most of the day is a blur of repetition that includes sleep, sipping water, runs to the toilet, sips of broth, more runs to toilet, more sips, more sleep. I make sure I answer the phone so Beth and her mother Jean won't worry. Beth was planning on taking me out with her and some friends for drinks and a meal after work. In disappointment at missing out, I drift into a dreamland where vicious dogs chase me for food scraps and the girl with the dip-dyed hair at the beach is forcing my hands over her large breasts while trying to kiss me. 'Touch them,' she screams. 'Go on, touch them. They're real.'

Toward the end of the afternoon before Danielle returns from school – it looks like she lives in that cheerleading outfit – I gain enough appetite to eat two pieces of toast, then drink tea, followed by a quick Skype with Jon. I tell him about the slovenly state of the house, the nail clippings, the cleaning, going through all the photos, Dad cancelling, Dave, Revere Beach, the vomiting, but no mention of Uncle Ron and his dog. Afterwards when Jon pitches in, it's as though he's seen all my activity through a looking-glass.

'Maybe you shouldn't spend any more time sorting through your mother's stuff. I know you only have a short time there but, maybe it's just not good for you, you know, all at once like this. And you know what you're like with stress, what it does to you. I don't want you to get ill.' He throws in a reminder of how important it is to be kind to Dave. 'He's hurting too. In his own way.' Reminds me to get as much rest as possible. 'You know your body shuts down when you're not getting enough sleep. Stay away from greasy food and lighten up on the wine. You know what it does to you.'

There's a swimming pool just like the public one my brother and I used to frequent across town with our friends in the summer, and I, the middle-aged Jo, am swimming in a race. It feels like twenty-six miles instead of twenty-six laps. Two children, boy and girl, are ahead of me freestyling alongside each other towards a Buddha-like woman who waits for them at the other end, wrinkled face smiling, arms open, encouraging them. I'm working my hardest but I'm struggling and relieved to see someone else far behind me. I discover it's Tom Cruise. Hah! Even I, with my weak leg, can beat this pretty boy. But soon he's catching up and overtakes me. My strength ceases and I resign myself to snailing along. Smug Tom is all smiles and self-congratulatory, everyone patting him on the back. The two children are hardly visible as they huddle under the holding arms of the Buddha woman. She looks up at me coldly when I reach the end and mumbles, 'You're last.'

With a night of solid sleep behind me, I make a fresh start to the day with a gentle kick of sugary tea and check my work emails. Most of them I decide to ignore. I don't even open the ten or more from the undergrads I haven't seen all year, the ones who haven't signed up for any of the offered extra sessions or tutorials, the ones who have decided, near the end of their degree, that they should make their first visit to the library so they can make a pathetic attempt at writing something passable for their final-year dissertation. My outgoing message about bereavement leave is clear. In so many words, it says: *Fuck off, you little shits. Serves you right for waiting this long to contact me.* For now, they have my colleagues and the admin staff to deal with, then the Easter break will arrive, another way to stretch out some more time before I have to face work again.

And then I see a message from Nina Hayes. PhD student in her late twenties. Intelligent, committed, provocative. Intense Nina. Can I see you? the subject line reads. I linger, afraid to open it.

She started as a slow burner, an innocent intellectual flirtation.

'Be careful,' my colleague and friend, Tania, warned when I agreed to supervise Nina's master's dissertation a while back. 'I hear she's bad news. Smart one, yes, but needy. She'll suck up all your time and more. I heard there was some kind of weird clash between her and Peter, you know, the temporary guy who covered some teaching. I don't know any details.'

Misunderstood, I thought. A rumour did go around about this 'clash', but I assumed Peter just wasn't up to the job. She might have showed him up. I noticed Nina was a bit odd, isolated herself from other students, although in the earlier taught part of the master's programme she never failed to impress everyone with her wider reading. She'd rattle off endless references then challenge the European academic canon's deficit in 'really' original theories on taste beyond those that merely extended French sociologist Pierre Bourdieu's. The class wasn't sure what to make of her when she debated the futile nature of theorising about anything. What was the point of it all? she would ask. It was a game she said she wasn't sure she wanted to play. How could I, and the similarly sceptical Bourdieu, argue with that? She was the life of the seminar, the ideal future academic. In the end her distrust of the institution didn't stop her from

224

graduating with distinction, or from returning a year later and asking me to support her PhD application and to supervise her. And she was more than happy to accept that attractive studentship package.

Tania was right. Here I am now, more than half way into the first year of supervising Nina's PhD and she certainly has 'sucked up' lots of my time. At first I welcomed this when faced with other students whose lack of ambition prompted sinister thoughts. Nina's enthusiasm to set her ideas in motion has resulted in reams of pages that jump from one astute thought to another, without ever reaching closure. Her work has been a beautiful and thrilling mess.

Her PhD project weaves together feminist theory with her own photography practice which involves taking self-portraits of her naked body. Yes, it's been done before, but she has managed to make it her own with something new to say. Many of the images focus on her scars from the third-degree burns she suffered in a childhood accident. Some shots are close-ups of her fully made-up face and classic Hollywood looks, but the scars challenge any attempts at photographic perfection. Her body is a bas-relief of complex terrain. When we talked about the fire in our first tutorial she never revealed any details. It was just 'an accident out of my control,' she said. 'This study's like a way of regaining some kind of power again.'

'Yes, that's a positive thing, Nina, a way of telling your own story.'

Before responding she fixed her dark eyes on mine and smiled. 'But I have a right to be quiet about what I want to be quiet about,' she insisted. 'It's about having a choice, right?

Take that away and there's nothing.' She tilted her head to the side, then swivelled herself back and forth in her chair in a suggestive way. I had noticed her do this in our previous MA dissertation supervisions but tried to put it out of my mind.

'It's an interesting perspective,' I said. 'But it often feels like a fine line to me. In some cases, choosing to speak out or opting to remain silent will lead to the same result.'

She continued staring, smiling, swivelling. She wore a maroon satin camisole under a see-through blouse. It was hard not to admire the confidence she displayed in her soft, curvy figure, tummy roll and scars for all to see.

I saw her again that week after the Visual Culture talk I organised. The speaker couldn't stay for drinks and most staff and students dispersed after thirty minutes. It was still early and Nina coaxed me into grabbing a bite to eat nearby, followed by more drinks. Normally I would have said I was too tired, but Jon was away on a research trip across the country again and I didn't have to teach the next day. Along with a good appetite, I felt an unexpected rush of energy.

That's when it started. The power of a good tapas selection and sangria, how they take off the edge. The revelations that follow. There was a boyfriend a few months back, a girlfriend before that. Nina always knew she was bisexual.

'Aren't we all born that way? Isn't that what Freud said? I have some problems with Freud but I know he was right about that one.'

'Yes. Yes, you're so right,' I said, giggling, raising my glass. 'Let's not totally discount Freud. I'll toast to that!'

As the months passed we had more meals, exhibition trips, drinks. I hadn't considered any of this a problem at the time. My colleagues often socialised with PhD students, in particular the more mature ones. Their research overlapped with our own interests, they were sharing our undergraduate teaching hours and we treated them like colleagues. Over time Nina and I shared more friendly disclosures. Honesty about my MS, how it all started, the leftover effects.

'It was actually so awful, Nina. I really didn't know how I was going to get through it. And it was tough for Jon, too, at the beginning, but he's stuck by me all the way.'

'You're *incredible*, Jo. You're just *so amazing*.'

Inquiring chats about what it was like for me when I started as an academic. How 'inspiring' my work was. How captivating my teaching was.

'You just show up all the others in the department. You're way too good for this second-rate place,' Nina said, looking at me with those wide, admiring eyes. 'Why hasn't another top uni snapped you up? You should be a professor by now.'

I introduced her to Jon one evening in my office before he and I set off to see a film.

'So Nina's your PhD tour de force. I noticed she looked at you a certain way,' he said, lifting his eyebrows as we left the building.

'What kind of way?' I asked, with some trepidation, but knowing exactly what he meant.

'Let's just say she likes you, that's for sure.'

'Oh, she's young,' I laughed. 'It happens. Won't last though, the idolising thing.' In that second it felt good to think that someone might idolise me and I found myself flicking my hair in a silly gesture.

'No, Jo. I mean she *fancies* you. A lot. I can tell.' His expression and tone were serious.

'Hah, that's a funny one. I'm pretty much twice her age, not to mention *fat*, with an MS limp. Not exactly a great catch am I?'

'Look, I'm just telling you what I saw. I wasn't imagining it. And stop saying you're fat.' He slid his arm around me, pinched my love handle. 'You just need to lose a bit of weight, that's all.' He removed his arm, sped up his walk and I struggled to keep up.

It was the three-day conference in Manchester I attended before I flew out to see my mother at the hospice that confirmed Jon's suspicions. After dinner with others on the second night, Nina asked me to have a look at her slides as she claimed she was worried about her talk the next morning. Another PhD student she planned to share the room with had cancelled at the last minute and Nina had the room to herself.

With her sitting close to me on her bed, we went through her work in some detail. While I shared my comments I felt her move her arm under mine. I was surprised, although her touch felt natural and non-threatening. I smiled and continued to read. Then came the light strokes on my arm, then a kiss, just a little one, me stunned but not pulling away – her smiling, her waiting. After that, proper kissing, the eventual groping, me stopping, babbling about how wrong it all was – 'I'm your supervisor. I'm old enough to be your mother'; Nina whispering 'We aren't doing anything wrong';

more insistent groping, me refusing then giving in, refusing, and giving in again.

When I finally returned to my own room (Nina needed her sleep before her morning talk) I thought about Jon. I tried to convince myself that what happened didn't exactly count as cheating on my husband. No, it was a special intimacy shared between two women friends, that was all it was. Yes, we had ended up in bed, our imperfect bodies surrendered, but even so, this, I told myself, was not the same as going behind Jon's back with another man. What could be worse than that, the ultimate dagger in a husband's back? I went to sleep reassuring myself that what I had done was my business.

Yet when I met Nina at breakfast the next morning, something inside me had shifted. I wasn't sure if it was just nerves, but she appeared different, less appealing. Then it hit me, that boulder-hitting-the-bottom-of-my-stomach insight. Hadn't I joked with Tania about those male professors who abused their power and had affairs with their research assistants? Hadn't I sneered at those men who'd left their wives and kids after falling for an attractive female grad student? 'So typical. So *slimy*. They just can't control themselves, can they?' And there I stood, the morning after. Could I honestly claim complete innocence just because I was a woman?

When I delivered my talk that morning I tried not to catch Nina's eye. Her attention on me was unflinching and made me uncomfortable. She continued to stick by my side for the rest of that last day, embarrassing me by telling others how much of a 'stellar supervisor' I was. All at once, every word she uttered, every glance she threw my way, made me want to wince. At lunch when she asked if I could introduce her to yet another group of senior academics I noticed how quickly she moved in. I watched the way she inched closer to them as they chatted. I recognised the way she pulled back those silky blonde waves from her face and tucked them behind her ear at just the right moments. The way she tilted that head of hers, that coy smile. I remembered Tania's warning, 'Be careful…she's bad news,' as my body began to sense the gravity of the situation. And it frightened me.

Just be straight with her, I told myself. *No messing around. Strict supervisor/student meetings in my office from now on.*

'It has to be this way, Nina. I'm sorry if I led you on,' I said when we met in my office that week following the conference. It was a couple of days before my brother called and told me about my mother checking into the hospice. 'I shouldn't have let it go that far. I'm the one at fault here. I'm sorry.' I concentrated my eyes on a pile of papers that I was shuffling in front of me.

'Huh,' Nina said, and paused. 'Well, I don't think you're sorry at all. No, Jo, I'm pretty sure you're not sorry about what happened.'

When I shut down the conversation with, 'This has to be the end of it, Nina. Right here. Right now. Let's focus on the work. How far have you got now?' – well, let's just say Nina didn't take it very well.

I haven't seen her since she stomped out of the office that day.

Since then I've had plenty of time to worry about Nina and what might happen if she chose to complain to Richard smug-ass Appleton, the research committee chair, about me. How it would impact on Jon, on us. So I don't think about it. It does make me wonder, though, whether there is something lacking in my relationship; something that has been lost over the years.

I return to thinking about the pressure I'm under at work because of my lack of research output over the past year or so.

'OK, Jo. Your turn,' Richard Appleton said when the committee last met. 'How are things going with that article? Any progress? You know there comes a time when you just need to know that good enough is good enough. And we do need to submit our stats soon for the research assessment exercise.'

He wouldn't let me leave before I agreed to send him a timeline for the journal piece I should have finished a couple of months ago, the one about expressions of feminist politics in contemporary Western art practice, and the methodologies that academic prats like me use to analyse them.

For a few minutes I contemplate changing the entire premise of the journal piece so I can work in an argument that uses Michel Foucault's views on power. But I realise I don't have the strength and see I'm procrastinating again.

Instead, I look over the draft I've written for my mother's eulogy. It's all stiff and teacherly, although comforting in its orderly structure, a list of all the things that made her a perfect nurse, mother, and wife. She tried her best with what she had, I can't fault her for that. I fuss with grammar again, practise out loud adjusting my accent so I can sound more American, maybe even more like a Bostonian, like I did in the old days before fancy pants university sucked every last trace of street-talking townie out of me. I make the awful mistake of experimenting with my phone recorder so I can hear what I sound like, and cringe.

Later I get in the Mondeo and drive over to the house to meet Dave, before the old man arrives to talk about money.

Twenty Two

Dave's rushed over from a job and somehow looks right in his work clothes that show residues of dirt and dust. His eyes are a little tired, enough to reveal a reasonable level of work ethic respectability, a hard-working, middle-aged guy fitting in with what the world expects of him. But it's not too much; it looks like he's found the balance. I ask him again if he wants to add anything to the eulogy and he declines, insisting I'm the expert.

'Just don't overdo it,' he warns, smiling in a way that is intended to convey kindness but doesn't manage it.

'What's that supposed to mean?'

'No offense Jo, but, you know, just keep it short and sweet.'

After Dad arrives, Dave doesn't waste any time in sitting us around the kitchen table, freshly brewed coffee ready. His business ideas have progressed a lot since the evening we met at the grill place, I discover with some surprise, as he kept quiet about it last night at the beach. He and Karen have been looking into a franchise restaurant opportunity, a safer bet than building up from something new, we are told, and they've found out you don't need much investment cash to purchase the franchise agreement fee, although he's evasive about exactly how much. You also have to apply for a business loan for all the other costs.

'But you see Dad, that's the easier part because the banks want to help businesses around here and a franchise is so much less risky because the company offers training, gets people started, hooks them up with suppliers and all the rest. And of course, the less I have to ask for in terms of the business loan, the better,' Dave says with a surprising level of professionalism and confidence.

They've already located a space in the centre of town that looks good, just down the road from Dad's, and they're looking at applying for the BGR Burger Joint franchise. He's done some research and starts quoting a list of BGR success stories.

Dave stands over us with his empty cup, ready to pour another, and waves his free hand around. 'With all these other pizza places, Mexican, Chinese, Thai, Indian options, burgers, the right kind of burgers, can make a fortune here. People around here want a decent burger, a grilled one, with finesse,' Dave says, pinching the air between his index finger and thumb. 'And they've got the veggie options too, but red meat, you know, is still what everyone wants. It's a no-fail deal. A no-brainer.'

I watch our dad sitting still, his eyes lowered, his fingers tapping the side of his mug. Every now and then he looks up at Dave, nods, says, 'Uh-huh. Yup,' adds, 'OK,' and peers down again.

While Dave talks and I try to take it all in, I start biting the inside of my cheek again, then my lip, and can't seem to fight the temptation to feel for more chin hairs. Some of it is starting to sound a bit less scary, but who knows, they may not even get past the agreement fee.

Dad only interrupts Dave once with comments on how risky business is; that he should put a deposit on an apartment and stop renting.

'Well, Dad,' says Dave. 'Don't you remember back in the day when you put some money into that fish business with your friend and you cashed in OK when you had enough. Remember? If the business goes alright then I can still buy my own place.' We banter around it all, the hesitations, the possibilities.

'Things were different in my day. That fish place. That was small-fry stuff,' Dad says, and I'm thinking, yup, that's probably because it was a cover-up for Irish mob business. Not that I would ever say it.

'Come on, Dad. Put yourself in my shoes. How about giving me a break here? Just this once, will you? Can you just try to listen to everything I'm saying? How about cutting me some slack?'

Judging by the way Dad has closed his eyes and is tightening his mouth, I imagine his blood pressure is rising. He starts to laugh, still not looking at Dave. 'Hah,' he says. 'That's funny. Yeah. That's funny. Cut me some slack. Hah, hah.'

'I'm not joking, Dad. I'm serious.' Dave sends me a frustrated glare and I look away.

'Yup. Oh, I know you're serious alright.' Dad looks out the window, squinting into the sunlight. 'That's the funny thing. And you know what? The thing that's making me laugh is that you are serious. Yup. It all sounds great in your head and from your calculator.' He turns to Dave with an odd grin. 'But you know what? I've decided. I ain't gonna give you a *dime*,' he says slowly. 'Not a *penny*.' He shakes his head. 'Can't do it.'

'Oh, jeez,' I whisper, holding my head in my hands.

Dave slams his mug on the countertop. 'Jesus Christ, Dad. Jesus H fucking Christ.' With shaking hands he takes a cigarette from his pack in his shirt pocket and lights up.

'Yeah. Jesus Christ,' Dad laughs. 'Took the words right outta my mouth. Look, you can try to do whatever it is you wanna do, that's great. Whatever. But leave me out of it.' He raises his hands in surrender. 'I don't want any part of it. It's what Ma wanted. And she was right. Nothing you say is gonna change my mind. No point in talking.' He stands, looks at me and says, 'I gotta finalise things with this lawyer and if your brother wants any money at all we better get going soon.' He moves towards his bedroom.

Dave's cigarette smoke envelops me and I'm overwhelmed with a suffocating sensation. This is followed by an increase in body temperature that I know has nothing to do with my hormones. I could die here. Right now, this second, I could collapse and I know I can't let myself die here in this house. I reach in my handbag to find a wrinkled tissue and dab my forehead and upper lip. I examine the damp tissue, close my eyes, and dab again.

'That's it then, Dad? You're just gonna walk away from me? Sure you are. What the hell else is new?' He shouts, throws the mug in the direction of the sink, but it bounces off the edge, lands on the tiled floor and breaks into several pieces.

'You see? See that? There you go. Nice.' Dad shouts back, grabbing his jacket from the bedroom. 'I told you, it's in the will, there's no changing it.' He points a finger at Dave. 'You got plenty. I'm telling you to get a place of your own and I don't wanna hear anymore about it. We gotta go. I'm waiting outside in the truck.'

'But I can still do that,' Dave calls to Dad as the old man makes his way towards the front door, and there's a clear shift in tone. 'Jo, you can see how it works, right? I'm not crazy here.' He touches the top of his head. He begins pacing around the kitchen. 'I can make this thing work. I know I can. I just need someone to have faith in me. Please. Look at what you got. You worked hard. I'm no idiot, Jo. You had dreams, right? I got dreams too.'

'OK, OK. Just slow down, Dave. I need more time on this. I need to think about all this,' I say, feeling breathless. I don't know what's worse, Dave shouting or Dave ingratiating. I move to the sink to splash water on my neck and chest and start picking up the broken mug pieces. 'You can't expect me to make such a big decision all at once here. I need to see something like a business plan, that sort of thing. Actually, you know what, Dave? I can't even think about this now with Ma's memorial coming up. That's what we should be talking about right now. Not money. It's not right. It's Ma we should be thinking about. So don't push me.'

The three of us head over to the lawyer's office in Dad's pick-up truck in complete silence. You could cut the atmosphere in the cab with a knife. Outside the lawyer's office hangs yet another American flag. What's the relationship, I wonder, between respecting the flag and all this God-speak that everyone clings to around here?

'George's a good Irish lawyer, looks out for his own,' says Dad, as we open the doors.

Dave doesn't respond.

As we walk in, Walsh looks at the clock. He's near retirement age, is hacking away with a bad cough and we're twenty minutes late at the end of the day. We apologise. He apologises for not shaking our hands because he's concerned about passing on his germs.

I ask what we should do if I decide to lend Dave some of my share of the money.

'I can't change the staggered payments to Dave that your mother wants, but hey, whatever way you want to distribute the money between you and your brother is your decision. For a charge we can write up a legal agreement for the repayments you're talking about,' he says, wiping his nose with an old-fashioned cloth handkerchief with embroidered trim. 'Or you can go on family trust and be done with it.'

'Well, we're not doing anything just yet,' I say, avoiding Dave's eye, 'with everything going on, but we'll keep that in mind.' Soon we are signing everything and pass on our bank details.

'Your mother really struck it great with this investment. She wouldn't tell me anything about the stocks but when she came in that day about adding it to the will, specifying the three-way split and the conditions, I asked her why she didn't cash in earlier. Why didn't you set up a nice cruise for you and Jimmy? I asked her. She says to me, "George, by the time it started doing real good we didn't really need the money. We had everything. Yeah, we could've done a cruise but Jimmy would've got bored and hated it."' He laughs.

'Hah, yeah. She got that right,' says Dad.

'Then Terry said, "I just want to do right by my family now. They deserve it." So, you guys are lucky. It doesn't always work out this way.' George takes a break to cough and sniffle. 'If I were her I would've lived it up right to the end.'

Twenty Three

On the day of Ma's memorial, I get to the house just after 10am with plenty of time spare to collect the photo album I've put together and the rest of the framed photos then load the car. They'll look good in the restaurant where family and friends will be gathering for her send-off after the service.

Dave stands in the kitchen with Dad and my father's brother, Uncle Joe, the gambler who lost all his money. I haven't seen the guy for at least ten years. They're all finishing a round of shots with their coffee before setting off. After my uncle's laugh about my walking cane – 'How'd you hurt yourself? Oh, right, yeah, I forgot' – and some jokes about the sorry state of socialised medicine and British hospitals, I endure all the small talk. *It's good the weather held out for us. What a beautiful sunny day, just what Terry would want, probably a lot nicer than in rainy London, right? I couldn't live there with all that damp. The joints feel it as soon as it gets too wet. You sure sound like one of them now. I guess that's what happens after all these years, huh? But I remember you sounded like that a long time ago too when you first got over there.*

'Yes,' my brother pitches in, taking a stab at sounding like a royal. 'Just call her Princess Joanna.'

Wouldn't it be nice for once, just once, to be treated like a princess around here.

I get ready to leave for the church before them. 'It's a good idea to get there early, you know, to greet people,' I say. They look at me as though I'm speaking Mandarin. 'OK. So I'll go now and see you there. Don't be late.'

'Yeah. You go. Good idea,' Dad says and swigs the last bit of his shot.

Soon after I arrive, I see my niece, Amy, driving into a space with one of those newer Honda SUVs, her mother, Nicole, in the passenger side. (I think about the shitty little second-hand, fifteen-year-old two-door French thing that Jon and I share in London. And we're supposed to be respectable types.) It's been years since I've seen Nicole or Amy. The longer I've lived in London, the less effort I've made to stay in touch when I've returned for visits. Each later trip seemed to miss young Amy's visits to see Dave and my parents. Another year passes, everything else takes over; got to see my old friend Beth, off to New York for a couple of days with Jon, to the mountains up north to see that old college friend, anything but hang around here. The distance between Jo and the O'Brien family grows wider until the O'Briens are little specks on the horizon.

Amy is close to thirty years old, a mother herself now, so OK, maybe old enough to warrant her own SUV. Still pretty and slim, a fresh face and shy smile that works to good effect. She doesn't say too much, never did as she was always on the quiet side, although I knew all those years ago there must have been more going on in that head of hers. But her eyes offer genuine feeling, for a moment at least. The thing is, when I look down I notice she's wearing jeans, of all things. They're the dark-blue, nice-looking kind but shouldn't she know better? *Hey, this is your grandmother's memorial.* I try not to let these thoughts take over, such things shouldn't matter, all these outdated stuffy traditions; she's flashing those big, sad powder-blue babies, just like her father does.

Her expression takes me back to one summer afternoon at the beach in Cape Cod when Jon and I agreed to look after little Miss Amy who, for a kid who grew up near the coast, freaked out and screamed at the thought of going in the water. After several attempts, games and tricks, we gave up and suffered the humiliation of letting her bury us under the hot sand, slowly, one at a time, in the baking heatwave, as Amy quietly planned her next move. I can't stop myself coming back to the jeans when I glance in her direction. I blame it on the mother.

Nicole's hair strikes me first. Somehow she's perfected the dirty-blonde look with just the right amount of highlights, and her fine hair exudes a silky-soft sheen. I make a point to touch it and remark how gorgeous it is. She is much rounder than when I last saw her, but then so am I. We silently acknowledge this fact by saying how good the other one looks.

'How's your health, Jo?' she asks with a look of concern, touching my right arm. Sweet, how she wants me to know she's sincere.

'Could be better, could be worse.'

This routine repeats itself with others as I try to make my way to the front entrance and bump into more people I haven't seen in years. I catch sight of some friends of my mother's I saw during their visits to the hospice. Her best friend Rosie drives in, my second cousins arrive, those on my father's side of the family, the children of my grandmother's Italian sisters and brother. Al, the barber cousin who was well-known for his Elvis impersonator gigs in New Jersey, shows up, still sporting the side-burns and the harsh black dye job, but his balding scalp can't keep up with his performance intentions.

'Oh, I'm done with the show life,' he says, 'but I enjoy the karaoke down the road here. Like doing the early Elvis tunes.'

Another cousin, Marilena, is around my father's age. She's guided a bit by her daughter and when she gets closer I see she's got thin tubes coming out of her nostrils because she's hooked up to a portable oxygen tank that sits in her shoulder bag. Then I remember her lengthy chain-smoking habit and her characteristic hoarse voice which I thought sounded sexy when I was young.

'It's been around five years now,' she explains slowly, taking a breath, 'since they took the lung out. I'm part of a new treatment study now but after this round, that's it. No other chances. Your mother was a wonderful person. We had good times,' she says, and cries when we hug.

My first cousins, the two children of Auntie Josie, appear at different times. The oldest one, Steve, helps his old father, Phil, shuffle out of the car. While I still recognise Steve who is a bit older than Dave, his puffy face, marked with tired eyes and unsightly rosacea, gives the appearance of carrying a heavy burden, as if life's bullies have throttled him a few too many times. His sister Angela appears soon after with her teenage daughter, Kristen. Angela has a last drag of her cigarette, checks her lipstick in the rear-view mirror, exchanges a few words with Kristen, and they're off.

Then I spot Auntie Peggy's oldest son, Billy, from a distance, stepping out of a car with his father, Uncle Ron. He looks about as old and worn as he did the other day. A quick wrench passes through me and I feel a sudden desire to open my bowels. Why is he here? Why has he gone out of the way to pay last respects to my mother, a woman he hated and who despised him back, her jaw clenched when she talked about him, teeth worn down to the bone? *He's just such an asshole... Bastard.*

Beth and her mother Jean arrive, to my relief, and I try to forget that he's breathing the same air as me. My father, his brother and Dave show up about five minutes before the service commences and we all take seats in the front row. The smell of booze from the three of them is strong and I notice their glassy-eyed expressions show no clue as to any thoughts or emotions when my suspicious eyes meet theirs, except to say, *What the fuck, Jo? What'd you expect?* I guess if the situation was turned and Ma was at Dad's memorial she'd be knocking them back too. My father, every now and then, I notice, closes his glazed eyes, opening them again to reveal the same void each time. There are worse things than this numbing of the soul. The problem is the inevitability of the next day when you're right back in the same place again at square one. I avoid looking over my shoulder at the people filling up the pews just in case I find Uncle Ron and his son Billy sitting behind me.

It's good my mother isn't alive to witness the service. The old priest is on his last leg and he was probably offered the gig out of pity. Or maybe they just couldn't find anyone else. His voice never rises above a whisper, which accompanied by the

244

fast speed of his speech makes him incomprehensible. We can just about hear that he might have an Irish accent, but it's hard to tell.

The mass moves through the usual, plodding motions to which I remember being subjected in my youth, although none of us immediate family members, being reluctant and bitter Catholics now, have volunteered to read any of the Bible passages to help spruce things up a bit. After communion, the mass approaches its closing and Beth and I are looking at each other waiting for the priest to announce that I will deliver the eulogy. As he begins to head out of the church I step forward and halt him in the nicest way I can.

'I think someone must have forgotten that I was going to give the eulogy, Father. Can we do it now, please?' I say quietly.

There are some oohs and ahhs, oh my dears, wide-eyed looks of dismay from him and the two women church staff members. Finally he returns to the lectern, and after an introduction in which he refers to me as 'Jane', I'm up for the show.

I've got my written script, filled with red-pen edits and side notes in front of me. I slide into my usual lecturer's mode, hearing myself practically shouting in my efforts to wake up the crowd. I realise I do this to students to ensure all eyes are on me, so they'll take me and my subject seriously, as though it's the only thing that should matter to them in their sad, pitiful lives. *It's my gift of knowledge to you, and hard-earned it was, thank you, for which you should hold the upmost respect. That's why you are here, there is no other reason why you should spend your parents' money, if you are in doubt there's the door, right there, goodbye.*

A few minutes into my speech I hear myself rambling in a way I've done in the past when I'm teaching, but then I always managed to get back on track. Now I'm off-script babbling about my husband's Jewish family, how Jews wouldn't dream of firing themselves up in a cremation for obvious reasons, or are they obvious to this crowd? And then it's a thank you to so and so for visiting Ma when she was dying, and how nice it was to see so and so when I was at the hospice, how nice the place was. Then a surge of tears follows and I can feel my mouth quivering uncontrollably, turning me into a stuttering mess.

'She never wanted to hurt a soul,' I drivel on. 'Always thought about others. She was a good mother,' I tell them.

Then I look up and lock eyes with Ron who is positioned mid-church, and momentarily stutter to a halt. His eyes are focused on me. It's impossible to read him. Is he sympathetic? Hateful? Willing me to fail? *I'll show him what I'm made of, the bastard.*

'Ma offered nothing less than unconditional, unselfish motherly love to my brother and me. Her sisters, her brothers, they were everything to her.' No mention of the cheating husband. My voice is shaking but I'm on a roll, in full emotional swing, believing every word of my melodramatic nonsense. *Yes! Now you will all listen to me, won't you?*

Then I knock over my cane and lose my balance for a second; the sound of the object hitting the marble floor and rolling down the three steps sends a piercing echo throughout the place. Beth moves in quickly to take hold of it. My crying continues to interrupt my speech, which I try to remember to look at every now and then so I can get across the key points, but eventually the tears obscure my vision so much that I can't continue. Now all I'm doing is sobbing at the pedestal, first quietly in a dignified, contained way while the entire church is silent, waiting patiently for me to finish, then it's erupting out of my control. The sobbing grows into an echoing wail, so that I can no longer speak.

Beth rises to the pedestal and comes to my rescue, waiting for me to wind up. I manage to rein myself in for long enough to invite everyone to the buffet down the road where we can remember the wonderful, saintly Theresa O'Brien.

When I arrive at the restaurant I open the trunk and begin gathering up the flowers to take inside while keeping a look out for Beth and Jean. Dave approaches while Dad and Uncle Joe talk to one of their aunts. I sense that people are checking me out, so I turn to him with a look that says, *Please be sympathetic for your over-emotional, suffering, limping little sister. Please be a big brother who can make everything better. Please take some pity on me. Yes, this is my unapologetic objective.*

He stops, lights a cigarette and says, 'Hey, Jo, you OK? You want to try one of my Zolofts? It really helps panic attacks. Why don't you give it a try?'

Hesitation. Take a breath. 'I don't think that's a good idea.'

He insists. 'Hey, you know, there's nothing wrong with admitting you need some help when things are tough. Come on, try one?' He glances around us like he's doing a drug deal.

The conversation reaches a quick end when Beth and Jean step in to help take the photographs inside. There are some convivial exchanges between the three of them, with Jean offering her condolences. Amy's looking shy again.

'She may live up north in New Hampshire, but she's always here, right next to me.' Dave tells Jean, holding his fist next to his heart. 'And it's time I saw that granddaughter of mine. When you bringing her down?'

'Next time, Dad. Next time.' Amy may live in New Hampshire now but she hasn't escaped her Bostonian whine. For the most part Amy sticks by Nicole's side, a little too close in my opinion, and they are among the first people to leave later.

After setting up the photo display inside, Dave and I meet more of the staff from my mother's hospital who are drawn to comment on the pictures with recollections; young and older doctors, nurses whose names I remember her mentioning. Several nurses who were part of her gang and who visited the hospice remind us how special Terry was, a one-of-a-kind nurse who was always on the patients' side.

'And teacher, too. She was a great mentor for the nurses who were just starting. They really looked up to her,' her friend Maureen says. 'Although I can tell you there were a few times when nice teacher Terry lost it with some of those students who were slacking off. No way Terry was going to put up with their shit. Nope. She was good, Terry. Always set a good premise.'

Dave and I smile, nodding in agreement. My father sits at a distance with his brother and cousins having a beer.

Our mother, the admirable, respected, hard-working nurse. I know this side of Terry well, as does my brother. I'm filled with a sense of pride that her colleagues regarded her so highly, and also in acknowledging what she managed to accomplish out of what little she started with. And yet I'm still stuck with that silent and selfish yearning, with that wish that there would have been just a bit more of my mother left for my brother and me in those years when she was so hungry for her success, when she was so desperate for something better than what was on offer. There's no way around it, this cyclical motion in which I am trapped. It doesn't matter how much therapy I've had, I still end up in this same place. I can only feel some relief now, after the fate of my failed pregnancies, that I will never have to endure my child's unrealistic expectations of me. They want all of you, children do, every last expelled breath, no matter how weak it is, and even after you've sacrificed yourself in an effort to ensure their happiness in the world, they'll still demand more. *Is that all you got? Well, it wasn't my fault I was born, that was your doing.* Could I have done any better than Terry, especially given her circumstances? Maybe she was, after all, a saint.

'It's a hard job, but I'll be damned if I'm going to make the same mistakes our parents made,' my cousin Angela says. Her father, Uncle Phil, on the other side of the table, who suffered a stroke at the age of sixty after years of heavy smoking and drinking, suffers enough hearing loss that the comment goes unnoticed. We share a knowing laugh and I remember those summer days of our early childhood spent on Revere Beach with our mothers and brothers, each of us lathered in baby oil roasting in the sun, throwing ourselves into crashing, polluted waves, roaming the arcades, sneaking cigarettes and alcohol, living up the expectations our young bodies set out for us. Angie and I were a pair in those days, close in age and spirit, but when the junior and high-school years started, other friends' attentions took over and our lives separated. Before I leave the table I remind her to quit smoking.

They're lining up now, all these hospital people, to pass on their condolences, some quite important types; men wearing expensive suits and ties, women with tailored dresses, skirts and jackets. No jeans in this crowd. I step aside for a minute to take a break and refill my coffee.

When I return to the throng of mourners I find Uncle Ron standing in front of me. It's a shock: I'd almost forgotten that he was here, like a ghost whom I'd imagined had faded. My shoes have a low enough heel to keep me rooted to the carpet, but even so, I hover over him. With a boldness that surprises me he takes a firm grasp of my left hand, the one that's holding my cane, and locks it in his.

'I'm sorry for your loss,' he says, his voice emitting a rasping whimper. He is probably in his eighties now and close to the end like the others. But here I am, fifteen again, a stupid girl handing myself over.

I say without thinking, 'I'm sorry for *your* loss.' I realise how ridiculous this sounds since it's been at least four years since my aunt died.

He continues holding my hand, squinting at me, unblinking.

I want to pull away, but I don't.

Then Uncle Ron leans forward and I realise he has something he wants to share. 'Can we finally put everything behind us now? After all this time?' he almost whispers.

For some seconds there is a sense that my soul is being lifted out of my body and when it reaches full height at the ceiling it's looking down, pressing me to hold on to any last shred of sanity I might have left.

My loss. My losses. Does he know or even care how much I lost, what my mother lost, because of him? I think I know what he did to me, but what about *her*? He stole her goodwill, her trust, the sisterly relationship she once had with Peggy. *Sorry for your loss, my ass.*

What am I supposed to do now, sit down with him and have a laugh about the good times when I was a kid ?

A slow ache that's begun to feel too familiar starts to move up from the gut to my throat.

Not far from where we are standing I spot all his sons; Billy at the table, now with his brother Matt who has brought his two young ones with him. The youngest brother Chris, that once sweet Chrissie, who doesn't look quite so sweet now, is sitting on the other side of the table talking to Dave. Billy casts a sombre look in our direction. What does he know? I'm the nasty one who stopped coming around, the one who ruined everything. His mother Peggy could have continued to enjoy her bowling nights if it wasn't for me. Everyone would have been happier. If it wasn't for me.

Maybe Dave's Zoloft isn't such a bad idea after all. My mouth is open slightly but there are no words. Ron lets go of my hand after a last hard squeeze, which I struggle to interpret, and snails away from me back to his family.

I stare after him, still feeling the imprint of his hand on mine.

After coffee I give in to my impulses when no one is looking and find the bar to settle down with a double gin and tonic. The drink hits the spot, nice and strong. I have another double soon after and feel it slide down easier the second time. It feels too good to turn down a third. The tonic, the extra crushed ice and lime, buffer the alcohol enough to fool me into thinking I'm just indulging in a refreshing citrus cooler. In the meantime I meet more of my father's cousins and others who are refilling and I allow myself to get carried away in an addictive, dizzying laughter. The population outside of this family may think all this daytime drinking is strange – it's only just past 1pm. By the time I finish knocking back the last one (a fourth?) and positioning myself into a new, comforting place that beats the Zoloft option, guests are starting to leave, abruptly it seems. The party's over. Time hasn't stood still for them because of my mother's death. Business as usual. The land of the living resumes, all back to their Saturday routines, rushing off to kids' soccer games where it's all blue jeans and casual athletic wear.

Dad's looking flummoxed when settling up with the manager. My mother always sorted out restaurant bills, the right tips, remembered who ordered what, how many alcoholic drinks were drunk. He looks out of his depth and I decide to save the day, but when I move away from the bar stool I know it's too late for that. My head is light but my body's heavy enough to feel like it's going to topple over. A fit of giggling escapes from nowhere. My more than tipsy state brings on a new-found boldness when I spot Ron hovering nearby, his eyes on me again. I lift myself off the stool slowly and sway, cane holding me up, in his direction.

'Hey there, Ron. You're right. You know, you're so right.' In my mind I'm speaking carefully in a low voice. 'We need to put it all behind us…OK, let's do that,' I slur. 'Does that make you feel better? Huh? Tell me,' I shout. Surprise, surprise, the crying starts again, causing even more slurring. 'Because you know… we wouldn't want you dying an old man feeling bad about things, would we? And, hey, you know what? Maybe I just won't put everything behind me… Tell me, Ron. Why don't you tell me, huh? Tell me everything about everything, about what you did. What did you do that day? What did you do to me?'

'Come on, Dad,' says Billy, moving in with a look that worries me.

'Hey, Billy.' I grab his arm. 'Billy, you need to know. You *have* to know…I didn't do anything. You know that right? Tell, me, Billy. Tell me you know that. I'm not leaving…I can't leave before you see that.'

But he refuses to look at me and shakes me away. Before I know it, after more has been said that I will go on to forget, Beth and Dave are pulling me aside, trying to hold me upright, but next the floor is spinning before I crash. The cane bounces away, too fast to catch. I shout 'Ouch,' as I land hard on my knees. 'Goddamn it.'

'Come on, Jo, time to go. Don't get upset now, come on,' Dave says. 'Can someone get that fucking cane?' he shouts.

'Hey, don't be telling me not to get upset and don't you say anything bad about my cane. I'll get upset when I wanna get upset. I'm tired of not getting upset. My mother's dead…and, yeah, I'm…I'm fucking upset…just let me be.'

Then there's the faint sound of my father's voice. 'Shit. Is she alright? She gonna be OK?'

Beth and Jean offer to take me back with them but there's the issue of my mother's car and I don't want Beth to be driving all the way back the next day because I've lost control. They all agree I'll drive with Dave to the house only a few minutes away, rest, sober up and collect the car later. The O'Brien men have had more than just a few between them, but somehow, Dave claims, he's just fine behind the wheel, and in my half-conscious drunken state I want to believe him. Right at this moment in time I'm willing to hand myself over, melt into the cracks of his surface and dissolve until there's nothing left of me.

Dave loads all the photos back into his car. Dad drives with Uncle Joe and they meet us back at the house but soon disappear again to visit the local bar, their usual hangout that is a short walk away. Dave holds me steady as we go upstairs to our old bedroom where Uncle Joe has left his bag on my bed.

I push everything to the floor with a hysterical laugh, fall backwards and I'm off on a trip into la la land.

Twenty Four

I'm moving through a doorway into a dark room with nothing but a double bed in the middle. My mother lies in it, her body on its side in her preferred comfortable position, covered in a colourful handmade quilt. Her face, with its cold grey hue, betrays a look of death. Her eyes are closed, her dry, cracked lips open slightly. But then she changes. She's younger, resembling the beautiful Terry in one of the black and white photos I displayed at the memorial. She's flawless, like an overexposed image that washes out all the unsightly details. I move in to look closer and suddenly she's in a coffin, looking back at me with stiff features and a dazed expression. She extends her arm and appeals to me in a soft, broken voice. 'Don't, Jo. Don't go upsetting things.'

I wake to the sound of Dave's voice rising from the kitchen where he's talking on the phone. 'OK, sweetie, yeah, I'll get over there in a little bit and we can go then. Sure, sounds great, yeah, OK sweetie, see you soon.'

I walk down, taking my time, careful not to worsen the thumping ache in my head or the pain in my foot and leg.

Dave pauses to look at me as I enter. 'Hey, look at you. You feeling better?' He sounds genuinely sympathetic.

'Well, OK, I guess.' I don't want to have to explain myself, or worse, make small talk. 'The head hurts. A lot.' I notice from the clock that a few hours have passed and I catch sight of Uncle Joe, sleeping on the couch, drooling.

'He's out cold. Dad too. They got back a little while ago. Here, have some coffee.'

He pours me one and a glass of water, makes me a piece of toast to have with some Advil. He tells me, in a way that is a bit too proud, that he never gets drunk anymore, never suffers from hangovers. 'I can keep steady because I've built up a tolerance. That's what you need to do, Jo. If you just drink a bit more throughout the week you'll probably be fine.'

I'm stumped, trying to make sense of this. My weak, feeble, intolerant body can't hold its own. I need to drink more and toughen up is my brother's solution.

'Hey, I know it was the drink talking earlier,' he says in a tone that's meant to sound supportive. 'But all that stuff you were shouting at Ron in the restaurant with everyone around. I don't know. All that happened a long time ago, Jo.'

All that happened. I mull over his choices of words, wait before responding. There are too many gaps. The details are fuzzy. What exactly did Ron say before Billy showed up? I remember seeing his mouth open, moving with sounds coming out. Then I remember what it felt like years ago, his wet mouth on mine.

'You're right, Dave. You don't know,' I say, and hesitate. I'm exhausted now. I ask myself if I am ready to tell Dave about what probably happened when I was fifteen, that thing I don't remember after I let Uncle Ron get me stoned, then drunk. I take a deep breath and am surprised by an unexpected desire to purge. 'It was worse than you think. What he did.'

Dave stares at me. 'What do you mean? He made a pass at you, right?'

'It was more than that. He took me for a long drive. Got me stoned. At the time I thought it was fun, great, let's get high. Then he got me drunk on whisky and Coke. But it was more than just booze. I didn't think about it then, but I didn't see him mixing those drinks. I think he might have spiked mine with one of Auntie Peggy's sleeping pills because I passed out soon after. The last thing I remember was him kissing and touching me.' Although I remain composed, tears are beginning to stream down my face. I don't wipe them away. My voice begins to shake. 'Then later…later when I got home I saw I was bleeding.'

He is quiet for a bit, scratches his chin, purses his lips. 'Shit. Are you sure?'

'Am I sure?'

I see a confused look in his eyes.

'Did you really just ask me that?' Is his ignorance a reflection of some kind of shock or is he really doubting me? 'Yes. I'm sure, Dave. That's what I remember anyway.'

'Jesus.' He covers his mouth with his hand. 'Did Ma know?'

I wait until my voice has recovered a little. 'I didn't tell her everything. I told her about him kissing me later that week when I babysat for them. Then Peggy found out and that was enough for her to disown Ma for a while. Then years later Peggy made Ma sign that stupid piece of paper saying I lied. So, yeah, I said he kissed me. That was enough to cause the damage.'

The kitchen is silent for a minute. The only sound is the ticking of the wall clock and the faint hiss of Uncle Joe's breathing from the next room.

'You know,' Dave says, stops, and meets my eyes. 'I mean, that just sucks. But maybe the best thing to do is drop it, Jo. Auntie Peggy's dead. Ma's dead. Ron's going soon. Who cares now? We can't change this stuff. You'll drive yourself crazy trying to do that.'

He stretches and rubs his stomach, his way of finalising the saga of what Uncle Ron might have done once and for all so I won't rock the O'Brien boat, even after the mother ship's been blasted with so many holes it's been sinking for a long time. But maybe he's right. If I *drop it*, I'm letting it go, my hands will be free to hold onto something else. Whatever I do, say, or not say, drunk or sober, won't change anything. There will be no miracle, no saviour to make things better.

But that kind of logical thinking doesn't fix the way I *feel* right now. And Dave's expression is like the one he wore years ago when I confronted him about crawling into my bed. *Who cares?* Dave's business idea pops into my mind. How would it feel if, for the first time in my life, Dave was indebted to me? If I said to Dave, 'I will give you half of my share, and in return, you will never ask me for anything again. You might make a success of this restaurant or you might fall flat on your face. Either way, that's it. Our final deal.'

'This franchise thing,' I say.

'Oh, yeah. BGR. Burgers Grilled Right,' he says, eyebrows hopeful.

'It's got potential?'

258

'Jo, it has so much potential,' he says, smoothly changing tack. 'It's a great business. And franchising is a really safe way to go.'

'OK. I'm thinking I could give you $50,000 towards things. With some of your money and Karen's that should be more than enough.'

'That would be just right, I think.' Dave looks surprised. 'Oh my God, Jo, you won't regret it. Jo, I can do this. I'll show you and everyone else. And you'll get your money back faster than you might think.'

We pause again in silence. I can't even look at him. Right now, I can't bear him. *Who cares now? You can't change this stuff.* Half his shirt is tucked out. He sits down, slings one arm over the side of the chair. I'm envious at the ease he displays, his growing midriff doesn't hold him back, and I wonder if this self-belief comes across to the women he meets. Is this how he hooks them?

He sighs, closes his eyes, takes a cigarette from the pack in front of him and lights up. Sets his free hand to his forehead then rubs his eyes. He takes a deep drag and blows out noisily. 'Jo… You know what? I think you think too much. *Way* too much. How about enjoying what you got. Ain't so bad, is it?'

A reasonable point. When I'm home in London preparing lectures or a talk, gazing through our kitchen window at the view of the wisteria in bloom at the end of our garden, or spreading jam across Jon's home-made bread on a Sunday morning before I take it to the table where he says, 'It looks like it's going to be warm and sunny today,' I have to pinch myself, say, *this life you have is real, Jo. It's not a dream. It's not going to disappear unless you work hard to screw things up and drive your husband away with your neurotic head problems.* Even then he wouldn't go without a fight.

My life could have taken a different turn, a much darker one.

My head aches from the overdose of gin. From all the thinking. If only I could stop thinking.

'Hey, I was just on the phone with Karen. And we were talking about the restaurant and I'm thinking now I could drive you to see the outside of this place that's up for rent in the square, so you can see the potential. You know this area's on the way up, not like it used to be, people are coming here for excitement now. And you can meet Karen, I really would love it if you could meet her, you'll like her a lot, you know, she's very likeable, everyone loves Karen. We could have a drink, maybe a bit to eat, you can get to know her. And smart too, she reads a lot, has a good brain for lots of things, but especially business. She's got a great head for business, Jo. I know you're gonna like her.'

Uncle Ron: I can't get him out of my head. The sight of him shuffling around the restaurant, the feel of his old hand on mine.

'You don't have to worry about Karen, no, she's sensible, and she's already self-employed with her nail stuff, and she's got training too, knows how to do things. And with all her bar experience, you know she's done a bartending course too, she knows how to work with suppliers, knows customer service, she knows what she's getting herself into.'

Oh, does she really know what she's getting herself into? I wonder.

'OK Dave,' I say finally. 'Let's meet Karen. But after my headache's taken a walk.'

We use Ma's blue badge for easy parking and Karen meets us outside the vacant rental unit. When she arrives I'm surprised. I assumed if she was a nail and pedicure expert and serious gym goer, she'd have bleached hair, false eyelashes and wobble around on pin-skinny legs in sharp heels. Instead she wears her chestnut-brown hair at shoulder length and keeps a natural soft wave, unlike so many now who are slaves to straighteners. She's shapely with a large bust. No surprise her fingernails are pristine, but they're also her own. She smiles loads and offers the usual condolences.

'I'm sorry I couldn't be there earlier today. One thing after another came up and I just couldn't fix it. How you doing, hon?'

Dave sighs, closes his eyes for a few seconds. 'Oh, I'm holding up, you know. We got through it, right, sis?'

Dave has never called me sis. Am I supposed to call him bro and play out a fantasy brother-sister fun time so his girlfriend will assume we're normal? I try to imagine what sorts of things he's told her about us. About our family. 'Yeah, we just about got through it, Dave.'

'Your mother will always be with you both. She'll always be looking down wherever you are, whatever you do. You'll be sitting there outside on a bench and feel a sudden breeze,' Karen says, with a gentle wave of her arms. 'And that's it, that's her, always with you. She knows you'll be making her proud.' She nods her head and strokes Dave's arm.

Although she's talking loads of crap I find her steady voice soothing and try to imagine my mother's spirit floating around us in the wind. Karen displays only a little touch of the local accent which gives her a bit of charm. She takes a few puffs from his cigarette, noting how bad he is for her as she's been trying to quit.

'One day I'll get you off these things, Dave, you just wait.'

I admire her aspiration, but know only too well she probably has no idea what she's taking on.

We peer inside the windows of what could be the future Burgers Grilled Right, the only one in town, and there's a bit of shop talk about fixtures and fittings, my brother's area of expertise. It has great potential, not too big, not too small. It could work on so many different levels.

We go on to the nearby bar and grill where Karen was waiting before we arrived. She and Dave know the manager and the waiters. They exchange words, have a giggle or two and carry on like these people are part of the family. It's close to 5.30pm, so we order a nacho plate and drinks and Dave works hard to connect Karen and me.

'Oh, Karen, tell Jo the story about that drunk guy the other night who tried to pick you up, tell her how you managed that one, single-handed. Oh,' he shouts with excitement. 'And what about that other bartender you worked with who thought you made too many tips? It's a tough business you know, Jo, but Karen's the best, she shows them all who boss.'

The more Dave talks, the more his voice rises, which I'm convinced all can hear from across the restaurant, but I keep quiet. We move along through the friendly basics: *Where did you grow up? How old are your kids? What are they doing? What do you love about the restaurant business?* It's all about them, Dave and Karen. I don't give them a chance to bring up London and it doesn't look like they're bursting to ask. Within a short time I've seen that Karen emanates an impeccable patience. She's accepted that in order to survive, to get herself out of a bad marriage while her kids were still young, she'd have to work her hardest and make the best of her available prospects; bartending, nail work. She's always put her son and daughter first, worked a bunch of jobs with flexible hours, did everything she could to ensure her two would go to college. There are no shortcuts for Karen and there won't be any for her son and daughter. I listen to her, watch her closely, looking for signs of more wrinkles, there must be some laugh lines around the eyes, the mouth, considering all the time she smiles. But no, there aren't as many creases as you might expect in the face of a forty-something single mother who's had a rough go of things.

After an hour and a half, I plead that I need to get to Beth's. We say our goodbyes to Karen, with Dave promising he'll be back after taking me to my car. What's the verdict? He's eager to know.

'Isn't she great? I knew you'd love her. Don't you love her, Jo?'

'Yes, very sweet, seems a sensible woman,' I say.

How will I know anything about what's right for my brother? After marriage and divorce and all the other drama that's gone down in his life he still manages to attract women, younger ones even. In the past he's had many ups and downs, but somehow secured a couple of steady relationships that lasted a few years. This one may be a good one. And I hope, deep down, she'll stick with it, give my brother what he needs, that unconditional love that only my mother offered. *He's had some problems, yes, but he's my son. He'll always be my son*, she wrote in one of her letters when he was going through hard times. *And I'll always love him.*

When we return to the house after picking up my mother's car, I say a quick goodbye to my father who is having a wake-me-up coffee with his brother. I'll be back tomorrow afternoon to return the car and go to Logan for my evening flight. He's already booked Dino to take me. Goodbyes to my brother have always been straightforward and lacklustre, but this time I'm welling up, feeling as though so much more needs to be said, but I have no idea where to start. I give him a hug and hang on longer than usual. The strong cigarette smell on his clothes and breath reminds me of what it was like to say goodbye to my mother after our summer visits. I can't stop thinking that Dave, as he reminded me the other night, is heading in the same direction. *It's in the genes.* It may only be a matter of a few years when I'm standing here again, or sitting in a wheelchair by that time, for his funeral.

'You know you can always come stay with me the next time you visit,' he says. 'I got the futon and the location's good. I mean it ain't the best area, but not far from Teele Square in the car, or, Davis and Cambridge. It's great. You have to stay with me next time, you have to.'

I agree to it all, sounds great, yes, oh well, I'm not sure when I'll be back, we'll see. 'I'll call you tomorrow before you're off, wish you a good flight. Make sure you answer your phone,' he says. We embrace, but I can still feel the tension in his body. It wants to give something more but can't.

264

Twenty Five

When I was growing up, the Italian family next door had a little dog, a male Jack Russell called Tito. He wasn't neutered, barked loudly all the time and humped everything and every person he encountered. When my mother needed something like a spare egg, not for anything like baking, but when she wanted to fry it to have on toast for lunch, she'd send me, without any reservations, to their house to ask for one. After a while I grew tired of having to fend off Tito from sniffing my crotch and humping my leg. Finally I stood my ground and refused to go back. It was a battle I was tired of fighting.

I hear the sound of a gentle bark near Beth's front door as I enter. When I step in Beth is wearing her cleaning apron and has been wiping the glass cabinet, the one that holds the reproduction Fabergé eggs, after Stella, a pretty chocolate Labrador, has been slobbering around it exploring her new surroundings. She tries to take the cane from me. Beth shouts at her not to, but I give in, oh, what the hell, I say, and remind Beth it's not nice to raise her voice, she might scare her. As soon as I let go, Stella offers it back to me, then pulls when I take it again. We continue to play this back and forth scenario and for some strange reason it makes me laugh to a point where I feel out of control.

Beth's neighbour Pauline planned to take Stella with her to Rhode Island on a visit to see her children but the beach house didn't take dogs, so she asked Beth at the last minute if it was OK to have Stella until she returned. It hasn't taken Stella long to enjoy what Beth has to offer. A luxury memory-foam dog bed that Bailey used to use, is, I'm told, much better than what Pauline brought. Over-priced dog treats and biscuits from Whole Foods, all the outdoor space for running around. Endless amounts of attention. A new dog heaven.

Beth offers me some soup, herbal tea, and those tasteless coconut slices she always has in abundance. Beth shows me her new bedding set and I let myself stretch out on it, admiring the detailed bedspread stitching. Like our teenage days, we end up cosying together, Stella insisting on lying between us, and we recap about the memorial, the sad state of my drunkenness and my later introduction to Karen, the new woman in Dave's life.

'I was trying to find you and didn't see you anywhere,' Beth says. 'Then I got distracted in a conversation with one of your great-aunts, then one of your second cousins, you know, the one with the funny hair that looks like he's got a fur hat sitting on his head. Well, he tried to talk me into agreeing to get him an interview at my company because he's been laid off for a year, and then he asked me for my phone number, so I told him I had a boyfriend, but it was impossible to get rid of him. Next thing I hear is you screaming at that slime bag.'

I try to explain myself but words don't work, can't begin to make sense of anything. Beth understands this and we fall into a comfortable silence. Stella, especially, understands this, reaches her paw and touches my chest. *There, there, JoJo, it's OK*. My tears release again, but this time they're short-lived. I continue stroking Stella, and when I stop, she prods me just a tiny bit again, reminding me to keep going. I'm a little child with my first ever dog and all I want are her cuddles. *Oh, Stella. You are a good girl. I love you.* Beth reaches across Stella and strokes my arm.

In the end I agree with Beth that things are the way they are. How can it be so simple? I am impotent to change anything except what I have made for myself in London outside of the O'Brien world.

'I think I just need to get back to London now. I don't miss all the crap that's going on at work but I sure as hell miss Jon,' I say. For a second I tense at the thought of my supervisions with Nina. Lots of time has passed since that day she left my office in a huff and I know I'll have to face her. How will it play out? Could Nina ruin me? And what if it happens again with some other charismatic student? Am I any better than some of those loser professors I've laughed about in the past, those middle-aged fools who wish they could turn back time? 'God, I miss Jon,' I tell Beth.

'That's home now, Jo. Jon is your home. And he's good for you.'

Beth is called away to sort out Danielle. I shout good night, ready to shut down for an early sleep. I take another long look at Shawn Mendes. He's trying so hard with those eyes. If I could have five minutes with him, just five minutes. Oh, the things I could tell him about life.

Soon afterwards I hear Stella push the door open with her nose and see her saunter over to the side of the bed. In the dim light from the hallway I watch her stare at me, her expression saying, *Well, what did you expect? Did you think I was just going to leave you like that?* Then with a hip, hop, skip and a jump, she's up, circling awkwardly about three or four times, stepping on my legs, waiting for me to accommodate her. Soon enough we're spooning, me behind her, my arm resting across her smooth torso, her chest moving up and down rhythmically. How is it she can smell so nice? *Such a good girl.* As time takes us into the late night hours every now and then I feel her shake and shudder as she grumbles through a dog dream or maybe a nightmare.

'It's OK Stella. There there, girl.'

She exhales one last whimper and falls into a deep sleep.

Twenty Six

16 January 1993

Hi Jo and Jon,

Natural Bridge is just one of the beautiful sites on the island. This is our last full day here in Aruba and we've enjoyed every day. Sunny days and blue green waters. It's heaven. I'm wearing a #15 sunblock so no sunburn. Weather at home is 28 and snowy.

Love, Ma and Dad

It's quiet at the marina, probably because it's a Tuesday, a late morning in mid-September, and most of the men, that's usually who's around here, are already out trying to nab a good catch for the day, hanging on to the last bits of an Indian summer. From the bench near the parking lot where we wait for a friend of Dad's, a guy called Hank who's offered to take us out on his boat, a light breeze picks up hints of ocean; the smell of distant seaweed, fish just caught and filleted, a suggestion of something like sulphur. There's a sense of promise when you're near the water, I think, that great, never-ending vastness beyond. *Smell that, Jo. There's nothing like it, that fresh sea air*, my mother would have said when she finally found that perfect spot on the crowded beach and sunk into her chair. She'd close her eyes and say, *Don't you miss it?* It took so little to make my mother happy. All she needed was her mind to take her to places like Aruba, where she sent this postcard from, where for two weeks the problems of life belonged to other people. Where the sunny days and blue-green waters would have promised to release her soul from all earthly responsibilities. Where she could enter the gates of heaven.

At 75°F and the sun beating down on us, Jon lifts one of my father's old baseball caps as he wipes beads of sweat from his forehead. 'I can't believe it's this time in September and still so hot here,' he complains.

Dave laughs. 'You Brits are wimps in a bit of heat. Just wait, it'll all change soon. There's talk about storms coming in.'

'Luckily we'll be gone by then,' I say.

Around eighteen months have passed since my mother's death. In my middle-age that chunk of time can feel like a little hiccup, a quick skip of a heartbeat, before you remember that the weight of the world came stomping through your front door during that time and stayed for a long, unwelcome visit.

My brother ended up ditching the burger franchise prospect he had considered so carefully with Karen. The application wasn't so easygoing, he said, and the money needed for everything was more than he first assumed.

'They want robots, Jo. That's all they want, after they've taken all your money, and then they'll screw you.'

I wanted him to tell me more, so I pushed. 'What do you mean, Dave, they'll screw you? How exactly will they screw you?'

He shouted, 'They're big conglomerates and they hate the little guy. They promise you the world if you work a hundred hours a week and hand over your soul just so they can spit it back out at you. That's it. I'm done with that. No more to say.' There were other, more realistic business opportunities though – a pizza place in town was selling up and just needed a fresh, modern approach. Who could go wrong making pizza, a low-cost product with high profit? Easy money in the bank, another no-brainer.

A dingy little bar down the road from Dad's place, the Rosebud Lounge, was going out of business, finally, and was up for sale. I remember the interior well. It was the local dive where my paternal grandfather took me a few times when I was a child. I always thought it was strange that you had to walk down all those stairs to its lower basement level where the bar sat, dark and waiting with two pool tables, a jukebox in the corner. No windows. A ceiling fan swayed unsteadily as it attempted to circulate the smoky air. I couldn't see the attraction, but Dave, at least during that particular phone conversation, thought there was a hidden diamond lodged under every mouldy stone.

A friend of Karen's was selling her nail salon in Somerville. This friend was moving out to LA, the place of her and every north-easterner's dreams, where the sun shines every day, where it never snows or rains, where people don't grow old, where the hands and feet of every man and woman are groomed to porcelain-like perfection. Dave could buy the salon with Karen, the nail pro, the one who knew all the ins and outs of that world. They talked about extending the business, buying the shop site next door, to incorporate spa facilities and tanning. There would always be good business in hands and feet, massages and the golden-bronze look.

I wasn't going to transfer a cent into his account until I was convinced that Dave understood my intention – that this was to be the last time he called on me for help – but turned out none of it was to be. There was never enough money to get anything worthwhile started, Dave claimed. He always needed more, 'to do things right,' and it was always more than I was willing to hand over. If it wasn't money it was something else that halted the next move. Dave had too much work, too much stress and not enough time or patience to get all the details sorted. Karen grew ill, had all kinds of aches and pains and dreaded fatigue. Was it that thing called ME, he wondered, or worse?

'Jo, what's if it's MS? I don't know if I could fucking cope with that,' he told me in a panic during a surprise late-night phone call. Ah, yes. The dreaded MS. Who would want to be stuck with someone like me?

In the end, after a series of tests Karen was told it was fibromyalgia. Her doctor advised her to take some time off work.

After Dave let go of the business ideas he bought a second-hand but expensive sports car with money from his own first inheritance instalment, although he wouldn't tell me exactly how much it cost. And, Dave argued later on the phone with me, why couldn't he have a decent car? 'It's OK for people in your circle to have nice things but not the likes of me, is that it?' Before hanging up, he shouted, 'So just mind your own fucking business.'

Not long after that I heard he and Karen had a break on one of the US Virgin Islands, top-end, all-inclusive five-star resort. But the sun and fun was no miracle worker. A month or so later Dave and Karen were having problems. Her fibromyalgia wasn't cured and seemed to worsen around him. It all came on at once; Dave's long work days, too much forced overtime from his slave-driving boss.

'And that girl Karen,' Dad said, 'she's a nag, says to Dave he doesn't care enough, doesn't pay her enough attention, spend enough time with her. He doesn't need that shit. No, he's better off without her.'

But it was Karen, not Dave, who called it off when she reached the point where she said she needed some space.

'Hah, she doesn't know what she wants. He's better off,' said Dad.

Each month when we spoke long-distance, Dad's voice expressed a greater lassitude, as if his body was losing slowly what was left of its electric charge. His voice remained monotone, like he was reading from cue-cards. The conversation exemplified the decline of my father's mood since my mother died, from its usual disinterested state. I noticed his memory was deteriorating.

One afternoon when I called he was confused because he couldn't find his credit card and cheque book. He was convinced Dave stole them so he could rob Dad of his money and he told Dave this much.

'I keep telling him his instalment is enough and he's not getting anything out of me. And here he was sneaking around the other day making like everything was OK, but I knew. I knew he was up to something.'

A week later he found the items in the glove compartment of his truck.

On another occasion, he referred to his only grandchild Amy as 'the girl with that shady-looking boyfriend who needed a haircut and was a bad influence on her'.

Not long after this he confessed he wasn't getting called in for any more work. 'The boss says there ain't any work now, maybe nothing for a while and then he says to me, "How about retiring now, Jimmy. Take a step back, relax a bit. Take a vacation." What the hell is that supposed to mean? I don't need no vacation.'

He phoned me at close to 2am, London time, and opened with, 'There's some shit going down here.' But this conversation was not about him. 'The neighbours called the police. David was in the middle of the street there outside his apartment, naked. He was banging on people's doors, then screaming something about how the CIA was out to get him because they thought he was somebody else, like a case of mistaken identity. He wasn't making any sense. It's all screwed up, the mania, the craziness, like those other times. It's all happening again.'

I asked Beth to follow-up for me and she told me later that Dave was taken to a new state psychiatric hospital, a decent facility where he got back on track with his meds and was well enough to go home after a couple of weeks and back to work a week or so after that. His boss at the air-conditioning place was understanding, apparently.

Dad said, 'I told him he's gotta stay on those meds, that's what Ma always said. Thank God she ain't around to see all this.' When I asked Dad about how things were going at his end, his health, what he was doing to keep himself busy, he said that he thought someone must have broken into his house; the front door was wide open when he got home that evening, but nothing was taken. 'The bastards came in to scope this joint and took off quick when they heard me pulling up in the driveway.'

Did Dad maybe forget, I suggested, to close the door behind him when he left earlier that afternoon? I reminded him also about a couple of other odd things he had done, including his confession that he had put hamburgers and sausages in the bread bin instead of the fridge, only to find them rotting three days later. He only grunted in response. Then I heard an odd gasping noise escape him, which I could only guess was the start of his emotions threatening to overcome him, that dinosaur about to devour him again.

Quickly, as a goodbye, he said, 'That's someone knockin' at the door. Gotta go.'

I tried calling Dave to talk about Dad's memory when he was back into a routine at work, but he never picked up and didn't return my calls.

A couple of months later, Dave phoned out of the blue one Sunday evening, his voice uncharacteristically soft and light. 'I'm in a good place at the moment. Can't complain.' He told me he'd been going to church, one of those non-denominational ones in the city. A silent agreement, like so many other ones I had with him and my parents over the years, dictated that I wasn't allowed to bring up the subject of business, money or Karen. We talked about the weather, the current state of US politics, taxes, Obamacare, the National Health Service in Britain, the deadly state of our cholesterol levels and the wonders of statins. I tried to talk about Dad's memory problems again, but he didn't seem to think it was much of an issue.

Several months later the phone rang in the early hours, I opened my eyes wide with a strong sense of foreboding. I struggled to see nothing but darkness. I held my breath, felt my heart pick up a few paces and waited to see if I was dreaming. Jon sat up this time, turned on the light, and stared at me. I stared back. Funny time to notice that Jon had put on some weight. He had mentioned it a few nights earlier when examining his naked body in front of the mirror after a late shower before coming to bed. Without lifting my eyes from my book, I told him, 'Don't be silly. You have nothing to worry about.' But there he was at 3am in the dim light looking noticeably heavier around the neck and with a bit of extra flab that jiggled at the back of his arms when he moved. For some reason I thought about babies; the pain and yet inexplicable sense of relief I felt after that last miscarriage. I thought about how our plans can often not turn out the way we expect them, but can still end up OK, sometimes even better than we had ever dreamed. I thought about the nail clippings my mother left on her bedside. I tried to imagine what Jon would look like in his seventies.

'Answer the phone,' he said. 'What are you waiting for?'

It was Dave. 'Jo,' he said, then hesitated. 'Sorry to call you this late, your time. Look…I don't know. I don't know how to say this.'

'It's OK, Dave,' I said, half asleep, in the most comforting voice I could muster. I was getting better at practising patience. I knew I could sound like a genuine, caring person. 'Take your time. Are you OK?' I was waiting for him to tell me about another business brainstorm, the need for a loan, or worse, something about the CIA.

'It's Dad,' he said, then stopped again, took another noticeable deep breath. 'He shot himself.'

Twenty Seven

Dad had gone to the same marina on the morning of his death to rent his friend Hank's boat to do some fishing, near the cottage at the Cape. He had talked about maybe buying his own fishing boat again, but complained they were all over-priced, the mooring costs were too much, he'd take his time and look for a better deal and if one didn't come around he wouldn't bother.

He had his gear; fishing rod, hooks, bait, beers, and a bottle of whisky that was empty when they found him. There was no sign of any food, which he normally would have taken – no lunch bag, no snacks, not even a bottle of water. The boat was found anchored far out sometime that evening, just where he would have been if he were looking for sea bass, but the rod and bait hadn't been used. His body was located in the lower deck area among the mess of life jackets and other supplies. I wasn't sure I wanted to ask for details but Dave offered them anyway.

'He did it through the mouth so his face was intact. Right through the mouth, you know, makes it clean. Wonder if he had that in mind beforehand,' Dave said.

An image popped into my mind then out again quickly: what about the toothpick? I couldn't stop thinking about what had happened to the toothpick.

I pictured my father stepping up on that rickety kitchen chair, that stupid toothpick secure in its usual corner of his mouth, and reaching for the gun inside that shoe box, wrapping it in a towel before packing it. Maybe he would have left the $1000 'play money' behind; there would be no point in taking it, no play time for Jimmy O'Brien at that stage. A simple note with Dad's handwriting in blue ballpoint pen on an old grease-soiled receipt from a local fish and chips take-out joint was left tucked under the box of bait: 'Sorry,' it said. *After all these years*, I thought, when Dave told me about the note, *Dad was willing, finally, to offer us this much, but it had to be on his own terms.* Dad always liked having the last word.

I flew back to Boston with Jon a few days later, this time without the usual worries about work. At that point I had plenty of time to accept that my stint in the ivory tower was well and truly up. The university had been edging me out for a while, they were just waiting for the right opportunity for the final push. The news came not long after warnings from the university about brutal cross-faculty cutbacks, with the dead-weight senior staff being the first targets. Middle-aged colleagues like me who had been loyal for twenty-plus years, but whose research and teaching interests were no longer 'desirable', were 'invited' to consider early retirement. Managers told us the leaving packages were attractive but wouldn't stay that way if we waited too long. They didn't attempt to dress up the situation; if some of us didn't volunteer for early retirement, the university would no longer offer us a 'voluntary' option. These dead-weights, including myself, I was told, but in nicer terms by my line manager, Adam, had become somewhat tired and perhaps 'even a little bitter'. Maybe we had lost our passion for higher education, our love for the subject area, and needed to hand over our office to the younger (and presumably cheaper) generation of scholars.

Adam, who had been so warm and fuzzy with support when I took time off sick, when I rushed to Boston when my mother didn't die the first time, then rushed back after she did, now confronted me with a list of concerns. Apparently my so-called bitterness had affected my teaching, not to mention my obvious lack of research output. While student feedback over the last year showed vast improvements for others in the department, my positive feedback had declined significantly.

She kicked me and my mate out of a seminar because we hadn't done the reading. She's just out to get us, wrote one third year undergrad.

I tried to hold my ground. 'I told them to go to the library and come back when they finished reading the chapter. What's the use having them there when they haven't done the work?'

Another second-year student reported, *All she does is talk at us in lectures. Her slides suck. If we raise our hands to question anything she tells us to wait until the end, but by that time we've all fallen asleep and she's run over time and no one cares anymore. What am I paying for? I want to change courses.*

'Come on, Adam. That's just a perfect example of these kids wanting us to hold their hands and spoonfeed them. Higher education died with the invention of PowerPoint.'

'Well, Jo, I wouldn't say all the grad students are thrilled either. Anyway, look, that leads me to Nina Hayes. She's asked for another supervisor.'

The mention of her name made me shiver. 'Oh,' I cleared my throat. 'Go on.'

'She saw me about a week and a half ago worried that she's lost the focus of her project, that it's gone off in too many directions she never intended, and she says this is because you've confused her. Now I know she has a bit of a history of being difficult, but she does happen to be one of our stronger students.'

'Well, sure she's a strong one,' I chuckled nervously. 'That's because I'm the one who took her on for her master's dissertation back then when no one else wanted her. You haven't forgotten that, have you?'

'Just hold it, Jo. I'm not finished. I took the time to read some of her work and to be honest it's a shambles. Great ideas, great potential there, but all over the place. I asked her to show me copies of your supervision reports, the targets you should have set for her, and all she had was a few pieces of paper, not the official forms we use, some handwritten lines that hardly say anything. Like this one here.' He picked up a wrinkled yellow-lined A4 sheet. '*Getting there with great lit review, looking good so far but need to explore more.*' Adam gave me a look. 'We do expect to direct them a bit more at this stage, Jo, and for them to be putting something together that's cohesive. And she says you've ignored her emails. With her upgrade coming up soon this is close to a disaster.'

I took the sheet from him. Only Nina could have produced this as evidence of my incompetence. 'What about all the verbal feedback I gave her? And I told her I was going to re-write this note. My schedule was completely crazy and I just ran out of time, and then my mother was dying, then she died. And you know what Nina's like. It's delicate, finding that line between forcing too much direction and giving them the freedom they need, you know, to find their own way.' Adam's expression didn't change and it dawned on me how feeble I sounded. Those summary notes were written in cafes and restaurants, through all the laughing, joking, and flirting. Then I remembered the email she sent when I was in Boston. 'Can I see you?' I had made a conscious decision to ignore her request and it had gradually moved down my to-do list. Soon it became invisible, lost in a digital nowhere land where I had willed Nina to disappear.

'I've already decided to move her over to Rachel. And with Andrew, Dylan and Caterina completing this summer you won't have any more PhD students to worry about.' Adam closed his folder. 'The thing is this, Jo. There's no choice here. It's time to finish. You've done some great work, but now it's time to go.'

When I got home that evening Jon was preparing dinner. The sense of failure and defeat still emanated from my face. I poured a large glass of Merlot and tried to explain what had happened. I wasn't sure myself. All I knew was, my career had finally been shot down. The career I had worked for so hard and for so long.

'What about your PhD supervisions? Nina's the one you're really invested in. Maybe they can keep you on contract to work with her till she finishes. I know some people who've done that.'

'Oh no, no, no, Jon.' I raised my hands in despair, barely able to meet his eye. 'You were right about her.'

'I thought she was your friend. All that time you spent together, you saying how bright and talented she was.'

I could sense Jon looking at me hard. He knew me so well.

'So, what,' he said slowly, 'you finally realised she's had her eye on you?'

I pictured that night with Nina, the two of us in her bed at the hotel in Manchester, and I tried to convince myself again that I did not cheat on Jon. We'd both flirted with people in the past, but that meant nothing. Our many years together, that was what counted. And this was just a stupid indiscretion, not an affair. I could never lie to Jon. *I did not have sexual relations with that woman* hadn't worked for Bill Clinton – it wasn't going to work for me. Get it over with, that was the way forward. I took a big breath.

'OK, Jon. You were right about her. When you said she fancied me. OK, so when we went to the conference in Manchester, and that's when she made her move on me. And I'd been drinking, she'd been drinking and then, well, one thing kind of led to another. You know.' I stopped gabbling.

Jon stopped stirring his bolognese and stared at me, waiting. 'One thing led to another? What do you mean, "You know"? Oh don't tell me you and her,' he shook his head. 'Don't tell me you ended up having lesbian sex or something. No, do tell me, Jo. Tell me what happened,' he snapped.

'No. No, Jon. It wasn't like that.' How could I even begin to describe what I'd done? I barely understood it myself.

'What else do you call it then?'

I closed my eyes and sighed, 'I don't know. I don't know what it was.'

Jon's face grew stonier as he stared at me. 'No wonder you're in trouble. Oh boy, you dug your own hole with this one, Jo. What the hell were you thinking?' He threw the wooden spoon down and red sauce splattered across the countertop and cupboards.

'Oh, please, Jon. Oh, God. It just seemed so innocent like two friends getting close. Oh, I don't know. But then I realised afterwards it went too far and I told her later that was the end of it, that it was a big mistake. But she was upset, and then my mother died and I was away and had to go back again and I never had the chance to sort it out and I just hoped it would all go away, die down on its own and then she tells Adam I'm a crap supervisor. Then she told him she wanted someone else. I should have seen how wrong she was going with her project but I let it go, just lost sight of things. Oh, it's all so awful.' I sunk my head so I could blank out his accusing face and pulled at my hair. 'You're right. I've dug my own hole. It's all a big mess. Oh, Jon, please. Please don't be upset.'

'Please don't be upset? I don't believe this,' he shouted, making me jump. Jon left his pot simmering, grabbed his coat and left the house.

As the door slammed behind him, I sat in the kitchen wailing in regret, wondering if he'd ever forgive me. Had I done the unforgiveable? After a while I began to ponder about that email Nina sent. Had she sent others I had missed? I found the email and hovered the cursor over the words 'Can I see you?' for half a minute or so, then I pressed the delete button without opening it. I hoped it would wipe Nina out of my mind for good.

Jon slept in the spare room after returning home late.

At least two days passed before Jon showed a willingness to talk other than reminding me to set the burglar alarm when

I left the house, to clear up after he'd finished cooking, or to remember to pick up more milk. This silence was the worst punishment he could have inflicted. When he finally agreed to sit down one evening he said, 'I've seen you reach some lows, but this is probably the lowest. Now that you're looking at forced early retirement and you're going to have all this time on your hands, you'd better sort yourself out. Yes, we can move on, but the hard work starts now.'

I forced a hug on him and felt him tense up. I knew that the cyclone damage I'd caused was not reversible, but as I held on to him and cried into his chest I could feel his body begin to relax. Then he tightened his embrace around me and began to sob.

The following week the HR director, an eager beaver in his late-thirties with a trendy shaved hair cut at the sides, had offered me a coffee, a big Danish pastry and lots of his time. He was almost too polite to convey any real sincerity about losing me to early retirement. What did he really care about my future, my old age, the sad reality of my 'condition,' as he called it, that might require care later on? Gerald confirmed the paperwork that I had signed with him, which secured my nice retirement package. If I found some freelance work here and there to top up my university pension, my later state pension, my savings and the pot of my mother's investment money, then things looked like they were going to be OK. 'We've really valued your contribution and your commitment, Joanna. You'll be missed,' Gerald said with a mixture of forced sympathy and relief in his youthful eyes. I wondered at that moment if any bad things had ever happened to him. I guessed they probably hadn't, but there would still be plenty of time for that.

Before I left, he added, I guess in the way of small talk, 'Any exciting holidays planned?'

'Well, no, but there's lots of stuff I need to catch up with, let's just say that.'

Back home, Jon checked the numbers and said it all looked good. 'Get back to doing some painting and enjoy life again. You've paid your dues.'

'And us?' I said. 'Are we OK?'

Jon shrugged and gave me a small smile. 'Let's see,' he said. 'Let's see.'

After a few formalities, the police from the Cape Cod town of Sandwich concluded there was no foul play involved with Dad's death. Word about the nature of his suicide hit the local and state news and soon everyone in the old neighbourhood heard about it. All it took was one or two of Dad's cousins to spread the story around to the extended family and our job was made easy. Dave and I didn't have to spend too much time contemplating what to do. Dad made it clear, after Ma died, that he hated Catholic wakes, churches, priests, funerals and anything else to do with the stifling religion in which he was raised.

'When I go don't throw away money on some funeral parlour caking all that crap on my face. No funeral. No memorial. None of that shit. Just burn me. Have a few drinks and be done with it.'

With great relief that we didn't have to endure another Catholic memorial service, we abided by his wishes and invited family and friends to the same restaurant where we had held our mother's post-memorial gathering. I found a nice picture of Dad in his young, slimmer days on a boat with a few of his friends, standing proudly, a cigarette dangling from his mouth, holding a huge catch which Dave reminded me was a cod. That was one of his happier times, when his dodgy money was overflowing, when he would free himself of the burden of family, take off and hook up with any woman he wanted. One of those many times I had wished he'd indulge in a binge and never return.

'He was a handsome one even as he got older,' his cousin Marilena said before getting short of breath. 'All the girls wanted to date him when he was young, but it was your mother who won the prize.' She took some more breaths again before finishing. 'He must've been devastated when he lost her. I wish we could've helped, Jo…I'm so sorry we weren't there for him.'

I told her there was nothing she could've done, but it was clear to me that I was probably the negligent daughter. I asked myself how I could have responded when faced with a man who, in spite of any biological parental obligations, during my lifetime had created such an emotional distance from his children that any attempt at repair would have taken decades, time he'd never have.

Around two months before his death I had approached Dad again to get him to acknowledge his grief in losing my mother, but he kept changing the subject. 'Dad, it can take people a long, long time to get over the loss of their spouse. There's nothing wrong with admitting you might need some help. You sound a bit sad most of the time when I get you on the phone. It might be good to talk to about it.'

'OK, you made your point. Yeah, some days aren't so great but what're you gonna do? I keep busy enough. I help the guys over at the station with some cars and I see my friends down at the bar. We talk. Don't need any other kind of talking, thanks very much. Anyways, hah, speaking of talking, yeah, my brother likes to talk a load of shit. I heard from him the other day and you wouldn't believe what he told me. He says, "Hey Jimmy, I got a tip on a good winner at the races." Can't remember if he said it was the dogs or the horses. Whatever. Then he says to me, "It's a sure thing, you could double some of that money of yours." Then the next thing he says to me is, "You think you can front me something for this one, just this one time? I gotta a good feeling." Yeah, that's what he said. See? Everybody wants a piece of me.'

Dave and I talked again about Dad's increasing episodes of memory loss and unpredictable moods. We finally persuaded him to see his doctor and Dave agreed to go with him to the appointment.

'Yeah, I went with your brother and saw the quack. The doctor says it's probably just because I'm old, that's all, this is what happens to old people like me. We forget a few things. But he did some tests.'

So I asked him about the results.

'I did OK on some, not so great on others, but this guy, he's getting up there in the years too, you know. He ain't no spring chicken. I'm not sure he even knows what's going on. I think he said he'll do some more tests, then he said something about medication. He gave me some stuff to read that I put somewhere but I haven't looked at it. Ask your brother about it, he was there. Anyways, I'm telling you there's nothing wrong and now I'm getting tired of hearing about it all the time. Everything's just fine and dandy.'

Dave reported Dad's difficulties to the doctor in as much detail as he could. Dave told me the doctor had some concerns about early dementia but said at that stage Dad looked like he was still getting by. Dave went with Dad to another appointment but our conversation about it was cut short. My brother had been more stable overall since his last hospital admission but I still heard the fragility in his voice over the phone.

'Jo, Dad doesn't want to know, doesn't want to face it. And you know what? I really can't deal with any of this right now either, with work and everything else going on. This doctor asked if there was any other family and I said you were in London and he should talk to you on the phone about what's going on. Dad knows you'll probably call the guy.'

I called the office from London only a week or so before Dad shot himself. The doctor did sound like an older man in his late sixties maybe, but he was professional and clear. He accepted that family members would be concerned.

'It's obvious to me that your father's been depressed,' he said. 'I'm sure the death of your mother has been a major trigger. Then the gradual loss of his work, and with his history of depression it's not surprising.'

I was a bit stunned when he said this, but I said nothing. Later I recalled the time when Dad returned home after his long disappearing stint with another woman, that time I overheard him crying in my mother's arms, his glassy-eyed, sleep-filled days of recovery afterwards. Over the years my brother and I knew something wasn't right with Dad, but neither he nor my mother ever disclosed what the problem really was.

'I wouldn't say he's the easiest of patients but I'm used to those,' the doctor added. 'He did say that you urged him to see someone about the memory issues. From what I've been able to find with the memory tests, the scan, he is showing signs of early dementia but he seems to be coping in general at the moment. We talked about this and about possible medications. But like many patients when they hear the word dementia they shut down and go into denial. He's not willing yet to think about the future. That's where he is right now. Your brother did look a bit upset when I talked to him privately about future caregiving needs, that sort of thing. I know it's hard for family members.'

Dave was difficult to get hold of after that and when we did talk we made the decision to give Dad some time to adjust to the doctor's news before addressing what to do next. But before we found time to *do* anything else, Dave called me with the bad news.

I've wondered if Dad's apologetic note was, in fact, his way of saying, *I'm sorry but I just don't have anything I can offer you.* I always thought of my father as a selfish man, but maybe he was trying to save Dave from becoming a carer, surely a role that his son would hardly be best suited to. Aside from the despair he must have felt in losing his memory, could Dad have also just reached a point where he thought he couldn't carry on in his self-serving way anymore, but didn't know how else to be in the world? Is that why he was sorry? Or maybe there was a simpler explanation, as Marilena suggested: he missed my mother too much and couldn't live without her. Maybe he was just plain sorry, because he knew he was going to be leaving us in that bloody state with a mess to clean afterwards.

I made sure I didn't attempt a eulogy this time. Dave and I both thanked everyone for coming and for befriending our father. After the episode at my mother's memorial I was relieved Uncle Ron didn't show his face, but two of his sons, Matty and Chrissie came along. They apologised that Billy couldn't be there. They were polite enough not to mention my drunken outburst, and I decided it was only right to return their good manners.

'Sorry for your loss,' Matty said, extending his hand.

'Thank you Matty. Thanks for coming. I appreciate it,' I said.

'Sorry, Jo. Sorry you're having to go through this after what happened with your mother,' said Chrissie, who offered an awkward hug. 'Billy's working today. Couldn't get away.' He looked down, and clasped his hands together.

'I know it was hard for you guys too when your mother passed,' I said. 'It's really good to see you both.'

Neither of the boys mentioned their dad, and Chrissie gave me another hug. 'You take care of yourself, Jo.'

Beth, Jean and Beth's father, Brian, attended for support. Brian was a handsome older man for sure, not much changed since his younger days, I thought to myself when I saw them arrive. Silver-haired, still slim and keeping up with his jogging, he turned up looking pretty suave in that steel-grey suit of his. For a second, I'm not quite sure why, I imagined him catching the eye of a younger woman in her fifties, someone like me, maybe, sweeping her off her feet, in spite of his age, and leaving his wife Jean in a devastated mess.

Why do I think these things?

Jean was chatting away to Beth, but Beth's attention was elsewhere. She wore a fitted black blazer that appeared to stretch a bit too snugly at her arms, which were folded high across her breasts. Her eyes narrowed as they scanned most of the room. It looked as if this was her way of ensuring that everyone would behave themselves. Jon kept polite conversation going with the older relatives who, I could tell from a distance, were impressed by his British accent and Mediterranean-style good looks, even though he was developing a bit of a double chin. Dave spent a short time with Nicole and Amy, but mainly kept company with a few of his friends and some cousins.

Karen made a brief show and offered her condolences. I watched her and Dave share a long embrace in the foyer before she left, and for the first time in many years, probably since that night at the dinner table when my father thrashed him for complaining about his McDonald's burger, I witnessed my brother sobbing for real, his whole upper body shaking, while Karen wiped away his tears with the hem of her linen sleeve. For me, though, cry-baby Jo, the tears never came, although I was close, contagious as crying can be, when I watched my brother. I wasn't sure if this was a good or a bad thing. Is this what it means to *let go*, or was I, at last, able to pull myself together?

I had found the $1000, all in tens, in an envelope in the shoe box, and we used it to pay for an open bar.

'Your father would've liked that,' his brother Joe said with a tired shrug and bloodshot eyes.

I made sure I stayed clear of the bar, but others appreciated it, making quiet jokes here and there, reminiscing about the good times with Jimmy O'Brien. Unexpected tears filled the eyes of many of his male friends, including Dino, the limo driver, who took time out of his working day to pay his respects.

'Jimmy could bust balls sometimes but in the end he always did good business,' he said, wiping his eye. I never knew what kind of business my father did with Dino or the others and I lost interest in asking a long time ago. 'I'm so sorry for your loss, hon. Let me know when you and your husband go back to Logan. That ride's on me.'

Following the gathering for my father, Jon and I met up with Dave at the little cottage in Cape Cod that my mother bought. The realtor was positive there wouldn't be any problem getting a good price for it, that it would get snapped up straightaway.

Dave will take a lot of the furnishings, keep the fishing gear, all the tools; the Salvation Army will take the rest.

We haven't figured out yet how to get rid of the rifles Dad kept in the glass cabinet in his bedroom at the house, but I've insisted they have to go. Dave will have Dad's four-wheel drive and sell my mother's Mondeo and the sports car he just bought. He will live in my parents' house, the mortgage paid off years ago, and I will benefit from the sale of the cottage. Any profits from liquidising their assets will be split between us. Fair is fair, my mother would have said. Dave will now be able to pay off all his debts.

So here we sit on Hank's boat with my father's old fishing buddy, who offered to take the three of us out to scatter the ashes. It doesn't take us long to reach a quiet point where it feels right, somewhere around, Hank says, the usual spots where Jimmy used to fish. We don't ask where the boat was found that evening.

Before we do the deed Dave suggests we sit close together to hold hands and pray, with Dave sitting between Jon and me. 'You too, Hank,' Dave says.

Hank declines politely. 'It's OK. You're family. That's the important thing.'

We close our eyes and Dave's grip tightens gradually as he prays. Jon wriggles a bit in protest.

'Let's keep it silent, Dave. It's better that way,' I mumble, and Dave falls silent.

Hearing only the sound of the boat rocking gently with soft waves slapping against its sides, I welcome the quiet between my brother and me, Jon and Hank. The water hits the boat in such a way that it reminds me of the time I sat dozing in our garden sunshine recently and heard the bed sheets on the washing-line blowing hard against each other in the strong wind. There's something oddly soothing about that. The only thing I pray for, not to God, but to the ocean or any other element of nature that could easily take my last breath away in an instant, is that this peace with my brother can last long enough to create an enduring memory.

We've brought two metal urns – one is bronze with an embossed Celtic cross, and is filled with my mother's ashes. The other one – bronze with a pewter finish and an engraved image of three dolphins – holds my father's remains. Ma chose her own urn when she was planning her death. She wanted it to be special, she said, something that would always remind us of her. She requested to have her ashes released in the sea with my father's, 'Whenever that time may come. That way your father and I will always be together. Even when we're gone and in heaven.'

Dave leans over the side and empties half of my mother's urn, a slight wind blowing the ashes several feet across the ripples of water. I empty the other half, some of the ashes covering my hand, which I touch, examine, and smooth into my skin. We repeat the ritual with my father's and Dave and I stand next to each other, swaying with the slight rock of the boat, holding ourselves steady at the side, as we watch our parents dissolve into the abyss.

The following morning at around 4.30am, I wake up to the sound of Jon's loud snoring, which shocks me out of a dream. In the dream my parents and Dave and I are together. There's a strong sense of Jon's presence although he isn't visible. It's as if he's hovering over us, a spirit in the clouds, watching and guiding. In the dream we all know that Ma is going, on her way out with the cancer, but we accept this and we are all content just to be together in each other's company. My father is surprisingly affectionate with me, even though there's something about his actions that warns me it's only for a fleeting moment. It's maybe after he's said something he realises he shouldn't have said, or done something he now regrets. He goes out of his way to get me a beer and a snack from the kitchen and he brings them outside. I am settled in a wooden Adirondack-style chair next to Ma. It's the kind of chair my mother always loved but never bought for herself. We are in the back yard at their cottage and Dad creeps up from behind, sets his arms gently around my shoulders and leans over to embrace me, his stubbly face and the sharp point of his toothpick brushing against my cheek. I accept his hand, hold it and turn to Ma to see her smiling. She takes my other hand in hers and I think, *this is what a mother and daughter do.*

A trampoline appears out of nowhere and I decide I'm going to have a jump; no cane, no pain, only young, strong legs that are ready to bounce. I want to show them I have blissful energy and I want them all to marvel at it. And that's what they do. Dave, Ma, Dad and Jon in those clouds, all smile and giggle with me as I bounce up and down, struggling to contain myself, not wanting any of it to end. I wake up to the sound of Jon's snoring. For a second when I open my eyes I fear he's struggling for his last breath and there's silence, but it resumes again, his roaring declaration of life.

I nudge his shoulder to signal that it's time to turn to his side. I curl up behind him into the spooning position we enjoyed so much in our younger days. The heat of his body, the pace of his breathing, up and down, is steady and reliable. He takes hold of my hand and moves it next to his warm bare stomach. I close my eyes in an effort to return to a sleep in which I can pick up where my idyllic dream left off, but it doesn't happen. I orient my breathing to match Jon's, count each one up to twenty, then start again; one, two, three, four.

A few more hours will pass, morning will come, the day will resume, like any other and we will still be here together.

Acknowledgements

I want to thank the team at RedDoor Publishing, Anna Burtt, Heather Boisseau and Clare Christian, for their passion and faith in this novel. Thanks to editor, Sadie Mayne, whose insights opened my eyes to hidden narrative possibilities. Thanks to cover designer, Clare Shepherd, for capturing the heart of this story.

Thanks to my family and friends for the many encouraging words and confidence in me. Extra gratitude is extended to those who took the time to read critically and comment on early drafts: Lisa Lipman, Sheila Brill, Bernadka Dubicki, and Janet Thumim.

To my loving husband – thank you for your endless support of my creative endeavours, for all those times you told me never to give up, for convincing me that this effort was worthwhile. Thank you for loving me the way you do.

To my children – thanks for your patience during those intense moments when I was grumpy, when I was somewhere else, either glued to a notebook, the laptop or wandering around in a blank-faced daze. Thanks for always, always, saying how proud you are of your mother at those moments when she needed so desperately to hear it. Thank you for loving me the way you do.

About the Author

J.M. Monaco grew up in the northeast region of the USA where she studied English and Creative Writing at undergraduate level. She worked in a variety of areas before taking up postgraduate studies in England where she completed her PhD. She now lives in the South West of England with her husband and children.